FOURTH WORLD

J†M†J

FOURTH WORLD: Book One of the Iamos Trilogy
Copyright © 2015 by Lyssa Chiavari.

Published by Snowy Wings Publishing
www.snowywingspublishing.com

Cover designed by Najla Qamber Designs.
Model photos by Mosaic Stock Photography.

This book is a work of fiction. Names, characters, businesses, brands, places, events and incidents are either the products of the author's imagination or used in a fictitious manner. Any resemblance to actual persons, living or dead, or actual events is purely coincidental.

ISBN (hardcover): 978-1-946202-12-3
ISBN (paperback): 978-1-946202-10-9

Third Edition

FOR THE LEOPARDS:
reach for the stars.

FOURTH WORLD

the iamos trilogy , book one

LYSSA CHIAVARI

Snowy Wings
PUBLISHING

THE SKY LOOKED RED.

That was all I could think as I gazed out over the desiccated plain. The once-gray rocks and boulders, strewn about the old dry coastline, were now almost completely covered with rust. Orange-tinged clouds swirled above my head, the air thick with choking dust kicked up by the harsh wind that raked over the parched ground.

Even though we'd been forbidden to leave the safety of the citidome, I'd decided to take the risk that night. I had wanted to see the sunset—*really* see the sunset—for what could be the last time. It had been so long since I'd seen the sky, I couldn't remember what it looked like.

But I certainly hadn't expected it to be so *red.*

The oxygen was too thin. It made breathing difficult, painful. I couldn't believe how quickly it was depleting now, at the end. Last year on my annual we'd still been able to go outside. But now we had to huddle in our enclosed cities, looking out at the world through the tinted filter of smooth blue glass. And even that option wouldn't last much longer. The world really was ending.

It was much too soon. This was the first day of my eighth year, my *enilikin.* I still had my whole life ahead of me. I hadn't even completed my schooling yet, thanks to Gitrin. It would be at least another year, now, before I was ready to take my place in the ranks of the *geroi.*

But in their last report, the scientists said that our planet couldn't sustain us another year. My heart stuck in my throat at the thought. Standing here, looking at this, I knew it to be true. Sometime in the next six-hundred days the last of our atmosphere would be gone. The energy sources used to power the citidome would be entirely depleted. And if the colony on Hamos wasn't stabilized—if we didn't complete evacuation by that time—we'd all be dead.

I'd be dead. Before I even got a chance to live.

We needed more *geroi*. And still she told me I wasn't ready. Everything was so hideously unfair.

I shivered as the biting wind dragged over me, pulling wisps of colorless hair loose from the tight braid encircling my scalp. There was the briefest hint of the fragrance of flowers on the wind's breath, but it was overpowered by the dry, metallic scent of the ever-reddening earth. What if this was the last time I'd ever smell Iamos? The last time I'd ever see the sun, or the sky, without something in between me and it?

No.

I took a final shuddering breath, and, tucking a flyaway hair behind my ear, I made my decision. I was not giving up. It was not over. No matter what it took, this would not be my last annual.

It was only as I turned to head inside that I saw him.

I might have missed him otherwise, but the light from the setting sun threw his form into relief. A boy was sprawled across the ground. He wore no breathing apparatus. He was completely unprotected. And he wasn't moving.

Panicked, I raced to his side. I was out of breath by the time I reached him, even though he lay only a short distance away. "Are you all right?" I asked, wheezing. When he didn't respond, I rolled him over onto his back.

He was young—probably close to my own age. I realized instantly he couldn't be from my city; his traits were all wrong. He must have come from another citidome. But how? He couldn't have walked. All that way, unprotected? He would never have made it...

I reached for my earpiece, then hesitated. I was invisible right now—the System couldn't track me—but if I called for help, I'd be back online and the *geroi* would know I'd broken the edict. Not to mention that it could draw their attention to the fact that my earpiece had been altered. Ceilos would never forgive me.

But there was no way I could shift this boy's dead weight on my own, not when I was already feeling the effects of the thin air.

Before I could give myself a chance to change my mind, I pressed the button. "*Gerouin* Melusin," I called.

"Nadin?" Melusin's voice was soft in my ears, like the drip of water in the caverns.

There was no time for explanations. "I need help outside the dome," I said as calmly as possible.

"'Outside'?" she repeated, her gentle voice faltering almost imperceptibly. "What are you doing—"

"Just hurry," I interrupted her, breathless. "I found someone out here. He's injured."

The *gerouin* said nothing more, simply disconnecting. I turned back to the boy. He was still unconscious, but he was breathing—barely. I crouched to get a better look at him. His hair was coated with the red dust that the wind kicked up in swirling eddies, but I could see it was curly and dark. His skin, on the other hand, appeared bleached like an old man's, even though he was clearly young. Could unprotected exposure to solar rays have done this? The atmosphere was so thin now...

I inhaled shakily, my lungs burning. It was already painful for me to be outside, and I couldn't have been out for more than five minutes. This boy... how did he get here?

PART ONE
ISAAK

Tierra Nueva, Aeolis Province
Martian Colony
2073 C.E.

CHAPTER 1

· ₀ ∘ • ◯ ∅ ϕ ○

THE SUN'S WARMTH MELTED OVER ME AS I STEPPED OFF THE bus. I paused for a moment, blinking away the startling brightness of the open air after the dim confines of the school bus. It was near the end of April II—our spring April—of my junior annum, but it was weird for it to be this warm on Mars, even during the summer months. As my classmates filed off the vehicle behind me, I rolled up my long thermal sleeves. Here in the hills, the wind was stronger, with a cooling bite, but the undercurrent of warmth to the day was still unmistakable. I grinned in spite of myself.

"Right, right, everyone, keep clear of the steps, we need to get everyone off the bus if we're ever going to get moving with this," my homeroom teacher, Mr. Johnson, yelled over my classmates' chatter. "Henry, that means you. Isaak! Would you please do something about your partner in crime?"

I started at the sound of my name and glanced over my shoulder. At the foot of the bus steps, a stocky kid with long black hair and a faded t-shirt that proclaimed "FREE MARS" in what was once bold red text was streaming music on his earpod loud enough to be heard five meters away, seemingly oblivious to the world around him.

1

Turning back to Mr. Johnson, I shrugged. "I don't know what you expect me to do about him."

"I suppose it would be too much to ask you to make him behave for the rest of the day," said Mr. Johnson. "But for a start, you can move him."

I rolled my eyes and tromped back toward the bus. "Come on." I nudged Henry away from the steps.

"What? What'd I do this time?"

He looked up and caught Mr. Johnson's eye. They exchanged matching glares.

"That guy's got it in for me," Henry complained.

I opened my mouth to answer, but broke off as my other best friend, Tamara, elbowed her way between the two of us. "Well, maybe if you didn't get called into the principal's office every other day," she pointed out reasonably.

"I'm only in the principal's office every other day because *he*"—Henry gestured toward Mr. Johnson—"has it in for me."

"Right." Tamara's reply was more of a laugh than a word. "I'm sure it has nothing to do with your *conscientious homework objections*, or your habit of leaving class early, or the anti-government graffiti in the boy's bathroom that I heard about last week."

As she spoke, she glanced knowingly over at me, a smirk tugging at the corner of her lips. My heart lurched momentarily, and I—discreetly, I hoped—urged it to settle back into its regular pattern. For the amount of time I spent with Tamara on almost a daily basis, you'd think I'd manage to *not* go into full spaz-mode every time I saw her.

Yeah. You'd think.

Fortunately, she hadn't seemed to notice my suddenly red face. Henry certainly hadn't. He was too busy complaining.

"Tamara," he said solemnly, "as conscientious citizens of Mars, we have an obligation to future generations to prevent this world from falling into the cycle of imperialism that destroyed so many lives on Earth. I'm simply providing an alternative to the narrative being forwarded by the administration, to prevent the further spread of misinformation. Graffiti is the people's tool, you know."

He was off again. Tamara shot me a pained expression and I shrugged. She should have known better than to get him started on one of his rants.

I moved a few paces away, craning my neck to get a better look at the red hills around us. From up here, Tierra Nueva seemed to spread out before me: a small valley crammed with a rambling mishmash of tightly clustered buildings and, in the center of town where the rivers converged, the clump of high rises that made up the AresTec complex on Sparta Island. The valley was blanketed in a filmy gray haze from the factory district on the edge of town, blurring the details, but in the distance I could just see the sun glinting off the waters of Escalante Bay.

I jammed my hands in my pockets and breathed in deeply through my nose. It was nice out here, where the air smelled fresh and the acrid scent of the factory exhaust was just a wispy memory. Maybe today wouldn't be so bad after all.

"Okay, everyone, eyes and ears up here!" The chattering voices around me tapered off at Mr. Johnson's shout. "We've got a lot to get through today, so I'm just going to go ahead and turn this show over to Dr. Luna here, if everyone would *please*"—he

3

narrowed his eyes at the lot of us—"give her your attention."

A tall woman with black hair reaching almost to her knees stepped forward, smiling at us. "Hello, everybody, I'm Professor Clara Luna. Thank you for coming all the way out here to visit us today. I understand you're having Career Week at your school right now. How has that been going for you?"

The group grumbled noncommittally. Career Week was the week-long round of field trips that the junior class at the Academy had to take every year to help pick their study emphases for senior annum. All week, we'd been visiting different "high-need" areas in the peninsula, to help the undecided kids figure out what they wanted to do with their lives—the ones who hadn't had that predetermined for them by a scholarship committee like Henry and I had, anyway. On Monday they'd dragged us to the GSAF branch in the city, and yesterday we'd taken a tour of AresTec's newly-completed offices. Today, they'd switched things up by busing us out to this isolated site in the hills that divided the peninsula into its east and west halves. It would have made a great horror flick premise—*a group of teens brought to the middle of nowhere, only to be massacred where we stood!*—but it was nothing as exciting as that. Instead, they were apparently planning to bore us to death with a presentation from these Kimbal University professors who were doing some kind of geology survey out here. But at least it got me out of Earth Lit for a week.

Mr. Johnson rolled his eyes at my classmates' lack of enthusiasm, but Dr. Luna seemed undaunted. "It's good to see so many fresh faces out here today," she said, her smile never wavering for an instant. "What we're working on is a very exciting project that is helping us to learn more about our planet's past, which in turn will help us understand how to shape the future of Mars. I'm one of the co-leads on this project. My associate should be coming along any second—"

"I'm here, I'm here," a man's voice broke in, and a moment later its owner popped up over the top of the sloping crater behind her. He was tall and dark, with a head of thick black hair and a neatly trimmed mustache to match. My breath hissed in through my teeth, louder than I meant it to. Henry and Tamara both looked at me.

"What's your problem?" Henry whispered.

"That guy." I nodded in the direction of the newcomer. "He's—"

"Hello, everyone," the man said over me. He brushed off his dirt-encrusted hands on the sides of his pants. "Sorry I'm late. There's always so much to do on a dig like this. Anyway, my name is Professor Erick Gomez, I'm the head researcher for this field survey."

"Wait, *that* Erick Gomez?" Henry whispered. "That tool your mom's dating now?" Tamara winced sympathetically in my direction as I nodded.

Maybe I was being unfair. I suppose I hadn't really known Erick long enough to know, objectively, if he was *actually* a tool or not. Mom had only introduced him to me and Celeste a couple of weeks ago. Although, from the way they were acting, I suspected they'd been seeing each other for a while before Mom told us about him. I mean, they'd worked together as long as we'd lived in Tierra Nueva. They had plenty of opportunity.

And I couldn't really begrudge her dating again. After all, Dad was the one who'd abandoned us all so unceremoniously two annums ago, during my first term at the Academy. Considering the fact that he hadn't contacted me or Celeste once since he'd left, it was obvious he was only concerned with his own happiness. So why shouldn't Mom be happy, too?

It was just weird to have some new guy showing up at the house all the time. Especially since this one was so... *different* from how Dad had been.

"I'm sure most of you are wondering what exactly we're working on way out here in the middle of nowhere," Erick said, smiling with way too many teeth. "It might not look like much, but it's actually very exciting. This study is continuing work begun by the first Mars landers sent from Earth over a hundred years ago."

"Riveting," Henry muttered. I snickered.

"As you all know, we humans have not been on Mars for very long. There's still a *lot* to learn about our new home. And here, we're using geological methods to do just that. We're studying the planet's past, specifically its atmospheric makeup over the millennia and behavior of ancient and precolonial waterways. Our data will enable modern scientists currently working on Phase Three of terraformation to better understand what challenges to expect while adapting the planet for life now."

As Erick spoke, Dr. Luna started leading the group of us down a trail that wound between ditches of varying size. A few of these had groups of people working inside them with shovels and picks, but most were empty and roped off—to keep us from wandering around inside them, I guess.

"This site we're currently excavating is fascinating for two reasons. First of all, it's the site of an ancient stream bed, which provides us with information about how water behaved on Mars in the past, and what sort of organic material it supported. We've already found fossil evidence of early ancestors of the modern spider weed, as well as extinct forms of Martian flora, and even primitive fauna. We're hoping to uncover more evidence of other ancient lifeforms that might have existed here before atmospheric degradation set in."

My arms were still crossed, but I have to admit, he caught my interest with "fossil." Against my better judgment, I found myself paying a bit more attention to Erick's little spiel.

I might never have noticed it otherwise.

Erick had turned to face the group of us, walking backward and gesturing here and there like some kind of tour guide. "The second reason this site is so interesting is that the entire hills are pockmarked with craters from various meteor impacts over millions of years. The crater walls left behind can give us a snapshot of Mars' geological processes over time." He indicated a smallish crater to his right that appeared to have been widened by the dig crew. The sides of the hole were striped, with a variety of different-colored rocks mashed together. It almost looked like Neapolitan ice cream, I thought as I glanced absently down at the bottom of the trench.

Then I froze.

On the crater floor, carefully dug out from the dirt by Erick's crew, was a pile of smooth-topped stones stacked in the shape of an arch.

I cleared my throat. "Hey, Eri—uh, Professor Gomez," I interrupted.

He stared for a moment. Then recognition washed over him and he grinned at me. "Oh, Isaak. Did you have a question?"

He seemed so pleased by my interest in his project that I nearly didn't respond to him. But my curiosity got the better of me. I pointed to the bottom of the pit. "Um, yeah. What's up with that pile of rocks down there?"

"Oh, that. That's a natural rock formation. We've discovered a number of them throughout this site. We believe they were pushed into that formation by the movement of ancient waterways. Then they calcified, solidifying together like mortar. If you all will follow me, we'll see a few more of those 'arches' on the tour."

He turned to lead the group through a narrower part of the trail. The rest of my classmates shuffled off after him, but I hung back. Something wasn't sitting well with me. It may have been a "natural" rock formation, but I'd seen it before—on something that was definitely man-made.

"Isaak, come on," Tamara called when she noticed I was still hovering at the side of the crater.

I paused for a moment, still looking down at the trench floor. Then, resolved, I turned to her and Henry. "Hang on just a sec." I ducked under the rope surrounding the ditch.

"Whoa, what are you doing?" I heard Henry exclaim as I stumbled my way down the steep, rocky side of the crater.

"I just want to get a better look at it," I replied.

"Isaak!" hissed Tamara. "You're going to get in trouble!"

"Just keep a watch for me, then. Let me know if you hear them coming back."

She frowned down at me, her eyebrows knitted with worry.

Henry, on the other hand, had already pushed his way under the rope and was thundering down the slope after me.

Red dust settled in a cloud around me as I crouched at the base of the pile of stones. It was only about waist high, but otherwise it looked exactly like the design on the coin. I supposed it could just be a coincidence, but that would be too weird.

"What's so great about this thing, man?" Henry asked. "It's just a pile of rocks."

"Yeah, but the way they're shaped..." I reached out impulsively to touch the arch.

When my fingers brushed the rock, a deafening klaxon shrieked.

Henry cursed at the sound. I cringed, my head jerking up. I hadn't noticed the security drone hovering at the perimeter of the crater, but its camera was focused on us now, the red light on top of its body flashing.

In moments, our group was back at the side of the crater. Erick silenced the security drone, and in the stillness that followed, Mr. Johnson's voice echoed.

"Contreras and Sandhu. Why am I not surprised?"

After ensuring that I hadn't caused any damage to the site with my "reckless behavior," Mr. Johnson had hauled the three of us back to the bus while Erick got the rest of our classmates back on their regularly scheduled field trip. As we lowered ourselves into the front row of benches, I glanced over at Tamara and felt a twinge of remorse. Her normally tanned face was white as a sheet. Henry and I were more used to getting in trouble, but

Tamara had always managed to keep her nose clean. I hadn't meant to drag her into this as well.

"All right," said Mr. Johnson, leaning against the bus' emergency manual drive console and looking the three of us over, his arms crossed. "What was it this time, Sandhu? Now even scientific studies are a tool of Earth-based imperialism? Kind of a stretch, don't you think?"

Henry was aghast. "What makes you think this was my idea? I'm innocent!"

"Right. Like I'm going to fall for that."

"He's telling the truth," I broke in. "He really didn't have anything to do with it this time. It was my fault."

Mr. Johnson gaped at me, then began to massage the bridge of his nose in exasperation. "Really, Isaak? Being Henry's accomplice wasn't good enough for you? Now you have to commit the crimes yourself?"

"I wasn't going to *do* anything to it!" I protested. "I just wanted to get a better look at it!"

My teacher sighed. "Isaak, I don't know what to do about you. In just one annum, you went from being one of the best students at the Academy to having a C-average and being in the principal's office every other week. What happened?"

I knew it was true, but his words still stung. That didn't mean I had any intention to tell my homeroom teacher *what happened,* though—especially while he was sitting there all torqued off at me.

"Look, Mr. J," I said quietly. "I'm sorry. I wasn't trying to make trouble. I just wanted to get a better look at it."

Mr. Johnson shook his head. "Fine. But that doesn't mean I'm going to let you off the hook. All three of you are getting a one-week in-school suspension..."

"Me?" Tamara squeaked. It was the first noise she'd made since the drone alarm went off. "But Mr. Johnson, I wasn't—"

"You're on the drone's security footage just like the two of them," replied Mr. Johnson. "I know you're a good kid, Tamara, but you need to take responsibility for your actions. Maybe it's time to think about who you choose for your friends."

Tamara looked like she was going to cry. My stomach knotted with guilt.

"Andy?" a voice broke in from the bus's doorway. I turned in annoyance to see Erick standing there. "Sorry to interrupt. Clara's finishing the tour for the rest of the students. Might I make a suggestion?"

Mr. Johnson seemed as taken aback by the professor's interruption as the rest of us. "Regarding?"

"I looked over the crater, and there's no damage done to the site. And it seems to me if the students are really that interested in my team's findings, there's a more productive way for them to pay their penance than an in-school suspension."

Johnson folded his arms and nodded. "Such as?"

"We always could use a few more workers at the site. There's still quite a bit of digging to do. The three of them could volunteer here on weekends and put in a few hours of community service. They'd be helping out the GSAF science division, and they might learn a few things in the process."

It took all my effort not to leap to my feet in protest. I honestly would have preferred an in-school suspension over having to spend my free time with Erick.

Tamara looked down at the floor, her shoulders slumped. "I have voice lessons at Herschel on the weekends, though."

Mr. Johnson's grin was devilish. "I'm sure your schedule can be worked out. I know your parents will be willing to cooperate once they know the alternative."

Tamara nodded glumly, and my temper flared on her behalf. Was it really necessary for him to be so happy about this? I was starting to think Henry was right about Mr. Johnson—maybe he really did have it in for us.

"Of course, we can work around your other classes," Erick intervened. He smiled encouragingly at Tamara. "I know there was no harm meant here today. I think this can be a learning experience for everybody."

I was just starting to feel a grudging ounce of respect for him when he turned and grinned at me. The charitable feelings I had toward him dissolved. I could just tell he was going to make a huge deal out of us "getting to know each other."

I knew then that the rest of this annum was going to be hell.

CHAPTER 2

· ₒ ° • ◯ ∅ ɸ ○

THE REMAINDER OF THE TRIP HAD GONE PRETTY NORMALLY, apart from Henry giving me the cold shoulder on the bus ride back. Well, and Tamara. She wouldn't even look at me—or anyone else, for that matter. She just stared down at her rhinestone-studded sneakers like they were the most interesting thing in the world.

I felt really guilty for dragging them into this. Though, honestly, Henry didn't really have any room to complain. He'd gotten me into trouble way more often than vice versa. So it was an enormous relief when school got out that afternoon and I saw the two of them waiting for me out in front of the Academy as usual. Henry and I always walked with Tamara over to the pier, where she took the ferry over to Herschel Island for her music lessons, before catching the train down to the south side of town where the two of us lived.

I hurried down the first set of steps to meet them. "You're not too torqued at me?" I asked when I caught up with them.

"That depends on whether you're going to explain to us what all that was about," Henry replied. He led the way down the second set of steps. The Academy was perched among the flat-faced cliffs on the northwest side of town, and it was quite a trek down to the street for those of us who didn't qualify for a key to the elevator. There were some mornings when cutting class seemed a more appealing alternative than climbing all those flights of stairs. "Seriously, Isaak, what's so special about that pile of rocks that it was worth six weeks of Saturday school? That's a new record, even for me."

I flushed. "It's probably stupid," I admitted. "It's just... I really felt like I'd seen that arch before."

We were onto the second-to-last flight of stairs by now, and the street sloped down before us. The stopping zone was loaded, as usual, with a line of swanky cars sent by the richer parents to pick up their kids. Wyatt Ponsford—a particularly obnoxious classmate of mine, the son of the Lieutenant Governor—was just sidling casually into the backseat of his family's shiny black Tesla. Considering that the Ponsfords' bayfront mansion was probably only a five-minute walk from the Academy, it always seemed a bit ridiculous for Wyatt to get chauffeured back and forth while most of the rest of us had to hoof it. But I supposed it didn't matter to the truly rich if their legs atrophied.

"Where could you have seen it?" Henry scrunched his nose up. "You mean, like, online? Or in real life?"

When the Tesla pulled out, I noticed a rundown blue pickup truck had been parked behind it. The truck stuck out like a sore thumb in the midst of the usual luxury sedans. Its sides were caked with red-brown mud, and the paint on the roof was badly oxidized. I wondered vaguely what a deathtrap like that was doing parked outside the Academy. Maybe they were lost.

"Neither. You know that box of junk we found in my mom's garden after my dad took off? It looked like something I—" I broke off as I realized that the driver of the blue truck was

14

gesturing wildly at me. "Oh, geez."

I trudged up to the driver's side window. There was Erick, smiling with way too many teeth again. "Hey, Isaak. Fancy seeing you again so soon."

Yeah, imagine that. And I was sure it was a coincidence and everything. "What are you doing here?"

"I told your mom I'd give you a ride home today," he said blithely.

I looked at him in horror. "You didn't tell her—"

"No, no. Well, not all of it. I just said you'd decided after the presentation to volunteer to work at the site on weekends. I omitted the rest of it."

I suppose he probably expected me to thank him or something, but I just stared at him warily. After a moment— when he realized I wasn't going to say anything—he went on, with a bit less enthusiasm, "I do think we need to talk, though, Isaak. And I thought it might be easier to do it this way. You know, without your mother here."

I blinked at him, uncertain whether that was a threat or not. Probably better not to find out. I glanced over my shoulder at Henry and Tamara. "Uh, I guess you guys better go on ahead."

The two of them stared incredulously at me for a moment, Tamara's mouth drawn into a frown and Henry's burly arms crossed. I shrugged helplessly at them.

"Whatever," Henry said at last. "But you'd better be on Speculus later."

"Sure thing," I agreed, skirting around the front of the pickup and pulling open the passenger door.

As we pulled away from the curb, I realized that Tamara hadn't said a word the whole time.

The truck was a relic. Its vinyl seats were rough and cracked, and the rearview mirror had apparently fallen off at some point and been reattached with duct tape. Erick drove the vehicle himself, rather than relying on the self-steering mechanism. For some reason, this didn't surprise me. The truck seemed to fit his personality in a way I couldn't quite describe. Sort of old-fashioned, like a pioneer. I supposed it fit with the rugged-Martian-colonist stereotype you saw in flix, though I hadn't ever known anyone who was actually like that in real life: sun-baked cowboys who wanted to shape the new planet with their own two hands.

He was the polar opposite of my dad. Dad had always liked the modern conveniences. I don't think he even knew how to drive a car himself. I guess maybe that's why he wound up heading back to Earth, in the end. Building a new world yourself is too much work. That thought made me feel bitter, and I folded my arms and slumped down in my seat.

Erick steered the pickup in the opposite direction from the way Henry, Tamara and I usually walked, heading for the crosstown expressway. Through the window, red boulders and scraggy clumps of spider weeds gave way to ever-denser clusters of buildings. Before long, the blue of the bay disappeared behind the city skyline.

We rode in silence. He didn't even have music streaming. There was nothing but the constant, electronic hum of the engine and the swoosh of the tires over the pavement. It was only a matter of time before the quiet drove me out of my mind.

Finally, I shifted in my seat and blurted out, "Well? Aren't you going to ask me what I was doing in the crater?"

"Not unless you want to tell me."

That wasn't the response I'd expected, and it knocked the wind out of my sails. What was even with this guy? My mom would have been all over me—"*Explain yourself, Isaak!*" I supposed my dad wouldn't have pressed, but that's just because he wouldn't have cared one way or the other. This was an approach I was unfamiliar with. Now I felt obligated to say *something*, since I'd opened my stupid mouth, but for the life of me, I couldn't think of what to say.

So I just looked back out the windshield at the road in front of us.

After several more moments of silence, Erick said, "I understand you're very close to your grandfather. He's an archaeologist on Earth?"

This abrupt change of subject threw me even more than his prior reverse psychology crap. "I... uh, yeah?" I replied lamely. "Well, he used to be, anyway." Abuelo had retired five years ago, when the dig site on the eroding Veracruz coastline that he'd dedicated his life to finally crumbled into the sea. He'd known it was coming—that's what had made his excavation so critical—but it had still been a major blow.

Erick smiled but kept his eyes trained on the road. "I'm familiar with his work. Dr. Hector Garcia. You might not realize it, but geologists and archaeologists actually have a lot of overlap, professionally. We use similar methods. But that's not why I've heard of Hector Garcia, of course. He's quite famous on Earth. Or he was for a time."

"Yeah, since he's the one who finally translated the Cascajal

Block." It was sort of a Rosetta Stone, only for the ancient Olmec—a civilization that existed in Mexico over three thousand years ago. People had tried for over sixty years to decipher the writing on the block, which was the oldest written language in the Americas. But Abuelo was the one who had finally done it.

Erick nodded. "And I understand you inherited your grandfather's knack for languages. Your mother tells me you're a regular polyglot. How many do you speak, anyway?"

"Eight."

Erick swore.

I flushed. "Well, to different degrees of fluency."

"Still, at your age? That's impressive."

I stared down at my scuffed shoes. They looked embarrassingly at home on the mud-caked vinyl car mats. "I grew up speaking English, and my mom wanted to make sure I knew Spanish. Heritage and all. None of us really use it, though, apart from the EBCs."

"The EBCs?"

"Yeah, you know. Exclamations, baby names and curse words."

Erick laughed at this, a huge, bellowing sound that felt much too large for the cramped pickup cab. I squirmed in my seat.

"I picked up some Greek and Russian just from kids in our neighborhood," I went on, staring out the window at a group of pedestrians waiting at a crosswalk. Businesspeople in suits trying to ignore the tourists beside them, snapping pics of the AresTec tower on their palmtops. "Henry's mom taught me some Hindi... the rest are from the classes the Academy is having me take. Japanese, Mandarin Chinese, stuff like that."

That was the root of my scholarship to the Academy. The Academy had pretty much been founded as a place for government officials and GalaX execs here on Mars to send their kids to, since they'd sooner cut their own right arms off than see *their* precious snowflakes in a public school. But the Academy did recruit a few kids from the local middle schools every annum. They sought out students who not only had good grades, but who were *gifted* at something. Kids they knew, if they were given the opportunity, would grow up to be useful.

My usefulness was in my knack for language. I guess I could see why that stood out to them—all of Mars is kind of a mishmash of different Earth cultures, what with the simultaneous colonization process, but Aeolis province is an especially diverse area. See, the International Climate Treaty of the late 2040s had provided generous financial incentives for any Earth nation that reduced its carbon output, and most of the industrial hubs of the world had done that by moving their manufacturing plants to Mars. GalaX had started the terraformation process a decade before with their MarsEpoch project, but the planet was still basically a frozen popsicle at that point. Even with the McKay-Zubrin space mirrors melting most of the permafrost, Mars didn't have much of an atmosphere to speak of. It needed more carbon dioxide. And that was something Earth had in abundance.

With the jobs moving to Mars, and the government subsidizing most of the costs, people from all over Earth started flocking to Mars to find a "better life" in the new world. In less than a decade, Mars went from having just a few pockets of scientific outposts to major colonies all over the entire planet. That's when GSAF was established, to oversee the colonization process.

My hometown, Tierra Nueva, had been one of the first manufacturing towns in Aeolis. When it was first founded, it was mostly made up of immigrants from Mexico. You can see their fingerprints all over the south part of town, where most of the landmarks and street names are still in Spanish. But Tierra Nueva has gotten a lot bigger over the years. More corporations have shifted their manufacturing plants to the valley, and that's drawn large communities of immigrants from India, Russia, and most recently Greece, still reeling from its civil war back on Earth.

But the biggest change in Tierra Nueva came with the founding of AresTec almost ten annums ago. It was the first corporation ever to be based on Mars instead of on Earth. Their corporate offices are here in Tierra Nueva, and everything they do—from design to business to manufacturing their electronics —is done here.

I was only eight when it happened, so I didn't really understand what was going on, but I remember that no one in town could shut up about it. It was this huge opportunity for people on Mars, and here in Tierra Nueva at that. And I definitely noticed that things in town changed after AresTec opened its doors. It wasn't just that they'd built Sparta Island and the huge AresTec campus—the whole face of downtown changed. The older, kind of rundown areas in the business district got bulldozed, replaced with high-rises and tourist traps, coffee shops and kitschy boutiques. Then the mansions started appearing, dotting the cliffs on the northwest side of town. The Academy had opened not long after. In what seemed like a really short amount of time, Tierra Nueva got really, really big.

Actually, all of Mars was getting really, really big.

With so many people from so many different backgrounds coming and working and living together, GSAF had a lot of work to do to keep the new world in order. And that was the "use" that the Academy had seen for me. I was being groomed for a translating job with GSAF, the details of which I still didn't really know. But I guess the idea of a native Martian who could speak eight languages—and that wasn't even counting the dead ones, like Olmec and Mayan, that Abuelo had taught me—had been very appealing to the scholarship board at the Academy. So I'd been offered a full ride, with my linguistics emphasis already laid out for me as an incoming freshman.

My parents had been ridiculously pleased by this. I suppose they'd been a little bit worried about my future beforehand. My mom's a GSAF bioengineer—basically a hacker for plants, splicing them together like a jigsaw puzzle in a laboratory in the hopes that she can take a plant that had evolved for life on Earth and change it into one that can survive on a totally different planet. She loves her job, but it's not exactly known for its spectacular pay grade. My dad, on the other hand, had worked in a factory. They'd met here on Mars, and if my abuela's lengthy rantings about how they "always knew he was no good" are to be believed, it wasn't exactly a match made in heaven.

Either way, between the two of them we were comfortable enough, but I knew they were worried about my future. Dad was always telling me I was living my life wrong, rolling his eyes at me for being myself. Saying my identity was the product of an overly-active imagination, and if I didn't knock it off, I'd be sorry when I got older. The Academy scholarship had been like a dream come true—a guarantee that I would be successful, that maybe I *could* "make it" as an adult after all. My future was laid out for me.

I hadn't been quite as thrilled as they were, although I didn't say anything about it. Sure, I liked learning languages, but... the Academy's plan, it wasn't what I wanted to *do* with my life, you know what I mean? Working in some windowless cubicle in the GSAF building seemed like a complete soul-drain. I'd never told anyone, but what I really wanted, more than anything, was to be like Abuelo. To be an archaeologist. Working outside, digging in the dirt, uncovering hidden treasure. I wanted to hold the ancient past in my hand and uncover its secrets. I'd even hoped to maybe dig at the same site in Veracruz, even though I'd known there wasn't much time left before they'd have to shut it down for safety reasons.

But things hadn't been going well between my parents. And when I got the scholarship, that changed for a little while. Dad was proud of me for the first time since I started middle school. So I went along with it, happily believing that everything was going to be better. If it meant Mom and Dad would stop fighting, anything would be worth it.

The fighting hadn't stopped for long.

"So, do you like the Academy? And your program?" Erick broke the silence again. I was so preoccupied with my thoughts, it took me a minute to come up with a response.

"Yeah, I guess. I mean, school is school, right? And I'll get a good job out of it, at least."

Erick signaled to merge onto the bridge fording Santos Creek. On the north side of the river, downtown bustled with its typical fervor. The neighborhoods across the bridge seemed dead in comparison, rows of tiny duplexes with minuscule yards and peeling siding. "Naturally," Erick said, keeping his eyes fixed on the road. "That's important. People would say it's wise of you to have such a mature idea about your future at your age." His voice sounded odd, and I glanced sideways at him. "I've heard a lot of good things about the Academy, the way it structures its emphases like a college major. Career preparation at the high school level, rather than post-secondary. It gives kids an extra edge, which we always need in this economy. Of course, I would argue that seventeen is kind of a young age to have your whole life written in stone. You never know what direction your interests are going to lead you in."

I rolled my eyes. "I've been hearing that all week—AresTec, GSAF, you name it. Guys in cravats and ties telling me to *follow my dreams*. Kind of a moot point, though, isn't it? It's not like I can change my scholarship."

"That's true. Well, it's all academic, regardless. I guess what I mean is... I hope you'll go into this survey with an open mind, Isaak. I know Andy was looking to give the three of you a punishment, but that's not really my style. I honestly don't see any harm in pursuing your natural-born curiosity. The whole reason we're out there in the first place is to learn. We want to know the whole story behind Mars' geologic history. I'm as eager to learn about the processes that created that arch as you are."

Somehow I doubted that, unless he'd somehow come across my dad's coin, too.

Gravel crunched beneath the tires as the truck turned onto my street. "Like I said earlier, geology and archaeology have a lot in common. So I'm hoping we can turn this whole situation into something fun. I know it's been a rough couple years for you."

I bristled. I was getting tired of hearing iterations of that sentence.

"But I have to say," Erick went on, "I think I understand why you jumped into that trench. You're a bright kid. You're curious. I know what that's like, especially when you're maybe in an environment that's not challenging you in the ways your mind craves." When I stared at him, dumbfounded, he chuckled. "You know, you kind of remind me of me when I was your age."

I didn't respond. I couldn't. The anger building in my chest was too intense. It choked the words right out of me. Who the hell did this guy think he was? To think he knew me, after just meeting me a couple of times? To think he had a right to that, just because he wanted in my mom's pants? And to say I was like *him*. I could tell right then and there that he and I were nothing alike.

He was wrong. He had no clue why I had jumped in that trench.

I kicked the passenger door open before he'd even finished pulling into the driveway. "See you on Saturday," he called as I stomped past the garage up to the front door and jammed my thumb onto the keypad. I could still feel his eyes on my back as I slammed the door behind me.

It was four o'clock. Mom and Celeste wouldn't be home for a couple more hours, at least. It was time to dig out that box.

CHAPTER 3

· ₒ ˳ • ◯ ⊘ ϕ ○

I SEARCHED HIGH AND LOW FOR THAT DAMNED THING. MY FIRST thought was that it would be in Mom's lab, the converted garden shed in our backyard where she worked on her smaller projects. But I checked every drawer and cupboard, every nook and cranny, and found nothing. It wasn't in the garage, either, or in the kitchen. I looked through her dresser drawers, the back corner of her closet, everything.

It occurred to me, as I slumped back on my heels after feeling around under her shoe rack, that she might have thrown the box away when she took all of Dad's clothes to the recycling center. The thought made me sick to my stomach.

I closed my eyes, trying to remember what the coin had looked like. I was sure the arch engraved on its face looked just like the one out at Erick's dig site, but my memory was fuzzy. There had been other things in the box that had held my attention more, things that were more definitely *Dad's*, like his spare e-cig atomizer and his great-uncle's wristwatch. And his wedding band.

That's what I'd been looking at when Mom caught me. I still remember the way her face hardened when she saw that ring there, in a box of junk he must have buried in the garden before

25

he took off. I still don't know why he'd left that stuff there. I guess maybe I'd hoped he was planning to come back for it. But when Mom saw that ring, I think she knew once and for all that he wasn't coming back.

Mom had taken the box and told me she wanted me to forget about it. Fat chance of that.

I sighed and opened my eyes. It must be long gone by now, buried in some landfill where I'd never find it. I was just starting to get back to my feet when my eye caught on the hatch to the crawlspace on the ceiling of the closet. We'd never stored anything up there, since it was loaded with insulation and Mom was worried Celeste or I would get sick. But I shoved the hatch open now and, stretching up on my tiptoes, reached my hand inside.

I felt around for a few seconds, encountering nothing but dust and bits of fiberglass. But then my fingers struck something hard and metal.

I pulled the object out. It was the box.

It looked like some kind of vintage lunch box you'd see in flix, with the remnants of a painted cartoon character on its lid. I didn't know how old it was, but I knew he'd brought it from Earth. The hinges were rusty, which made opening the lid difficult, but I finally managed to pry it open. There was all the junk I remembered, all the weirdly personal objects that seemed strange to leave behind. Little knick-knacks and trinkets, and a handful of memory cards and flash drives.

And amongst all of Dad's *Dad* things, shoved up in the corner, was the coin.

You could tell right away that it was ancient. It was made out of some kind of metal, but it was all corroded and discolored, kind of a greenish hue now. Its reverse was engraved with nine circles, each differently sized. The front face of the coin, meanwhile, had three marks along the upper rim, but they were too worn for me to make out. They didn't quite look like writing; more like pictures, or maybe symbols of some kind.

And beneath these markings was an engraving of an arch. It looked bigger than the one that I'd seen at the dig site—that one was only waist high, and the one depicted on the coin showed a figure standing beneath it, as if passing through a doorway—but the pattern of the flat-topped stones was identical, sort of an upside-down-V-shaped archway.

I hadn't thought much about the coin at the time Henry and I found the box. We'd come across it, buried in the garden, while we were supposed to be yanking up spider weeds to get the ground ready for Mom to plant the new experimental seeds she'd developed to grow during the long Martian autumn. It had been clear when we'd got the lid open that it was Dad's stuff, but there was so much else in the box that I hadn't dwelled on the coin too much. I guess I'd figured he had probably gotten it from one of his friends at the factory. You'd never believe the kind of weird junk they'd brought with them from Earth.

Maybe arches like this were common. Erick had said it was a natural formation—maybe there were some like it on Earth, too. Or maybe it was just a coincidence. But something felt really weird about this whole thing.

I hadn't heard the garage door go up, but the slam of the kitchen door was unmistakable. My little sister Celeste's voice echoed noisily down the hall. She was chattering at Mom about something they'd done at her after-school program.

Crap. I slid my palmtop out of my pocket to look at the time.

It was already after six. Quickly, I yanked the crawlspace hatch closed and rushed out of my mom's room.

The idea had been to sneak the box into my own room, but as I turned the corner, there was Mom standing in my doorway.

"Oh, Isaak, there you are," she said.

"Hey, Mom. How was your day?" My heart was pounding so loud that I was sure she'd be able to hear it, but she didn't seem to notice anything amiss.

"Just the usual. You know, boring lab stuff." She grinned and nudged me. "But how about you? What's this I hear about you volunteering at Erick's geological survey? That was unexpected!"

"Oh, yeah, well, you know." My fingers clenched around the box behind my back. I hoped it didn't look too obvious. "It was... fresher than I thought it would be."

"But that's wonderful! To see you taking an interest and engaging in something..." I thought for panicked a minute that she was going to hug me, and how exactly would I be able to conceal the box then? But she got this far-off look on her face and sort of turned, looking off into nowhere. "Ay, niño, I was really worried about you for a while there. Well, I suppose it's only natural, such big changes at such a young age—everyone needs time to cope..."

I tried to take advantage of her reverie to creep backward into my bedroom. I'd forgotten, of course, about Celeste. I hadn't even noticed her standing in her own doorway, watching Mom fawn over me with her ever-sticky fingers in her mouth, until I heard her say, "Zak, what's in the box?"

Dammitdammitdammitdammit

Mom's eyes flicked over to me and her smile faded. "Isaak, what are you hiding there?"

"Nothing."

"*Isaak.*"

Her face left no room for argument. I sighed and reluctantly produced the lunch box.

She frowned momentarily, as if trying to remember where she knew the thing from. Then realization dawned. "Isaak, where did you get that?"

I hate when adults do crap like that. "*Where did you get that?*" You torquing know where I got it from, you're the one who put it there. What you really want to know is, "*What were you doing in my closet? Besides invading my privacy and defying my orders, that is.*"

I sighed. Might as well come clean. "It's just, I saw something at Erick's dig site that reminded me of something I saw with Dad's stuff—"

As soon as the word "Dad" came out of my mouth, Mom blew her stack. "That's what all this is about?" I wouldn't say she *shouted*, but she wasn't exactly quiet. "Here I was thinking you were just expressing an interest—"

"Well, technically I am. I'm interested in knowing why, exactly, Dad had something in this box that looks like something from Erick's dig site."

"Like what, a piece of equipment? He probably stole it."

"Not equipment! It was... like... a thing they dug up. There was a picture of it. Sort of. In here." It sounded completely insane, once I said it aloud. What was I expecting, aliens?

"Isaak," Mom groaned, "you know that's not possible."

"No kidding! But that doesn't change the fact that—"

"I hid this box for a reason, Isaak. I saw the way that you were looking at it the last time you found it. Your father is gone. He hasn't even contacted you or Celeste once since he went back to Earth. The last thing I want is for you to spend your time chasing the shadow of a man who doesn't want anything to do with you."

Her words stung like a slap in the face. I knew they were true, but to hear them spoken aloud hurt in a way I wouldn't have expected.

"I'm not chasing anyone's shadow, Mom," I argued. "But I just... don't you think it was weird, how he just... *disappeared* like that? I mean, leaving is one thing, but to take off with no warning, not even bringing any of his stuff with him?"

"No, Isaak. I don't think it was weird. It happens every day. It's a coward's move." Mom's voice went from livid with anger to just hollow, almost dead. Maybe she wasn't as over it as I'd thought she was. "We all knew your father was on his way out. It was just a question of when."

My shoulders slumped. "Okay, but... why'd he bury the box? Why not take this stuff with him?"

"That, I don't know. But there's no point obsessing over it. Sometimes you need to know when to just let things go. Let this go, Isaak."

So I let the box go.

She took it but didn't go back in her bedroom with it. She would have to hide it somewhere new, now, to keep it away from me. Maybe this time she'd throw it away after all.

It didn't matter. I wouldn't look for it again. The coin was in my pocket.

Neither of us brought it up again, but an awkward silence hovered over us throughout dinner. I looked down at my plate the whole time and poked sullenly at my *calabacitas*, stirring the small squash and tomatoes together with the beans and rice until they formed a wholly unappetizing brown lump. Celeste chattered excitedly about what she'd done at school today, and how this friend and that friend weren't speaking to each other again, and on and on and on, while Mom's eyes bored into the top of my head. Eventually I dumped my half-eaten plate in the sink and wandered back into my room.

I had no homework, what with Career Week and everything, and for the first time in my life, I actually found myself wishing that I did. Then I'd have something to think about other than the fact that I'd alienated my two best friends, torqued off my mother, and gotten myself roped into Saturday school for the rest of the annum.

I put on my Speculus headset and browsed the internet for a while, looking for... I don't know. Something to show that I wasn't crazy. But I couldn't find any information about that coin of Dad's.

Next I tried searching for the arch. This is how I learned that corbeled vaults, as they are apparently called, are a dime a dozen. Practically every civilization on Earth had built something that looked like that. There was even a similar-looking one in Veracruz, where Abuelo's old summer site had been. I couldn't find any natural examples that looked like the same—most natural arches were worn out of solid rock, not stacked in a pattern like that—but I was starting to think that Erick was right. It was just a coincidence, the coin came from somewhere on Earth, and now I was stuck spending my weekends with my mom's new loser boyfriend digging up rocks.

Way to go, Isaak.

Notification bubbles from Henry urging me to go on chat kept popping up in my peripheral, but I flicked them away. I wasn't in the mood to talk to him and have to explain away my stupid behavior. Honestly, the person I wanted to talk to most was Abuelo, but it was 2:00 AM in Berkeley where he and my grandma lived, so I figured I'd better not. Finally I took the headset off altogether and wandered toward the kitchen in search of something to fill my growling stomach with.

As I turned the corner past my mom's room, I heard her say, "I'm just so worried about Isaak. He's been... *drifting* so much since Raymond left."

I froze in front of the closed door. A second later, I heard the response, much fainter and somewhat tinny. My mom was using the chat app on her deskpad. She'd never been much of a Speculus person; she always insisted VR gave her motion sickness.

"It's natural, Jess. You need to not push him so much."

I recognized my Tia Mayra's voice. Mayra wasn't my *real* aunt, but she was my mom's best friend, so that's what we'd always called her. She lived in California—apparently Mom had been less concerned about time zone differences than me.

"I know, but his grades at the Academy are slipping. I'm worried about his scholarship. If he loses that, I don't know what we're going to do. It's so much harder to get into a university here with a public school diploma, and without a degree, there's not a whole lot he could do here. Apart from the factories. I don't want that to be his only alternative."

"What about a school here on Earth? He'd be a third-generation student at Cal, that must count for something. If his grades aren't high enough, he could start at a community college and transfer."

Mom's voice shook a little when she answered her. "I thought about that, but I don't know if I could bear him going back to Earth. I already had to leave behind my parents and my friends when I came here. And then Raymond... you know. So to lose my son, too?" She sniffled. "But if he can't get his act together here, what choice do I have?"

My chest clenched. This was ridiculous. Everyone had been planning my life out for me when I was a straight-A student, and now here they were, doing it again when my grades slipped. Was I ever going to get to have any input on anything?

"Have faith in the kid, Jess," Tia Mayra said. "He's going through a lot of crap in his life. He still has another year of high school left. He's smart, and you said his grades in his language classes are fine. He's probably just bored with his G.E.s. Happens to the best of us."

"I know. You're right. Maybe I'm just stressed. My last round of crops didn't come out any better than the ones before, and there's pressure from GSAF..." She sighed. "I just... deep down, I worry. Isaak is so much like his father. I just pray he's not like him in the ways that count."

I couldn't listen to any more of this. All thoughts of snack food forgotten, I rushed through the kitchen and out the back door. I clumsily made my way across the small yard, taken up almost entirely by Celeste's playset and Mom's vegetable garden and orchard of fruit trees, and vaulted the waist-high fence. My mind was a blur as I stormed down the alley behind our house. I tried to keep it focused on the sound of the rolling waves in the bay, to let it drown out the echoes of the conversation I'd just overheard. The disappointment in my mother's voice. The crushing guilt that I'd been trying to avoid all day.

Why'd she have to compare me to Dad like that? I was nothing like him. For one thing, I'd never abandon her and Celeste the way he did.

But I was nothing like Erick Gomez, either. Why did all these adults keep trying to stick me into some kind of box, like they couldn't make sense of me without comparing me to someone else? Why couldn't they just let me be myself? Make my own choices, do what I want to do? Maybe my grades at the precious Academy wouldn't have dropped so much if everyone in my life wasn't hell-bent on giving me so much shit all the time!

My feet unconsciously led me down to the wharf that lined the water's edge. There were lots of people out tonight, couples on dates and families out to dinner. A large and noisy group of Earth tourists clamored past me to get down the stairs to the beach. They nearly collided with four girls coming up from the ferry docks, and I stepped back to give them some room. The tourists were chattering to themselves about wanting to catch a glimpse of "authentic" Martian life, rather than sticking to the more upscale and artificial areas the northern waterfront had to offer. I snorted. If they wanted to see the real Mars, they should take a tour of the factory district. That would dash their little sci-fi dreams in a nanosecond. The idea was almost funny enough to snap me out of my bad mood.

I was so preoccupied, I didn't even notice one of the girls detach herself from the group that had just come up the stairs. I nearly jumped out of my skin when Tamara clapped her hand down on my shoulder. "Isaak, what's the matter?" she asked. "You stomped right past me back there, you didn't even notice when I said 'hi.'"

"I'm sorry, Tam. Nothing's wrong, I was just... thinking."

Silence hung heavy between us, and I thought back to what had happened on the field trip this afternoon. One more thing I'd screwed up. More than anything, I just wanted to wake up and find that this day had never happened, that I could have a do-over.

"Look, Isaak," Tamara said. "I'm sorry about earlier."

I blinked. "Why are *you* sorry?"

"I was acting like a brat, not speaking to you after what happened with Mr. Johnson. I guess I really am a goody-two-shoes, like everyone says."

"You're not—" I started, but she held up a hand.

"No, seriously. It was lame of me. So can we just pretend it didn't happen? And you can just tell me what's wrong? Because, seriously, you're not fooling anyone. I can tell you're torqued. You've been acting weird all day, and I just..." She trailed off and shrugged. "I just want to help you."

The breeze off the bay picked up, biting at my face and playing at the wisps of hair around Tamara's face. A couple of meters away, the girls she'd been walking with—probably classmates from Herschel—were watching us pointedly. One of them tried to cover a giggle with her hand.

Awkwardly, I turned to face the water. The smaller of our two moons, Deimos, was setting in the west. It hovered over the bay like a bright star. The lights of the city glinted off the waves, vibrant dashes of white and gold.

"Okay," I said. "But it can wait, honestly. It's a long story. I'll tell you tomorrow before class or something."

Tamara rolled her eyes. "I don't think so. Where are you headed, the beach?" When I nodded, she said, "I'll go with you."

CHAPTER 4

· ○ ° • ○ ∅ φ ○

SOMETHING ABOUT ESCALANTE BAY HAD ALWAYS BEEN VERY calming to me. I loved the rhythmic motion of the rolling waves washing over the dull red sand on the beach. The wind was strong and fresh, its briny scent masking the memory of the acrid stench of factory smoke. Just being here by the bay made my problems seem to disappear.

Beside me, Tamara had yanked off her shoes and rolled her leggings halfway up her calves. She sat close enough to the shoreline that occasional waves lapped over the tips of her toes. Neither of us said a word, but Tamara hummed to herself, running her fingers across the sand beside her like she was playing a keyboard.

"Did I tell you that I got my first official gig?" she said suddenly.

"What? No! Where at?"

"Museum opening. That big building they've been building on Sparta Island, the one with all the columns in front. It's an art museum, but I heard they're opening with an archaeology exhibit—'classical art of the ancient world' or something." She grinned at my dumbstruck expression. "Up your alley, huh?"

I nodded, rubbing the back of my neck with my left hand. "You know it. But what about you? You're singing?"

"Yeah, they're having some kind of hoity-toity Grand Opening banquet for the board of trustees in June. Supposedly the Governor's going to be there. They want me to play and sing." She wiggled her fingers, miming the keyboard again. "I think they just invited me because of my parents. Mom is one of their donors."

"Come on. You know that had nothing to do with it. You're one of the most talented musicians in Tierra Nueva. How do you think you got into Herschel?"

She looked down, her long brown hair hiding her face, but I thought her ear looked sort of red. It was hard to tell in the near-darkness. "Well, I'd argue my moms again, but it's nice to have a vote of confidence. I hope I don't blow it."

"You won't. You'll be stellar, for sure."

Tamara's toes dug into the silty sand, so fine that it was more like dust, really. She kept her gaze fixed on her feet as she said, "Do you want to come? With me? To the opening? I mean, not just to hear me sing, there's the exhibit and stuff, too. They've got some Olmec artifacts, they might even have some of your grandpa's..."

My heart jumped. I could barely hear my own voice over its hammering. "Of course I'll come. Not... not just for the exhibit. For you." Oh, *Cristo*, did I really just say that? Could I be any more embarrassing?

But then she grinned at me, and I couldn't help but grin back.

Tamara leaned back on her hands. "So. What were you saying earlier? You thought you'd seen an arch like that before?"

I flushed. For a minute, I thought about just telling her to forget it—it was stupid and crazy. I knew that. But deep down, a little, tiny piece of me wanted to hear someone tell me that I wasn't crazy. That maybe my mom was the one who was wrong, and that there really was more to that box of Dad's than just a collection of Earth junk.

I shifted, digging down into my pocket to pull the coin out. "It's probably stupid, but I thought it looked like this."

I handed her the coin. She shifted onto her knees, holding the coin up to examine it in the glow of the fluorescent lamps on the wharf behind us. She squinted as she turned it over and back. "It does look the same. Look at the way the stones are stacked."

"Right?" Eagerly, I scooted closer. "I mean, it's probably just a coincidence, but still."

She'd flipped the coin over again and was frowning at the markings on the reverse. "Where did you find this, again?"

"Henry and I found a box of my dad's junk buried in the garden at the end of last summer."

"This was your dad's?"

"Yeah. Well, I think so. It was in this metal box that had a ton of other stuff that I know was his. I'd never seen it before, though. I figured he won it off one of his buddies at the factory or something."

Tamara hesitated. "Maybe. But..." She stretched out her hand, the reverse side of the coin facing me. "Look at that."

I peered at the nine engraved circles again. Looking more closely, I realized one of them was actually a star, not a circle. The other eight had oblong rings coming out of them, stretching around the coin. Eight circles, each of various sizes. The fourth from the center was a different color than the others. I took the coin back from Tamara and scraped my fingernail across it. It was tarnished, but it almost looked like gold.

I looked back up at Tamara. "The solar system?" I said.

"Right. And the central planet isn't Earth. That's Mars."

I flopped back down on the sand. The breath had left my body entirely. "Mars?!"

Tamara snorted. "What are you acting so shocked for? You're the one who thought it looked like the arch at Professor Gomez's site."

"Yeah, but... I thought I was crazy!"

"Congratulations, then—you're as sane as I am." She grinned like a Cheshire cat. Deimos winked over her shoulder, completing the effect.

The wind picked up, and a large wave gushed over the sand, soaking my shoes. The water was freezing, but I barely noticed.

Mars was a dead planet. There was no one here before us. Nothing but spider weeds, and weird little fish things, and underground germs. I knew that had to be true, because GSAF had done a study before they approved the planet for terraformation, to find out if the planet could sustain life or if there was anything here that could harm humans. I'd been hearing about it my whole life just from listening to Mom talk to herself while she worked. We all had to learn about this in sophomore biology class. Everyone knew this.

But what if they were wrong?

Santa torquing Maria.

Tamara got to her feet shakily, brushing the red sand off her leggings. She held out a hand to help me up, as I was none too sturdy myself.

"You know what, Isaak?" she said. "I don't think I'm going to mind missing my weekend classes at Herschel after all."

✦

"So that's why you didn't go on Speculus last night, huh?" Henry asked. We were standing on the platform of the South Gateway station, waiting for the 7:20 train that we took to the Academy every morning. Groups of factory workers and commuters shuffled around us, yawning and taking huge swigs from plastic travel mugs. One scraggly-looking old man was vaping by the trash can, even though there was a huge sign a meter away from him prohibiting both vaping and smoking on the platform.

"Pretty much. Sorry, man. Not that I didn't want to talk to you, but I kind of had too much on my mind to even think straight, let alone articulate."

"Understandable. So, did you kiss her?"

I choked on my own spit. "I'm sorry, *what?*" I managed between coughs.

Henry shook his head, his sleek black hair flipping back and forth dramatically. "Ta-ma-ra. Did you kiss her, you moron?"

"Of course not!"

He sighed. "I don't know what I'm going to do with you, Zak. If you don't get your act together, someone else is going to make a move on her, and you don't get to say I didn't warn you."

I spluttered indignantly. "I made a date with her, what more do you want? It's not exactly like I had a chance to get super romantic, considering the fact that the very fabric of our existence has been challenged."

"Blow it out of proportion, why don't we?" said Henry. "We haven't even seen much of that dig site, other than getting up close and personal with one hole—and GSAF's security system. We can freak out *after* we find the underground kingdom of the Little Green Men. Let me see that coin."

I'd already shown him once, but I dutifully produced the

tarnished coin from my pocket once more. Henry frowned down at it. "Yeah, I guess it does look like that arch. But they had vaults like this in India, too, I know that much. So it could be from Earth." He flipped it over to examine the solar system on the back. "This, on the other hand..."

"What's that you have there, boy?" a throaty voice interjected. I looked up with a start. The vaper had wandered over to us, and he was leering at Henry now over the top of his hawkish nose.

Henry, ever polite, replied, "None of your business." He accompanied this with a gesture.

"Don't get testy, now," the old man said, powering off his e-cig and buttoning it into his shirtfront pocket. His hair was white and unkempt, sticking out every which way in longish clumps like an even-crazier Albert Einstein. He wore a gray factory uniform like my dad's old one, with the name *Emil* stitched onto the lapel in cursive writing. "It's just that that looks like something of mine that went missing a few years back."

"Pretty sure it's not. Because we found it at *his* house."

Henry pointed, and the scruffy man whirled on me. He narrowed his eyes for a long moment, and then said, "Contreras."

The air left my lungs. "W-what?"

"You're Contreras' kid. You look just like him. Where's your daddy, boy?" He moved close enough that I could smell his breath, a sour combination of cheap apple e-cig flavoring and tooth decay.

"He's gone," I replied shakily. "He left Mars two annums ago."

"Don't answer him!" Henry interjected.

I turned to respond, but Emil beat me to it, snapping, "Keep out of this, Paki!"

Henry moved faster than my eyes could keep up. One second

he was standing on my left, the next he'd charged forward and his fist was sailing briskly toward the man's jaw. Emil must have expected this reaction, though, because he ducked with practiced skill. He had good reflexes for someone who appeared to be in his seventies.

I grabbed onto Henry and attempted to drag him off the man, but it was difficult to keep my grip on him. Even though I was taller, I was also pretty skinny. Henry, on the other hand, was built like a tank—sturdy and strong.

"Henry, you can't just beat up an old guy in the train station!" I shouted, pulling him back. "Do you want to get arrested?"

Henry replied by yelling something in Hindi at the top of his lungs. Mrs. Sandhu had definitely not taught me that phrase, but its meaning was pretty easy to figure out. The throngs of commuters had all turned their eyes on us, and a couple of men in business suits came rushing over, trying to help me break up the fight. Between the three of us, we managed to separate Henry and the factory worker.

"Take it back, you racist bastard," Henry snarled.

"I will not. You need to keep your nose where it belongs. My business is with the Contreras kid." Thrusting his jaw toward me, Emil hissed, "That coin of yours is stolen, boy. It belongs to me, and I want it back. And I want the key, too."

One of the business suit guys looked up from straightening his cravat. "Look, buddy, if you've got a problem with these kids, you need to take it up with ADOT security. You can't just go picking fights with teenagers on a train platform."

As they argued, I heard the telltale clacking of the train on its way down the tracks. "Come on," I said to Henry, and we hurried to the platform's edge. The train coasted to a stop and we rushed through the sliding doors. I could hear the business suit guys calling after us, saying that security was on its way, but I didn't want anything to do with that. I just wanted to get the heck out of there.

"What the actual..." Henry panted as we slumped into our seats.

"I have no clue. That guy was a fruitcake and a half."

"You shouldn't have told him anything about your dad."

"You're the one who told him we found the coin at my house!" I flopped back against the roughly upholstered seat, exasperated. "What was I supposed to do? He was all up in my face with his nasty-ass breath! And he knew my dad, *and* about the coin. He might have known where it came from. And what else was he on about? A key?"

"Gee, I dunno, do you want to go back and ask him?" Henry suggested snidely.

"Of course not. And I think we'd better find another train to take to school if that weirdo's going to be there every morning."

"No kidding. I just hope he doesn't know where you live, dude."

I hadn't thought of that. He obviously had known my dad, but I didn't know how well. The thought of Emil turning up on my doorstep was enough to give me nightmares for the rest of my life. I pulled up my palmtop's phone app just to make sure it had emergency services saved on speed dial.

This stupid coin was causing me nothing but trouble. Maybe my mom was right—I should have let the whole thing go. But it was too late now. I was in it up to my neck.

CHAPTER 5

· ₒ ° • ○ ∅ φ ○

POSSIBLY THE WORST PART OF THIS WHOLE WEEKEND detention thing, I decided as I rolled blearily out of bed Saturday morning, was losing my two days of sleeping in. It was obnoxiously unfair to have to get up at 6:00 AM seven days a week.

The valley was blanketed in a thick fog as I walked to the train station—I was going to the one on Port Street now, a full kilometer farther to walk, but hopefully one that would be free of Freaky Emil. Henry was waiting for me when I got there, wearing a green short-sleeved t-shirt with no jacket, even though it had to be close to freezing out. This one said *Freedom is life's great lie* in white text, and he'd crossed that phrase out with black Sharpie and written DISSENT in capital letters below it.

I didn't know why I was ever surprised by anything he did, at this point.

We caught Tamara up when we transferred to the high-speed maglev terminal on Sparta Island. The maglev had a direct line to Kimbal University, over in Curiosity Bay on the far side of the peninsula. It was kind of out of the way, but we didn't have a way to get to the dig site on our own, and since Erick's project was being run through Kimbal, there was a shuttle to take the college students out to the site every morning.

By the time we got to the Curiosity Bay station, the fog had mostly burned off. Erick had told us to meet at the bus stop just past the front gates of the school. A group of students clustered in front of a short, carved marble sign that read *Kimbal University and Institute of Science and Technology* in gold letters. Henry, Tamara and I awkwardly positioned ourselves a couple of meters away from them and waited for the shuttle to appear.

It didn't take long before one of the college kids meandered over to us, a tallish, relatively curvy Asian girl with black hair in a pixie cut. "Hey," she said, "are you guys here for Professor Gomez's survey?"

"Yup," I answered.

"Fresh! I was hoping we'd get some more people signing up. It's been getting really hard to manage all the digging with just the group we had." She thrust her hand out at whichever one of us would take it. The three of us stared for a moment before Tamara finally moved to shake her hand.

"I'm Scylla," the girl announced.

"Is that the name your mama gave you?" asked Henry.

Tamara jabbed him in the ribs with her left elbow, hard enough to make him flinch. The girl, on the other hand, seemed unfazed.

"Technically, it is. Priscilla. But I shortened it in high school, because, hello! Did you know there's a huge monster named Scylla in the Odyssey? She's got six arms and four eyes and she devours all the unwitting sailors that venture into her realm. And her best friend is a monster whirlpool. I mean, what's not to love there?"

Henry nodded agreeably, apparently deciding that Scylla had passed the test.

"So, are you guys freshmen? Do you know what you're majoring in yet?"

I looked from Tamara to Henry before finally saying, "Actually, we're high school students. We go to the Academy in Tierra Nueva."

Scylla grinned. "Fresh! I graduated from there last annum. Hey, hey, does Mr. Aguilar still do the announcements over the intercom every afternoon? Like, '*Haaaave a nice day!*'?" Her voice squeaked on the last word, in imitation of our vice-principal. Then she laughed, and, not waiting for an answer, chattered on, "Aw, I'm so glad you guys are here! I didn't know they were opening the dig up to high school students. I guess they couldn't find anyone else from Kimbal to volunteer? We really could use some more people. I wonder if they'll open it up to other schools. My sister goes to Central—"

"They're not here because they volunteered, Priscilla."

A blond guy standing with the rest of the Kimbal students had apparently been listening in on the conversation, and he took a couple of steps closer to us now. "I was working with Professor Gomez on Wednesday while he was giving their class some tour, and these three set the alarm off."

"Not on purpose!" I protested.

"Yeah, well you'd better be more careful from now on," he snipped. "The work we're doing out there is invaluable. If you damage anything, you're damaging the whole of Mars."

Henry scoffed. "Calm down, man. It's just some rocks. I'm pretty sure the planet won't explode if we accidentally drop one or something."

"You can't possibly comprehend the scientific significance of this—"

In what could only constitute as an act of God, the shuttle rolled into the parking lot and over to the bus stop just then, sparing us the rest of the blond guy's diatribe. He still spent the whole ride down to the site fuming and glaring at us, but at least he didn't talk to us again.

Scylla sat next to Tamara in the row ahead of me and Henry. "That was Grant," she explained in a low voice. With a complete disregard for all seatbelt laws, she had gotten up on her knees and turned entirely around, leaning on her elbows over the back of her seat. "One of Professor G's grad students. He's insufferable. No one can stand him. I don't even think Professor G likes him, and he likes everybody."

My nose wrinkled involuntarily. "So do you think Erick—uh, Professor Gomez—is a good teacher?"

"Oh, he's stellar! Everyone loves him. He's one of those laid-back professors that doesn't care if you eat in class and won't throw a fit if you have to leave to go to the bathroom or something. He's super nice."

"Right," I murmured.

Scylla kept chattering and swiveling around in her seat for the whole rest of the hour-long drive over to the dig site. I was already worn out by the time we finally got there and started unloading equipment from the back of the van, and it wasn't even noon. We still had a good six hours of hard labor in front of us.

The other students who had taken the shuttle with us already had assignments, and they quickly dispersed to their usual trenches, which left Henry, Tamara and I standing awkwardly next to the van, wondering where we should go. A power tool whirred noisily somewhere in the distance, making a grinding sound that echoed off the hills around us. I wasn't sure whether we should follow the sound or wait for someone to come get us. I was just contemplating getting back in the van and hiding out in there for the rest of the day when Erick bustled up, fiddling with something on his palmtop as he walked.

"Hello Isaak," he said. "Tamara, Henry. Glad you could make it. Since you're new to the project, I'm putting each of you with an experienced group, to show you the ropes."

Our first day on site, Erick spent most of the time showing us the ins and outs of the dig. Henry and Tamara both were assigned to Trench 21, one of the bigger pits the project had excavated out thus far. Even though one of the other professors was technically the supervisor in that area, it appeared that Grant had appointed himself the unofficial lead. I would have felt sorry for them, except I noticed that Erick had placed me in Trench 17, an area that he was supervising personally. Coincidentally, that would give us plenty of opportunity to get to know each other better. Perfect.

The good news was that Scylla was also working Trench 17. Her friendly exuberance was a bit intense, but it was far preferable to Grant's imperiousness.

The site was much busier than I'd expected it to be, based on how quiet things had been the day of our tour—although, that day had been a weekday, and most of the workers were students. The machinery sound turned out to be emanating from Trench 6, where they were using a massive rig to drill core samples.

"This will enable us to get a more generalized look at the changes in geological strata over time," Erick explained. "But we also want to get a more detailed, up-close look at what's going on out here, and that's where you all will come in. Trenches 17 and 21 are being excavated by hand, which lets us examine the different areas with a bit more finesse."

He gave each of us what he called an "Earth Science starter kit," which comprised of a rock hammer, a brush, a hand lens, a magnet, and, of course, gloves and safety goggles. Each of the trenches had been marked off with laser grids, and our job was to each take a square and dig it out, carefully documenting everything we came across. Erick had sent us a link to an app for our palmtops that would let us record every find and map its exact position with GPS targeting. The app even had a built-in compass and inclinometer that would let us determine every feature's angle and orientation. Every detail would be captured and preserved exactly, and all our data together could be downloaded to any computer later on for analysis.

By the time Erick was done showing us the ropes—and since just about every task at the site had ultra-rigorous protocol assigned to it, that took awhile—the rest of the team had stopped for lunch.

"Hey, partner," Scylla said, tossing me a water bottle from the plastic cooler. Then she pulled out a second and wiped it across her sweaty brow. "Ready to get your hands dirty?"

Surprisingly, I was. As much as I hated to admit it, seeing the trenches all gridded out actually made me excited. So many of the tools they were using out here were just like the ones Abuelo's team used on his digs. I used to visit him for a month every Earth-summer—which corresponded with summer here some annums, and winter others—when he'd go down to Veracruz to excavate. When I was really little, I used to come home and grid out the backyard with kitchen utensils and dental floss, since Abuelo had told me they used to use string before the laser grids got more common. Mom would protest that she'd never get any gardening done if I had the backyard roped off like a spiderweb, but she always played along with it.

I had given up on archaeology. I knew it was an unrealistic, implausible fantasy. I couldn't afford to chase down immaterial dreams when I had a solid future in front of me.

But as I sat there in that trench that day, my jeans caked in red mud and the sun beating down, with nothing but a trowel and the observations on my palmtop... for the first time, I *felt* like a real archaeologist. Sure, I wasn't uncovering lost civilizations or exploring ancient pyramids, but when I dug up that first little stone seashell—Erick said they'd found dozens on the site already, evidence of primitive aquatic life—I felt like I'd just uncovered King Tut's tomb.

So as much as it irked me to lose my weekends, and as crazy as Erick was driving me, I started thinking that day... maybe this project wouldn't be so bad, after all.

CHAPTER 6

· ₒ ° • ○ ∅ φ ○

OUR FIRST FEW WEEKENDS AT THE SITE WERE PRETTY STRAIGHTforward, just a whole lot of digging and recording. It got to the point where I could recognize the different colors of rock and soil, and had somewhat of an idea what they meant—some of them formed only in conditions where water had been present, others were evidence of volcanic activity, and so on. And I started to recognize the fossils, too. We dug up dozens of those little spiral seashells I found my first day on site, which Erick said were similar to the cephalopods that were common on prehistoric Earth. There were fossilized plants, too; not just spider weeds, but beautiful ferns with curled, wispy fronds. Every fossil we uncovered gave me a thrill of excitement as I'd imagine how ancient Mars must have looked, so different from the pseudo-Earth we'd terraformed it into.

Apart from the fossils, the things I dug up most frequently were shards of glass. It seemed like every day I was uncovering one of these broken, blue-tinted fragments. The first time I found one, I thrilled at the thought that we'd finally found a sign of, as Henry put it, my Little Green Men.

"Don't get excited, Isaak," Scylla said as I held it to the light. "There's glass like that all over the site. Professor G says it's tektite. That's natural glass that forms from the heat of a meteor impact. And there's probably a billion impact sites here. Mars was like a meteor magnet or something."

I frowned down at the smooth fragment in my hand. "Is tektite usually as clear as this? I always thought it was more like rock, or crystal. And look how flat it is. This looks man-made."

Scylla hesitated, then took the piece from me, running a gloved finger over it. "I dunno. I've never seen tektite in real life. But Professor G ought to know what he's talking about, right?" She tossed it back to me. "I mean, how else would this much glass have gotten here? We dig it up almost every day. It's not exactly like *Martians* could have put it there." She shrugged. "Maybe it's because the chemical makeup of the ground is different here than on Earth."

That same nagging feeling I'd felt the day of the field trip hovered in the back of my mind, but I have to admit, I got so wrapped up in the work itself that I soon forgot all about it. The only time the coin crossed my mind was when Tamara or Henry off-handedly mentioned it. The two of them were more diligent than I'd been in the search for any clues about the coin. Tamara had tried to grill Grant about the arch a few times, but he'd been dismissive. It wasn't important or interesting, as far as he was concerned. And after three weekends of digging up several pieces a day and nothing else of interest, even the glass started to seem commonplace to me.

The last weekend of May-II, I woke up to the sound of rain pelting my window. When I pulled the blinds up, I saw that this wasn't just a little spring shower; water was pouring down from the sky in buckets. Along the hedge, a gnarled black spider weed that had popped up during the week and had already grown a meter high—one of us needed to get out there and chop it down before it overtook the whole yard—was bent over sideways from the force of the wind.

I wondered if the dig would be canceled in weather like this. Part of me was hoping it would so I could go back to sleep, but a shockingly larger part of me was disappointed by the thought of missing a day on site.

What had I become? Seriously, I was losing it.

My palmtop buzzed at an incoming group text from Erick. *Storm's less severe in the hills than the valley. See you all at eleven!* He followed this with a dorky grinning emoji. I sighed and grabbed a pair of windbreaker pants from my gym bag.

I was heading out the door, rain slicker in hand, when my mom's voice stopped me. "Isaak, you're not planning on walking to the train station in this weather, are you?"

I found her in the kitchen, still in her pajamas, sipping coffee out of her favorite chipped mug. "Well, yeah," I said, "unless you want to lend me the car." Even though I didn't have a driver's license, anyone over the age of thirteen was allowed to ride by themselves in a self-driving car; it was just that Mom usually needed the car herself, to get to and from work, or to drive Celeste around.

She set her mug down and looked out the kitchen window. "I think I might. It's awfully stormy out there." But before I could get too excited about having the car on my own for once, she added, "I've been wanting to get out to see Erick's project for a while now. Today's as good a day as any."

"But it's raining out!" I protested. Although I have to admit, I was less concerned about my mom getting wet and more about her turning up on site at all. It was bad enough having Erick around all day when I was working. The last thing I needed was my torquing *mom* showing up, too.

"Exactly. You're going to get soaked enough working all day. You don't need to deal with walking and changing trains and waiting for the shuttle on top of it. Message Henry and Tamara and see if they'd like a ride, too. I'll drive you all straight to the site."

I tried arguing with her, but she wasn't having any of it. So an hour later, there we were—me, Mom, *and* Celeste—parked in the circular drive outside Tamara's house.

Tamara lived on the northwest side of town, not far from the Academy, in what bordered between a large house and a small mansion. Tamara always prided herself on not living in the sprawling "smart house" compounds some of our classmates lived in, but it still was a stark difference compared to my family's duplex, let alone the apartment Henry had grown up in. Tamara's moms were about as high up at AresTec as you could get, so they weren't exactly short of funds. They'd been with the company since its startup and had even worked at GalaX for some time on Earth before relocating here to Mars when Tamara was a baby. Bryn was now the chief marketing officer for AresTec, and Mama D—her name was actually Delia, but she always insisted that Tamara's friends call her by that nickname—was some kind of technical whiz, responsible for designing all their latest gadgets. She'd actually designed the A-Top 8, the newest model of AresTec's palmtop that most of the kids at the Academy were using now.

Coming here always served as a reminder that, no matter how close we were, Tamara and I really came from two totally different worlds.

As my mom's sedan rolled up the driveway, Tamara came dashing out, the hood of her jacket pulled tightly over her head. Mom had opted to sit in the back, next to Celeste in her carseat, which left the front for me and Tamara. "Thanks for the ride, Professor Garcia," Tamara said, slamming the passenger door.

"Hi, Tamara!" Celeste shouted, grinning her gap-toothed grin. "We're going to watch Isaak and Dr. Erick dig up rocks for science."

"Oh, do I not count?" Tamara teased.

"No! You count most of all. I was going to say you. How many rocks are you going to dig today?"

"At least a thousand." Tamara looked at me. "Where's Henry?"

"He's coming later. He had to go in to the Academy. Apparently, he got busted for more graffiti, so he's got Saturday detention."

She groaned and slapped her palm to her forehead. "I should have known. What are we going to do with him?"

"Don't ask me. I'm not his boss."

She rolled her eyes and looked out the window at the rain.

With the shorter travel time thanks to the car, we wound up getting to the site almost an hour before everyone else was scheduled to show up. It looked like Erick hadn't been there for long himself. He and Dr. Luna were still unloading equipment from the backs of their pickups as our car pulled up to the site. A light drizzle was falling, leaving tiny droplets on their rain slickers, but it was nowhere near the storm we'd had back in

Tierra Nueva.

"Now, this is a pleasant surprise," Erick said, opening the passenger door for Mom. She leaned over to start to unhook Celeste from her carseat, but my sister had already unbuckled the seatbelt and was shoving the lap bar off herself. Erick laughed as she scrambled out of the car and leapt into his arms.

"Well, I'm not on any deadlines right now, and it's such a lovely day for an outing," my mom teased. She gave him a quick peck on the lips.

It's not like they were full-on making out or anything, but my stomach still knotted at the sight of it. The easy affection between the two of them, the way my sister clung to Erick like a beloved relative. I felt like an outsider in my own family.

There was a gentle squeeze on my arm. Tamara smiled reassuringly up at me. Warmth spread from the spot her fingers had touched. I grinned back at her.

Erick put Celeste down, but she was still holding onto his hand as he turned to address me and Tamara. "Well, gang, there's still another hour before the shuttle gets here, but I don't know how long this weather is going to hold out. Do you want to start working early? Clara and I are working over in Trench 9. You're welcome to keep us company."

Tamara's elbow jabbed into my ribs. I nodded, a barely perceptible movement. Trench 9 was the pit that the arch was in. We hadn't been back to it since starting at the survey. This might be our chance. It was too bad Erick, Dr. Luna, *and* my mom and Celeste had to be in on it as well—it would be harder to move toward the arch unseen.

As we slipped and slid our way down the muddy slope, I

noticed the drone that had caught my first investigation of the arch was still buzzing around Trench 9.

"You keep that thing on even when you're working, Erick?" I asked.

"Oh, that one's not ours," Erick replied. "It's GSAF's. They have a few security cameras set up on some of the high-priority trenches at the site." When I looked at the drone again, I could see the words *Global Space and Astronautics Federation* painted on the side of its body.

Tamara perked up. "What makes Trench 9 a high-priority area, Dr. Gomez?"

He grinned at her. "Well, not the arch, even though I know the two of you love it. It's because of some other stuff we've found in this area. Every once in awhile we'll uncover fragments from old satellites or probes, mostly from NASA and the Soviet space program and such. Those are GSAF property, so we have to turn any we find over to them."

"GSAF is that interested in retrieving broken pieces of junk from abandoned missions?" I asked doubtfully.

Erick shrugged. "This is their land, Isaak. This whole mission is on their terms. If they want broken pieces of junk, that's what I'll give them." As he spoke, he fiddled with something on his palmtop. The laser grids in Trench 9 flickered, then powered on. "All right, if the two of you could work on this quadrant, please."

The area he'd marked off for us was further down the dried streambed, just about as far from the arch as we could get while still working in the same trench. I looked at the rock formation longingly.

There was nothing we could do about it, though. We'd have

to wait for Erick to get distracted before we could move closer. I slid on my goggles, pulled out my spade and started digging.

Two seconds later, Celeste was standing over my shoulder. "Zak, can I help you be a arky-ologist?"

I sighed. Had it really been necessary to bring her along? "I don't think so, twerp. This isn't a game. We have to be really careful."

"I can be careful!"

"Yeah, right. You can't even play with your Barbies without one of them winding up decapitated."

"That's not true!" She didn't even know what the word *decapitated* meant, but obviously my tone had gotten through, because her face was red with indignation now.

"You can help me, Celeste," interrupted Tamara. Celeste beamed and raced over to her like a puppy. "Here, can you hold my kit for me? Okay, so when I dig, I need to put the dirt from my shovel into this box. See? Then we bring it over there"—she pointed to a pile on the side of the trench—"for Dr. Erick to go through later. That's called *backdirt*. We have to go through it again, in case I missed anything when I was digging here. It's *really* important, so I need you to be careful when you carry this, okay?"

"Okay!" Though the bin was nowhere near full, Celeste eagerly picked it up and rushed over to the backdirt pile to dump it. She poured the soil in as delicately as if it were a pile of diamonds.

"You have a way with animals," I said.

"She's just a little girl, Isaak. You don't need to be so hard on her."

My face reddened, but I scoffed. "You're not the one who has to live with her. It gets old real fast."

The ground was soft and slick from the light rain. My spade cut through it like a knife through butter. I worked methodically, waiting for Erick to turn his back or move away or something, but he and Dr. Luna stood talking to Mom smack in the middle of the trench, blocking Tamara and me from the arch. There was no way either of us could move without him noticing.

About twenty minutes into digging, my tool struck something hard. A rock, or maybe another cephalopod fossil. I dutifully switched from shovel to brush, so as not to damage the object. It was a bit muckier than usual, with the ground being wet from the rain, but the ochre soil cleared relatively easily.

It wasn't a rock. It was something metallic. I gingerly pulled it from the ground and looked at it in bewilderment. The object almost looked like an earpod, but I didn't recognize the model. And it was old—*really* old. The metal had turned a sick, seafoam green, and the edges were rough and worn. The part that fit into the ear looked like it was made of some sort of synthetic material, which started crumbling into my gloved hand the longer I held it.

"Hey, Erick," I started to call, when an unfamiliar voice interrupted me.

"Well, son, what do you have there?"

I looked up. On the walkway above the trench, a middle-aged man in a black suit with a peacock-patterned cravat was peering down at me. Despite the gray day, he was wearing mirrored sunglasses.

"I'm not sure. It looks like an earpod. Erick?"

Erick lifted his head and saw the man in the suit standing

over us. "Joseph, what are you doing here? I didn't think GSAF had an inspection scheduled for a few weeks yet."

The man cautiously made his way down the slope. "I had the morning free and thought I'd drop by and see how things were going." He took off the mirrored sunglasses and shot a glance in my direction. His eyes were a very pale blue, almost like ice, and they pierced right through me. I shifted uneasily. Something about this guy made me feel almost guilty, even though I hadn't done anything. It was like he could read my mind, and knew I was up to something, somehow.

He turned crisply back to Erick. "It's a good thing I did, too. Looks like one of your diggers there found something of interest."

Erick moved over to me. I held the object in my gloved hand, but I was careful not to move; the location of the find still needed to be recorded. Erick looked down and frowned. "Yeah, I see that. All right, Isaak, we're going to have to turn the site over to Mr. Condor and his men now."

"What? Why?"

"It's GSAF property. Our contract agreement states that any non-natural finds that turn up have to be excavated by GSAF officials."

I was taken aback. I knew he said that any objects like this we found had to be *given* to GSAF, but I thought we would still be the ones to do the excavating. "We just... *leave*?" I sputtered. "I mean, how do you know they're not going to do anything to damage the site while we're gone?"

The man in the suit turned those freaky blue eyes back to me. His graying hair was thin and cut close to his scalp. "I'm sorry. I should have introduced myself properly. I'm Joseph Condor, GSAF Director of Land Use for Aeolis Province." He held his hand out for me to shake it. I stared at him, unsure how to respond; I still held the earpod-like object in my filthy, gloved right hand. Eventually Condor frowned and put his hand back in his pocket. "This land is unincorporated, and as such is GSAF property. That makes it our responsibility to administer. In a way, we could be asking, 'How do *we* know *you* won't do any damage to *our* site?'" He smiled, his lips thin. "But our partnership with Kimbal University is built on trust, er..."

He trailed off and looked at me expectantly. I replied, "Isaak."

"Yes, Isaak. So you see, it's important for all parties involved to cooperate."

I glanced over at Tamara, who still knelt in the mud a few meters away. Celeste stood behind her, holding Tamara's backdirt bin and looking nervous. It had to be bad news when even Celeste was put off by the guy.

"Okay. I understand," I said.

Erick turned to Dr. Luna. "Clara, put in a call to the other students that today's dig is canceled. Joseph, I'll have everyone else out of here in ten minutes."

Condor nodded amiably, his narrow lips still twisted up into a smile. I started gathering my tools and then stood up, trying to wipe the dirt off my knees but just smearing mud everywhere instead.

"I'm glad you're cooperating, Isaak," Condor said in a low voice, not turning to face me. "After what happened the first time you were here, GSAF was a little concerned about your continued presence on site."

I froze. This guy knew about what I'd done on the field trip? I suddenly remembered that Erick had said the security drone was manned by GSAF, not Kimbal. Had they been watching me, this whole time?

Maybe Condor showing up on site today hadn't been a coincidence after all.

He turned to clap a hand on my shoulder. "But if you continue to work with GSAF, I don't foresee a problem."

Then he strode away, following Erick and the others out of the trench. I realized that I was alone now, just meters from the arch; but the security drone still buzzed, watching my every movement with its unblinking camera.

I tossed my tools back into my digger's kit and left Trench 9 behind.

Chapter 7

· ∘ ° • ◯ ∅ φ ○

"THIS WHOLE THING STINKS WORSE THAN PAHARGANJ ON A Tuesday morning," Henry announced, propping his feet up on the velvet ottoman in front of him. "I mean, we're supposed to buy that they shut down the entire site for a broken piece of seventy-five-year-old junk?"

The two of us were in our custom guild hall on Speculus, our favorite hangout. Henry had designed it himself. Some of the decor was loot we'd picked up from the various games we'd played over the years, but most of it was hand-coded by Henry. Programming was second-nature to him—that was how he'd gotten his scholarship to the Academy, and why they kept him around despite his somewhat checkered disciplinary record. There wasn't a better coder on Mars than Henry, and everyone knew it. Our guild hall was a work of art. What with the VR headsets and our figuscan avatars, it was basically like being there in real life.

Well, except that Henry was wearing chainmail. Not that he wouldn't dress like that in real life given the opportunity, but I doubted his mom would let him out of the house if he tried.

I said, "Erick claims that it's because the pieces are the property of whatever Earth government launched the original satellite."

"Yeah, but who would want it? Space junk is a dime a dozen. Not to mention the fact that half the governments that sent probes and satellites to Mars don't exist anymore. So why is this stuff so sensitive that they have to kick all the trained excavators off-site to dig it out?"

I shrugged helplessly. "I don't know. The whole thing was completely bizarre. And the way that Joseph Condor just popped out of nowhere like a torquing spider weed or something..." I still felt anxious, remembering the way those piercing blue eyes had stared right through me. And had he really been watching me from the security camera? Or was I just jumping to conclusions?

"I'm telling you, Zak, they're up to something out there. The way those drones go over every two minutes? I never see that many drones in Tierra Nueva. Do you seriously think they'd be paying that much attention to some college teacher's boring little science project? GSAF is covering something up."

"Even if they are, though, what are we supposed to do about it?" I asked. "It's their land. Why is it any of our business what they're doing with it?" It was a stretch, but I needed to be sensible. The last thing I wanted was to end up like Henry, constantly looking over my shoulder or, worse, posting rambling manifestos on the internet.

"Because GSAF is supposed to represent *us*! Do you not listen to anything I've been saying all these years?" He stood up and started pacing, his chainmail clinking with each step. "Everyone on Earth is all patting themselves on the back for making such an egalitarian new world, where everyone's supposed to be equal, blah blah blah. Look at how pretty and diverse it is, people coming from all over Earth to live and work together. But who's in charge? That's right. White Europeans and Americans, as torquing always. Do we have any say in who our governors are, or what the laws are, or anything? No. All the decisions come wrapped in a nice little bow from GSAF headquarters on Earth, with a built-in police state to enforce it. Has Mars ever had an election? No. Are there any native-born Martians in the GSAF government? No. We don't even have a voice on the Council. If that's not the textbook definition of imperialism—"

"Henry, calm down!" I said. "We haven't even been here that long. It's not like torquing Columbus sailing in to enslave and pillage the Native Americans or something. Everybody who's here now *came* from Earth. GSAF represents all Earth nations equally. We're all in this together."

Henry whirled on me. "You know what, Isaak? I am so tired of you making excuses for them. Every time I try to talk to you about this, you always laugh at me or try to shut me up. Even now, when you and I both know something huge is going on out at that dig site. Or did you forget about that coin and your Little Green Men?"

My face colored. I hadn't forgotten it, exactly, but I'd gotten so wrapped up in the day-to-day dig activities. I guess I was having so much fun playing archaeologist, I stopped thinking about what we were supposed to be looking for in the first place. But no way was I going to admit that.

"Of course I didn't forget," I said. "Tamara and I were going to try to look at the arch earlier, before Condor showed up. I just—"

"If something on the level of *precolonial life on Mars* is going on at that dig site, we have a right to know about it," he interrupted. "This is *our* planet! What makes GSAF think that they have a right to access that information, but actual Martian scientists like Erick don't? Why are we okay with leaving it up to them and their Top Men to cover everything up and keep us in the dark? Not to mention that if they're doing that, what else are they up to that we don't know about?"

"Henry, you're being paranoid."

He balled his fists. "Why are you so eager to kiss GSAF's butts, anyway? What have they ever done for you? Apart from completely deprive you of your rights as a citizen?"

Joseph Condor's creepy eyes stared me down in my mind's eye. *"I'm glad you're cooperating,"* he'd said. *"GSAF was a little concerned about your continued presence on site. If you continue to work with GSAF, I don't foresee a problem."*

What has GSAF ever done for you?

"Um, well, for one thing, they employ my mother," I said, only half in response to Henry.

"I knew it." Henry jammed his hands into his pockets, but since the figuscan's chainmail design didn't include pockets, his hands just sort of disappeared at his sides. "You get a handout from them, so everything is hunky-dory. Typical."

"It's not a handout!" I jumped to my feet in protest, thoughts of Joseph Condor forgotten. "My mom is working her fingers to the bone to ensure that the people on Mars can even live here to begin with! Or do you not like eating? Because I'm pretty sure if you're eating, you've got my mom to thank for it."

"You know what, Zak?" Henry snapped. "I don't know why I'm even talking to you. Obviously you like living with your head buried in the sand. Or maybe you think that, since your mom works for GSAF, you're in a different boat than the rest of us. That it doesn't matter if GSAF keeps trampling all over us. But I have news for you. Guys like Joseph Condor don't care where your mom works, or the fact that she was born in California and not in some slum in Mexico City. You're just as brown as the rest of us, Isaak, and even if you lick their boots, it's not going to make you one of them."

My knuckles were white with fury. "Henry, what the *hell* are you talking about?"

He looked down, his mouth drawn in a thin line. "I'm talking about Tierra Nueva. I'm talking about people like my parents, slaving away day in and day out in a factory for the rich a-holes on Earth. My parents break their backs to line the pockets of someone who will never know them, but has no problem dictating their lives from a hundred million kilometers away. They have no voice, and if we let GSAF keep on the way they have been, they never will. We never will. Sure, maybe things aren't too bad right now. But you know the funny thing about power? Once someone has a little, they always want more. So if we don't raise our voices now, we might not have a chance later."

He glared at me. "And if you ask me? That's the real reason your dad left. Maybe that coin just proved it to him."

I barely noticed Henry's figure flicker and disappear as he signed off chat. I just stood there, fists clenched, shaking with anger. I'd always known Henry was a radical, but he'd crossed the line. He had no right to say those things about my mom, or about me. My mom had worked her butt off to get this job with GSAF. Space travel had been her dream growing up. Henry had no right to disparage her for taking a job that would give her that dream, and help millions of people in the process.

And Abuelo! Did Henry think he'd had it easy, coming to the United States when he was just five years old? Having to fight for citizenship? He'd told me time and again that deciphering the Cascajal Block had been *pan comido* compared to dealing with the US immigration board. My family had worked just as hard to get where they were as Henry's parents had. And we certainly hadn't taken handouts from anyone, regardless of what Henry seemed to think.

I wasn't trying to make excuses for GSAF—how could I, after this morning?—but what did he want me to do? Lead a damn revolution?

I didn't want to deal with any of this. I just wanted my life to go back to normal.

I pulled my headset off and flung it onto my bed with as much strength as I could muster. I stared at it, laying sideways on my crumpled covers, for a full minute. Then I turned to my nightstand and yanked open the drawer, where I'd hidden the coin after the incident at the train station.

But the coin wasn't there. In its place was a piece of yellowed paper. It looked like a page that had been ripped from an old book. Across the faded print of the original text, a message was scrawled in black marker. My blood ran cold as I read the messy handwriting.

"Thanks for the coin. I still want the key. You know where to find me. -E.H."

Chapter 8

· ○ ° • ○ ∅ ϕ ○

THE STORM HAD PASSED, BUT THE FOG WAS THICKER THAN USUAL the next morning as I stood alone on the train platform. The tracks seemed to disappear into a blanket of white on both sides. It was so cold that my breath came out in steamy puffs that merged into the swirling mist.

This early on a weekend, only a couple of other people waited alongside me. Henry was nowhere to be seen. I doubted he'd show up at the dig site, either. He'd be sulking. That was fine with me. If I saw his face again before next annum, it would be too soon.

I'd barely slept the night before. When I wasn't stewing over the argument with Henry, I was having anxiety attacks that crazy Emil was going to show up in my bedroom in the middle of the night, wielding an ax and demanding that I hand over the mysterious key. How was I supposed to give him something if I didn't even know what it was? Had my dad left a key in the lunch box? I didn't remember seeing one, but I couldn't exactly check, now that Mom had confiscated it. And how was I supposed to ask her for it? *"Hey, Mom, I know you told me to let it go, but I didn't, and now there's a serial killer after me. Help?"*

I was relieved when the train rumbled up to the platform, and even more so when I found no one waiting for me onboard. But I didn't relax entirely until I reached the Sparta Island stop and met Tamara at the maglev station.

"Where's Henry?" she asked, looking around. "Not detention again?"

"Who knows? He's probably out defacing GSAF headquarters or recording a new manifesto to stick up in his precious anarchist chatspace. Probably a better use of his time."

Tamara furrowed her brows, but didn't say anything.

Scylla was waiting for us when we pulled into the Curiosity Bay station. I could see her as the maglev slowed, perched atop the university's entrance sign, swinging her legs. She was wearing a neon-yellow t-shirt that said *Eat People, Not Animals* in black letters huge enough to be legible from the passenger window. She stared at the train with such intense ferocity that Tamara laughed out loud and waved, though Scylla couldn't have seen her through the reflective glass of the window.

As soon as she spotted us crossing the pedestrian bridge leading from the station to the school, she pounced.

"Where were you guys yesterday?" she demanded. "The rain scare you off? The dig actually did get canceled, but not until we were all already on the shuttle and halfway out to the crater."

"My mom gave us a ride straight out to the site," I explained, "so we were there when GSAF showed up."

"Really? Fresh." She looked between the two of us expectantly. "Well, give me the dirt!"

So Tamara and I told her what all had happened the day before. This time in the retelling, I found that my mind dwelled on the stranger details more than it had before I spoke to Henry. Especially how quickly Joseph Condor had appeared. Had he really planned to drop in on the site all along? Or was GSAF actually watching us?

Scylla nodded as we finished explaining. "Yeah, that's happened a few times just this semester."

"Does it make sense to you?" asked Tamara. "I mean, I get that if these things are GSAF property, we need to return them, but why are they shutting the entire site down for the whole day over pieces of scrap metal?"

"That's been bothering me, too," Scylla admitted. "You know, some of the things we've found... I've never really gotten a chance to get a good look at them, but they never really look like anything that would come off a satellite. They're just weird, random things, like coins and stuff."

I nearly choked. *"Coins?"*

"Yeah. I mean, not exactly, but the thing I dug up was flat and round like that. It was super corroded, though, so I couldn't really tell what it looked like. Joseph Condor snatched it right out of my hand before I could even blink." She swiped at me, her fingers curled like claws.

"The thing we found yesterday looked like an old earpod," Tamara said. "I mean, I suppose it could be an antenna, but..."

Scylla said, "You know, I've been thinking about what you said, Isaak. About the glass not looking like tektite. I looked it up online and you're right, natural tektite is all dark and rocky looking. I think something's going down. Do you think it's a GSAF coverup?"

I thought back to what Henry had said last night. On the one hand, it just seemed so crazy conspiracy-theory. But on the other...

"I don't know. But I think we should keep our eyes open."

When we got to the dig site, we split into our usual groups and started working. It was a bit surreal, to see how normal everyone else was acting when I felt so on edge. Between Joseph Condor, everything that Scylla had said, my fight with Henry, and then finding that Emil had been *inside my house* without any of us knowing, my skin felt prickly with nerves. Every sound made me jump. Every shadow that passed over my head was sure to be a GSAF drone, surveilling my every move.

Across the trench, Scylla smiled tensely at me. I wasn't the only one on edge.

The ground was soft from the rain the day before, but not overly muddy. We dug for over an hour, Scylla starting from one end of our gridded-off workspace and me from the other, working methodically across the area, gradually moving closer together. By noon, we were about a meter apart and caked in mud. She was close enough that, when her trowel hit something in the dirt, I heard its metallic thud, softly.

She stared down at it for a moment. Then she glanced over at me, expression urgent, and looked pointedly down toward the dirt-encrusted object beneath her fingertips.

"Did you find something, Scylla?" asked Gilbert, one of the TAs supervising in our trench.

"Not sure," she replied, her voice wobbling slightly. "I think it's just a big rock."

Gilbert pulled out his palmtop and took a couple of steps forward. Scylla's wide eyes shot over to me. Before I could react, though, a shriek rang out from Trench 21.

The three of us leapt, startled. The radio at Gilbert's hip

crackled to life. "Dr. Gomez," a staticky voice intoned, "we need you in Trench 21 right away. And we need to call GSAF out here ASAP."

Gilbert's eyebrows furrowed. "The hell?" he breathed, and moved away from us, gingerly climbing up the slick, muddy slope out of the trench.

Distantly, I heard someone crying in the next trench over. What in the world was going on?

"Isaak, quick," Scylla hissed, dragging my attention back to the matter at hand. "Help me get this out of the ground."

The object she'd uncovered was a flat, trapezoidal thing, about fifteen centimeters across and five centimeters thick. It was completely coated in red mud, but as she brushed at it with her fingers, I could see that beneath the dirt it was at least partially metallic, and covered in symbols and markings that were eerily similar to those on the missing coin.

"What do you think it is?" I whispered.

"I have no clue. But you know what? I'm sick of GSAF taking everything from us before we get a chance find out. I want to get a better look at this thing."

"How are we going to do that, exactly?" The rumbling sound of an approaching helicopter echoed off the hills around us. "That's probably GSAF now. You heard the guy on the walkie."

"We'll have to hide it," Scylla said matter-of-factly, thrusting the muddy object toward me.

I stared at her, dumbfounded. "How am I supposed to *hide* it?"

"Stick it under your shirt!" She had to shout, now, to be heard over the near-deafening sound of the looming chopper blades. I looked skyward. A black-and-white police helicopter was bearing down on us. They'd called the *police?*

"Hold on!" I yelled back. "The cops—"

Scylla rolled her eyes and, without a moment's hesitation, shoved her hand down her own t-shirt and tucked the filthy object into her bra. The cannibalistic urgings of her t-shirt stretched until the words were barely recognizable.

I looked down, my face red and hot with embarrassment. Her glare burned into the back of my head as she grumbled, "Good thing I've got plenty of storage in here for the girls, since *some* people are too chicken to do their part for the cause. I'll never complain about wearing a D-cup again."

Tamara burst over the side of the trench just then, sparing me from processing that completely unnecessary piece of information. "Guys," she yelled over the noise of the helicopter, which was touching down on the flat expanse that doubled as a parking area. "Get over here, quick. One of the people in my dig group, they found..." She swallowed, struggling to get the next words out. "I think they found a body."

Erick was standing in Trench 21, visibly pale, his fingers raking through that thick black hair as he looked down at the half-buried object at his feet. The dig site was total pandemonium, TAs and student diggers jabbering over each other incomprehensibly. Some people were crying, others dashing around in excitement, everyone overcome by the shocking nature of the find.

I only managed to get a brief look at it before the GSAF suits swept in and ushered us all away from the site. It was undeniably a human skull. There was no mistaking the dark holes of the eye sockets, the eerily toothy grin. The bone was discolored, cracked and red as the earth around it. It reminded me of the fossilized skulls I'd seen at the history museums Abuelo used to take me to when I'd visit him on Earth.

I wondered how long it had been buried here. And, more importantly, *why*. Why was there a human body buried out here, in the middle of nowhere?

The GSAF agents escorted all the undergrads, and me and Tamara, over to the parking area where the shuttle van was waiting for us. I was expecting them to interrogate us or something, but they were really adamant about getting the group of us off the site as quickly as possible.

"We'll contact each of you individually for questioning in the next few days," one of the agents explained, practically shoving me into the van. "Please make sure you have some time available when we contact you."

"What's going to happen to the dig site?" I heard Grant, standing across the parking lot, ask. He spoke in his typical demanding tone, but his quavering voice gave him away.

"That will be determined based on what our investigation turns up. But I wouldn't expect to be back here for the next several weeks."

Grant looked crestfallen. I tried not to betray anything with my expression, but I suddenly found myself glad that Scylla had shoved that thing down her shirt, after all.

Nobody talked much on the ride back over to Kimbal. Everyone who'd been working in Trench 21 was pretty shaken. The person who'd actually made the find had stayed behind so

GSAF could question them about the events of the find.

"Poor Schlessinger," a girl I didn't know murmured at one point, her face shiny from tears running down her cheeks. "They were so freaked out, and now they're stuck out there all alone with Joseph Condor and the cops. I mean, what the hell? Rocks and crap are one thing, but I never signed on to dig up a crime scene."

"I wonder who it was," the guy sitting next to her said. "It would have to be a missing person, right? Has anyone heard about anybody disappearing from Tierra Nueva the last few years?"

My heart shuddered to a stop in my chest. The chatter of my classmates faded, inaudible over the deafening roar in my ears. *Oh, God, what if it's...*

My throat tightened. I thought I might throw up.

"Isaak? Isaak, are you okay?" Slowly I became aware of Tamara's hand on my shoulder, peering into my face. Her expression was grim. "You don't think it's"—she swallowed, and added in a whisper, "your dad?"

"I don't know. Ayyyy," I groaned and shoved my face into my hands. I wanted a do-over. I wanted this day to go away. All this time I'd thought he just left, abandoned us. But none of us had heard from him at all in over two annums. I knew he and Mom had been having problems, and he'd talked so many times about leaving and going back to Earth, but what if he hadn't? What if he'd actually been killed?

What if Emil killed him?

And Emil had been *in* my house, where Mom and Celeste were right now. Who knew what he might do to them?

I needed to get home. Now.

"I have to call my mom," I said, pulling my palmtop out of my pocket. "I have to make sure she's okay."

On the other side of Tamara, Scylla frowned. "Dude, what are you talking about? Are you seriously saying you might know who that stiff out there is?"

"I don't know." I didn't want to believe it, but it seemed like my dad had some sort of weird connection to the dig site—the coin, the arch, crazy Emil and his cryptic warnings. And then his disappearance. It was all way too much.

My palmtop buzzed in my hand. A text from my mom. *Erick called me. Celeste and I are on our way over to Curiosity Bay right now. I'll meet you at the bus stop on campus.*

They were out of the house. They were safe.

I'd never been so relieved in my life.

Chapter 9

· ∘ ∘ • ○ ∅ ϕ ∘

"ZAK?" CELESTE ASKED IN AN UNCHARACTERISTICALLY SMALL VOICE. I looked up, blinking a few times as my eyes came back into focus. I'd been sitting on the worn, faux-leather armchair in the living room, staring intently at my feet, for over an hour.

Celeste stood before me, holding Mom's deskpad out and smiling hesitantly up at me. "I drew you this. To make you feel better."

On the deskpad's screen was your usual kindergarten masterpiece, a stick figure whose arms came out of their ears. But I recognized the characters as ones she'd drawn before—it was me and Abuelo, wearing matching *Indiana Jones*-style hats.

"You're in the pyramid," she explained. "You're going to find the mummy and the treasure, and then you'll be a famous arky-ologist, like Abuelo."

I smiled in spite of myself. "Thanks. That's pretty fresh. Can you send it to me? Remember how?"

She flashed her gap-tooth grin at me and nodded, running her fingers across the deskpad's screen. The doorbell rang just then, and I nearly jumped out of my skin. Who would it be? The cops, come to ask Mom to ID the body? Or crazy Emil, come to finish the job?

"It's Dr. Erick. I saw his blue truck out the window," said Celeste, her eyebrows drawn. I could tell my reaction had worried her. She didn't really understand what was going on, but Mom and I had been visibly upset all day, and it'd had an effect on her, too.

I never thought I'd find myself relieved to see Erick, but I was dying to know what had happened at the site after we'd left. I leapt to my feet and hurried into the entryway. The front door stood open, and Mom and Erick were embracing. I wasn't sure who was comforting whom, honestly. They both looked as shaken as I felt.

When Erick saw me standing there, he quickly dropped his arms from around Mom. "Hey, Isaak. What a day, right?"

I couldn't think of a sufficient response to that. I eventually just twitched up a corner of my mouth, noncommittally.

"Were the police able to figure anything out?" Mom asked, her hand on Erick's elbow. "I mean, about the *thing* you found? It wasn't..." She trailed off and looked over at Celeste, who was standing behind me, peering around my legs and solemnly watching everyone's reactions. "Isaak, maybe you and Celeste should go watch flix in my room or something."

"Mom, I'm not a kid!" I protested. "I was there, I deserve to know!"

"Isaak—"

"It's okay, Jesica. It wasn't him. Isaak can hear."

Mom folded her arms. "Fine. But I'm not putting a six-year-old through this. Celeste, *mija*, come on. You want to go play Speculus? Maybe watch Mickey?" She took my little sister's hand and led her into the master bedroom.

I awkwardly wandered into the kitchen, slumping down onto one of the chairs in the breakfast nook. Erick followed, helping himself to a mug from the dish drainer and pouring some coffee out of Mom's eternally-plugged-in coffee pot. He took a swig and grimaced. The thing had been on all day, so I was sure it was probably lukewarm and stale.

A moment later, Mom bustled into the kitchen. "All right. Spill. So you're saying the body was *not* Raymond?"

Erick shook his head. "Definitely not. It's not... well, fresh enough." I winced, and he glanced apologetically in my direction.

Mom sighed and leaned against the counter. "How long has it been out there, I wonder?"

"It's hard to say. I wasn't able to get a very good look at it before the police closed the site off. That skull was definitely old, though. It almost looked... fossilized. I'd have to actually study it to be sure, of course. But that's how it looked to me."

I sat up. "How could a *fossilized human skull* be buried out there? On *Mars*?"

"I don't know. This whole scenario is so bizarre. It could be that the illegal antiquities trade has gotten a foothold here. There has been quite an increase in the amount of"—Erick paused, trying to think of a tactful way to put it—"wealthier people here in the peninsula over the last several years. And that is your typical clientele for black market dealers."

"So you're saying that smugglers might be using the survey site to stash their goods between buys?" I wrinkled my nose. "But why? Not only is it really far from town, it's also an area that people are *digging* at, every single day. I mean, that's like asking to get caught!"

Erick nodded, gnawing his lip. "I can't say. Maybe the site was in use as a cache before we started the excavation, and that's just an item they missed when they cleared out." He shrugged. "It sounds far-fetched, but I can't think of a better explanation."

I looked down at the table and started scratching at one of the myriad dried coffee rings with my fingernail. There was one person who might know for sure, but I sure as hell didn't want to track him down to find out.

I just wondered how long it would be before he came looking for me.

After Erick left, Mom came and found me in my room, where I was lying flat on my back on the bed, staring intently up at the popcorn ceiling.

"Hey, *papi*," she said from the doorway. "How are you feeling?"

I shrugged and rolled onto my side, my back to the door. A few seconds later, her footsteps scuffed across the tile floor and the door closed behind her.

Softly, she said, "I know today must have been hard for you. It was even hard for me." She laughed half-heartedly. "And it got me thinking." The mattress shifted beneath her weight as she sat at the foot of the bed. She placed a warm hand on my ankle. "You know, not everybody copes with things the same way, or at the same rate. Maybe I was bitter, but I shouldn't have taken that out on you. I shouldn't have tried to control your feelings just because I thought I knew my own."

I turned slightly to look at her over my shoulder. Her eyes were red-rimmed like she'd been crying, but she smiled at me.

"I'm sorry, *mijo*. You have a right to process things your own way. And if this is going to help you..." She gestured to an object that she'd set on the chest at the foot of my bed—the dirt-encrusted lunch box. "It's not my place to take that away."

"Mom, I—" The words caught in my throat. I tried to swallow the lump down, but my voice still did not return.

"It's okay," she said. She stood up and moved to the head of the bed, brushing my hair off my forehead like she used to when I was little. "We'll get through this, I promise." She squeezed my hand and left the room.

After a minute, I sat up and pulled the lunch box over to myself. My fingers ran across the grungy lid, but I didn't move to unlatch the clasp. A few weeks ago, I would have been thrilled to have it, but now I was too scared to open it, terrified I'd find something else inside that would bring Emil back knocking on my door.

But then again, the key that he kept going on about might be inside. If I could find it and give it to him, maybe he'd finally leave me and my family alone.

Before I could open the lid, my palmtop buzzed in my pocket. I froze in horror. *Emil?*

Reluctantly I slid the palmtop out and looked at it. A text from Tamara. *How r u feeling?* she wrote. *Everything ok?*

Yeah. It wasn't dad, I texted back.

A buzz again, almost immediately. *Good. I need to show u something. Can u come over?*

My eyebrows furrowed. It was kind of a weird request; usually if we needed to talk "in person," we would just go on Speculus and save each other the trip across town. Before I could react, a second text came in. *Plz. It's important. We can't talk online.*

Realization dawned as I remembered the object Scylla had found during the dig today. All my fears about the identity of the skeleton had completely wiped it from my mind. Henry's constant rants about GSAF data tapping suddenly rang in my ears. Yeah, I definitely did not want to discuss removing a classified object from GSAF property on the internet.

Ok, I texted back, *I'll be right over.*

CHAPTER 10

· ∘ ∘ • ○ ∅ φ ○

MOM HADN'T MINDED WHEN I ASKED HER IF I COULD SKIP DINNER
to go over to Tamara's house, which was pretty impressive. *Cena*
was the most sacred meal of the day at our house—Mom always
was trying out new recipes with projects from her garden, and if
she was going to go to the trouble of making it, we were going to
go to the trouble of eating it—so I figured that she probably still
felt bad about today and was going easy on me. "Just make sure
you're home by nine," she said, which was an astounding lack of
instructions from her, especially on a school night.

I certainly wasn't going to complain. Especially not after the
day I'd had.

"Hey," Tamara said as she answered the door. "How are you
doing? Is everything... you know, okay?"

"Yeah, it's fine," I replied. My voice echoed off the high ceiling
of the entrance hall. A sleek black chandelier hung over my head,
its clear crystal globes reflecting pink from the sunset glinting
through the tall windows over the front door. "Erick said the
skeleton was too old to be a, um, recent murder victim. He
almost thought it looked fossilized, which is even crazier than the
other idea."

Tamara shut the door thoughtfully. "That whole torquing dig

site is crazy. That's why I called you over. Come here."

She bustled through the arched doorway on her left, leading into the living room. I followed her and stopped dead in my tracks. Henry was sitting on the white sofa next to Scylla, who held the mystery object from the dig in her lap.

"Oh, great. What are *you* doing here?" I grumbled.

"I called him," Tamara interrupted. "I wanted everyone in this together. It's more important than whatever stupid thing you're arguing about this week. Look."

She took the artifact from Scylla and thrust it into my hands. It looked like she and Scylla had cleaned it; it was corroded and full of dust in the crevices, but the markings were clearly visible now. It was a flat trapezoid-shaped object, made out of a material I didn't recognize. There were bits of metal attached, and what looked like hinges on all four sides. On one side there was an engraving of a corbeled arch, just like the one at Erick's dig site. The same unfamiliar symbols as on the coin formed a triangle around the arch. In the center of the trapezoid, inside the archway where the human figure had appeared on the coin, was a shallow indentation, a few centimeters around, and coated with a discolored metal casing.

"It looks like something would fit here," I said, running a thumb across the indentation.

Tamara nodded. "But look at this." She flipped the object over. Its reverse was covered with etched lines and circles. In the lower left corner of the trapezoid were three interwoven letters: DRT.

"A monogram?" I asked.

"Sort of. That's Mama's maker mark. She uses it on her

designs and stuff she makes with her 3-D printer."

"*What?*" The word came out like a hiss. Tamara's mom Delia was the lead hardware engineer at AresTec, but that company had only been around for a few annums. She'd worked at GalaX before that, but this thing looked older than Mama D herself. It looked... ancient.

I flipped the trapezoid back over, running my thumb over the green metal coating of the indentation once more. "Did you ask her about this?"

"She's not home yet," Tamara said. "She and Mom are at a fundraiser."

"Now do you believe me about something fishy going on at that dig site?" Henry asked.

I glared at him. "I never said I *didn't*," I snapped, "but that doesn't mean—"

"Yeah, can you guys figure this out later?" Scylla interrupted. "Because I'm more interested in figuring out what the heck is going on out in those hills. Let's rewind." She stood up and started pacing, counting on her fingers as she talked. "One, I've been digging out there for the whole semester. Lots of rocks, lots of little dead fish, lots of weird hunks of metal and glass that GSAF freaks out about and won't let us look at. Two, you guys show up on a field trip and immediately get in trouble because Zak here wants to get up close and personal with that rock formation in Trench 9, which Erick *claimed* was just some kind of river rock thing but is suddenly turning up all over, Three, mysterious relics from Atlantis or some garbage? That, Four, at least two of *your* parents are somehow coincidentally connected to?"

"I wouldn't say *Atlantis*," I said. It was the best I could come up with. A throbbing pain was forming just behind my right eye.

"Henry here would."

I gaped at Henry. "What? Henry, you've got to be kidding. Government conspiracies aren't good enough for you, now you need aliens and fictional ancient civilizations?"

Scylla rolled her eyes. "Zak, shut up. Hank, tell him."

Henry glowered at her. "Do *not* call me Hank." Then he shifted his glower to me. "Since it seemed like *you* had lost interest in the *whole reason we were out there to begin with*, I took to the 'net to try to figure out what the deal was with that coin of yours. Granted, I only had the low-res scan from Speculus, not the real deal, but I started asking about it in a few counter-institutional chatspaces. You'd be surprised the sort of connections people on there have."

Never put it past a conspiracy theorist, I thought, but I kept my mouth shut.

"Anyway, this morning I got a DM from a guy who said he's seen coins like that before turn up in private auctions. The one he saw most recently actually was apparently discovered in—you'll like this one, Isaak—Veracruz, Mexico."

"What?"

"Yup. But they're not specific to central America. Coins just like it have been found all over the damn world, and most of them have been uncovered near arches just like the one we saw out at Erick's dig site. That kind of arch has picked up a little nickname in the antiquities business—the Atlantean Arch. They call it that because it's a link between civilizations. Like they say Atlantis was supposed to be." He leaned forward, his elbows on his knees.

"Now, I'm willing to buy that sort of thing being a coincidence on Earth. But on *Mars*? So. You try telling me that there's not something weird going on here."

I sank down into an armchair. "What the *hell*?"

Henry smirked. "I thought as much. So, we've got the arch, the coin, and this." He gestured at the object in Tamara's hands. "Add it together with the fact that GSAF seems to be surveilling the site, and all signs point to a Class-A cover-up."

A cover-up that both my dad and Tamara's mom—two people I'd never even seen talk to each other—were somehow involved with. And where did Emil factor into this? It was all way too much to take in.

"My source said he can give us more information, but he wants to see your coin, Isaak," Henry said. He shifted on the couch, and gave me his best conciliatory expression. "Do you think you could go on Speculus with us after school tomorrow?"

My stomach lurched. "Um, about the coin. I don't... exactly... have it anymore."

"What?!"

All three of them stared at me in horror as I explained how it had disappeared from my nightstand drawer. How, somehow, the factory worker who'd attacked Henry on the train platform had found my house, broken in, and left me the threatening note.

Scylla jutted her lower lip out and sighed, blowing her choppy bangs off her forehead.

"Right, well, who even knows what the *key* is. So the coin's a dead end. And everything else we've found on site, GSAF has now. But, Tamara, what about this thing with your mom's mark on it?"

Tamara looked it over once more. "There's a 3-D scanner in her workshop. If whatever this is has been saved on her computer, scanning it should bring up the file on her deskpad." She glanced at me hesitantly, as if looking for reassurance.

I shrugged. "It's worth a try. I think we're in too deep to do nothing, now."

Over our heads, there was the slam of a door. "We're home," I heard Tamara's mom Bryn announce. "Tam?"

"Down in the basement," Tamara yelled back.

The basement doubled as Delia's workshop and her unofficial museum of technology. Collecting old tech had been Mama D's hobby for as long as I'd known her, and her collection was pretty impressive. Plexiglas cabinets lined the walls, their shelves laden with more electronics than I could count. It seemed like every time I came down here, there was something new—a lime green iMac, an Atari gaming system, a brick-sized cellular phone. Some were just for show, but a number of them still worked, and Delia had modded them herself to make them compatible with newer technology. The room was crowded and would probably look haphazardly cluttered to an outsider, but I'd been around Mama D long enough to know there was always a method to her madness. Each and every one of these gadgets had been cataloged in great detail, I was sure.

In the center of the workshop, the four of us sat on stools around Delia's workbench, which was piled high with a clutter of tools. There were wrenches, pliers and screwdrivers, blank motherboards, lidless Tupperware containers filled with pins and random pieces of metal, and countless other things I couldn't even guess at the function of.

On the far end of the table, a new-looking A-Top was hardwired into Delia's 3-D printer. Tamara was scrolling through this now, searching for any files that might be related to the artifact. We'd already tried scanning it, but there was no record of it in the device's memory.

I looked up at the thud of footsteps coming down into the shop. Mama D stood on the stairs with her hands on her hips, her frizzy red curls falling out of her messy bun in three different directions.

"Ah, sure look it!" she exclaimed, then turned to call up the stairs, "Bryn, she brought the whole school home with her again for dinner."

Tamara retorted, "Not the whole school, just the junior class."

"And a junior-plus-two-annums," Scylla added with a grin.

Bryn appeared behind Mama D. Even standing two steps above her wife didn't quite make her as tall as Delia, but what Bryn lacked in height she made up for in authority. Her shock of platinum blond hair stood in stark contrast to her tan skin—not to mention the black eyebrows over her dark eyes. She looked us all over, her mouth drawn in a mock frown. "I guess I'd better put the kettle on. I wasn't counting on quadruple the mouths to feed."

"Oh, don't bother—" I started, but she silenced me with an appraising glance.

"Isaak, did you have *cena* at home?"

I shook my head, and Bryn nodded. "I'll put the kettle on," she repeated. She disappeared back up the stairs, and Mama D hustled her way into the basement.

"All right, so who do we have here? I know this love already," she said, coming up behind Henry and propping her elbows on his shoulders, resting her chin on the top of his head as he squirmed, "and Isaak of course. But here's a new face!" She grinned at Scylla and stuck out her right hand, nails manicured in five different colors. "Nice to meet you, my dear. Delia Randall-Torres."

"Scylla Hwang. I'm a friend of Tamara's from the weekend project."

"Ah, a collegian! Lovely. So, what are you four up to down here, fiddling with my very expensive and highly off-limits equipment?"

Tamara slid off her stool and opened the lid of the 3-D scanner. "It's about something we found on the site today, Mama."

Delia frowned. "Are you supposed to be bringing those things home, Tam? I thought I read something on the permission slip that said everything on the site was GSAF property."

"I know, but I'm not so sure about this one." Tamara held out the object and pointed to the DRT maker mark in the corner.

Delia took the artifact and stared down at it, her eyebrows furrowed. "Now what in the bleeding..." She stormed over to the workbench, yanked open the rightmost drawer and pulled out a magnifying glass and a tool I didn't recognize. "Tamara, baby, hand me my glasses?"

After a few minutes' inspection, she looked up at the four of us. "You found this out in the hills?"

"Yeah."

She pursed her lips and scrunched her nose, thinking. "I have never seen this before. But I'm sure you've surmised by now that, yes, that is my maker mark. And that makes me very concerned that someone is either helping themselves to my equipment"— she looked back at the scanner, rubbing her neck—"or is trying to associate my name with something that I am not a part of. And I don't like either one of those scenarios."

"You're sure it's not something you made a long time ago and forgot about?" Scylla asked. "I mean, look how worn that thing is. It had to have been buried for a few years, at least. If not a few centuries," she added under her breath.

Mama D replied, "Definitely not. Every time I upgrade my devices, I change my maker mark so I can keep track of when something was made. See these curlicues here?" She pointed to the monogram in the trapezoid's corner. "I added those when I got this printer"—she pointed to a machine against the back wall—"about three months ago. So it would have to be newly made." She pulled the glasses off her nose and tucked an errant hair into her bun. "Though it sure doesn't look like it, does it? I suppose it could be a coincidence, but I don't like it."

She narrowed her eyes at the four of us. "Would you mind if I held on to this for a few days, so I could get a better look at it?"

We all looked at Scylla. She was the one who had found the object, so it was as close to being hers as anything else.

"That's fine," she said. "We need to make sure GSAF doesn't find out that we took it, though. After today—that is, we technically aren't supposed to take things off-site, like you said. It's just that there's been some kind of weird things turning up, and after Tamara saw that mark..." She omitted the part where we'd smuggled the object off-site *before* Tamara had seen the monogram, of course. But it wasn't necessary to tell the *whole* truth there.

"Right. Then we'd better make sure no one tells Bryn." Delia's voice was severe. "She's uptight around GSAF enough as it is, but with AresTec applying for a grant to expand into Tharsis Province, Bryn'd probably have an aneurysm if she heard about this."

"If I heard about what?" Bryn asked from the top of the stairs. My stomach jumped up into my throat, but Delia didn't miss a step. Before I could blink, the object was back in the scanner and the lid shut.

"That Tamara's planning on dropping out of school to join the circus," she said evenly.

"Yeah, sorry, Mom. I was going to tell you, but I was *waiting* until after my eighteenth birthday passed so you couldn't tell me *no*." She shot a very convincing glare at Mama D.

Bryn rolled her eyes. "Right. I'm not even going to ask. I've got chicken and rice going, for whoever wants it."

My stomach growled. We didn't get real meat very often at home—it was expensive and hard to come by on most of Mars. Most food we had, apart from the few crops that actually could grow here, came out of a can. I felt kind of bad; I didn't know what Mom had been planning on cooking for dinner, but it definitely wasn't chicken and rice.

"Actually, I probably ought to get going," Scylla said, getting to her feet. "I have to take the train back over to Curiosity Bay, and I don't want to wait until it's too late." She winked at me and Tamara and pulled a face when Mama D wasn't looking. Based on her t-shirt that morning, I assumed she wasn't as thrilled about the prospect of real chicken as me.

Henry stood up as well. "Yeah, I think I'd better go, too. I'm technically grounded this weekend, so I suppose I should get home before the 'rents find me out and flip their shit."

I stared incredulously at him. "Being grounded has never stopped you before."

"Yeah, well, I'm trying to turn over a new leaf."

He shuffled up the stairs after Scylla. I shook my head. Henry, turning over a new leaf? That would be the day. I wondered what he was really up to.

"Well, I hope you're not planning on sneaking out, too, Isaak," Mama D said, turning on me. "Bryn'll have a fit if she cooked a meal for no one."

"Oh, no. I'll stay," I assured her.

Tamara's nose crinkled as she smiled at me across the workbench. As always, that had the effect of tying my stomach into a square knot.

In my pocket, my palmtop buzzed. A text from Henry. *How much of a dumbass r u? Make ur move on Tamara, moron.* This was quickly followed with, *& sorry I was a dick last nite.*

The corners of my mouth twitched. This, I supposed, was the closest Henry could come to an apology. It was pretty noble of him to give up a chicken dinner to help me out, I gave him that. But how exactly was I supposed to "make my move" on Tamara, especially with her moms hovering over us? Henry had some unrealistic expectations there.

Still, his words from before echoed in my mind. "*If you don't get your act together, someone else is going to make a move on her, and you don't get to say I didn't warn you.*"

He was right. I frowned to myself. It always felt like I was making excuses when it came to Tamara. "The time isn't right, maybe another day." It wasn't like I didn't *want* to, you know, "get with her," romantically speaking. I'd liked her *that* way for over two annums—since around when I'd figured out that the way I *liked* people was different from the way others *liked* people.

But I'll admit it: I was scared, too. Tamara had been my best friend since we were, like, eight, when her family moved to Tierra Nueva and my mom met Bryn at a GSAF fundraiser. As much as being around her made my heart race, I also didn't want to ruin our friendship. What if she didn't like me the same way?

But if I didn't do anything, I'd never find out.

CHAPTER 11

· ○ ° • ○ ∅ φ ○

I TRIED TO FOCUS MY ATTENTION ON CHOPPING THE VEGETABLES for the salad, but it was practically impossible. I mean, Tamara was standing so close to me that her shoulder kept bumping mine while she mixed the salad dressing. So close that I could smell her hair—a mix of berries and something really pleasant I couldn't quite place, but that was distinct to Tamara's scent—over the tart vinaigrette.

It would have been wonderful had I not been freaking out inside about what to say to her. I shook my head, trying to focus instead on Mama D's voice as she chattered in the dining room.

"Come on, slowpoke," Tamara teased, sweeping the tomato and avocado bits off my cutting board into the salad bowl. "I don't know about you, but I'm starving."

I laughed my agreement, though at the moment my stomach was so nauseous that I probably couldn't eat if I tried. I wouldn't be half as anxious if it hadn't been for Henry's not-so-subtle hints. It was nervewracking enough to be alone in Tamara's presence while under the close surveillance of her mothers—whom under normal circumstances I loved, but come on, who wants to be watched when they are trying to make a move? Especially by the girl's *parents*?—but now I had the added pressure of knowing that if I *did* chicken out tonight, I would never hear the end of it.

Yup, this evening was going to be fun.

To my surprise, though, once I'd taken my seat at their large dining table—Tamara's family often had dinner parties, being with AresTec and having a musical prodigy and all—I found I was able to relax, really *relax*, for the first time all day. Mama D always had a way of lifting everyone's mood, making worries seem like they were light years away.

"So this fella at the luncheon today," she said, "he just *would not* take the hint. Bryn sidestepped him a couple of times, but he just kept going after her like a bulldog with a rawhide. Flirting, compliments, double entendre, the whole shebang. It was almost enough to make me jealous, 'cept I know my gal better than that."

Bryn's cheeks reddened, and she swatted at Delia with her napkin. Delia grinned, swatting her right back.

"So *then*," she went on, "she puts her left hand on her hip to show off her wedding ring. Like, she's trying to be nonchalant about it, but..." She gestured, sticking her elbow up at an unnatural angle in imitation of Bryn. "It was so ridiculous! I thought I was going to keel over laughing. And he still didn't get the message! So, finally, I came up to them to try to bail her out, and Bryn says real loudly, 'Oh, Mr. Jørgensen, I'd like you to meet *my* WIFE.' And he just looks from her to me and goes, 'Ah. Shall we make it a threesome, then?'"

Mama D's boisterous bellow of a laugh echoed off the high ceiling of the dining room. Bryn rolled her eyes. "Really, Delia, what kind of story was that for the dinner table?" Her voice was scolding, but her own laughter betrayed her.

Tamara caught my eye, our eyes locking for an intense second before hers crinkled with a grin and she dropped her gaze. After another second I lowered my eyes, too, and took another bite of chicken. I assume it was delicious, though I certainly couldn't taste it.

"So, Isaak. How has it been at the dig site?"

Bryn's question nearly made me choke on my rice. I shot Tamara a panicked look before clearing my throat, swallowing, and stammering, "Um... okay, y'know, good. Shells and fossilized teensy fish. Spider weeds. Dirt." I laughed, trying to come off nonchalant. "Pretty boring, unless you like that kind of thing." Well, I *did* like that kind of thing, but I wanted to get us off any line of discussion that might lead to the artifact currently residing in the basement.

"Tamara, sweetpea," Mama D interjected, leaning over to refill my still-mostly-full water glass, "have you told Isaak about the museum opening yet? Star of the show here."

Tamara ducked her head in embarrassment, her cheeks getting the faintest rosy tinge to them. "Mama, I'm not the *star* of anything." She glanced at me quickly, then dropped her gaze to her lap.

"She did tell me a little," I jumped in, eager for the change in subject. "Something about playing and singing at the opening?"

"Oh, more than that," Bryn said. "She wrote all the music for the performance."

I blinked and turned to Tamara. Her face was red as a tomato now. "Seriously? I didn't know that! Tamara, that's stellar!"

"It's no big deal. They're not very good."

I nudged her with my elbow. "Come on. You can't fool me.

I've heard you sing at church, remember."

Delia stood up, a devious glint in her eye. "I know, love. Why don't you play one of them for Isaak now?"

Tamara's head shot up, gaping at her mother in horror. "Oh, no, Mama—they're not ready—"

"Bollocks."

"I'd like to hear it, Tamara," I said earnestly. "I mean, I know I'll hear it next month, but... I'd like to hear it now, too." I could feel my own cheeks turning red, now.

She looked at me and smiled. "Okay, fine. Let's go." She stood and held her hand out to me. I grinned and took it, hoping she wouldn't notice my sweaty palms.

"The dinner was great, Bryn," I called over my shoulder. Mama D caught my eye as I rounded the corner, and I nearly stopped short. Did she—did she *wink* at me?

Oh, no torquing way. Not them, too.

Tamara let go of my hand when we got to the music room. My skin tingled where her fingers had been. In the center of the room was a big grand piano. She sat on the bench, and patted the spot beside her. "It's not, um, you know, done yet," she said. "I still have some work to do on the bridge."

"I'm sure it's stellar," I said.

She placed her fingers on the keys, then hesitated. She closed her eyes and took a deep breath. And then she began to play.

The melody was lilting and slow. For a minute, there was nothing but the piano chords, casting their spell as they echoed around the room. Tamara's long, brown hair fell in cascades over her shoulders as her hands danced effortlessly over the keys. I almost didn't notice when she began to sing, her voice blending seamlessly with that of the piano. The words were whimsical, a tale of a drowned blackbird and an Irish princess. I didn't really understand it much, but the melody made my arms prickle with gooseflesh.

Too soon, the song ended, the last notes hovering in the air around us like mist over the bay. She lifted her fingers from the keys and sighed. "So?" she asked, her eyebrows furrowing with worry. "What do you think?"

I swallowed. "Tamara," I finally managed, "that was incredible."

Her face got red again. "Really? You don't think it was too choppy in the middle or anything?"

"Of course not! How did you come up with all that stuff about the bird?"

She laughed. "It's from an old book of Gaelic poetry Mama's nan gave her. 'An Lon Dubh Baite.' It's not actually a real bird, though. The blackbird represents the lady's lover who died."

I colored. "Ah. I thought she seemed kind of upset over a bird. No wonder I'm flunking Earth Lit. Allegory goes right over my head."

Tamara laughed, tucking a strand of hair behind her ear.

"Seriously, though, Tam," I said. "That was really beautiful. Everyone at the museum is going to be blown away."

Tamara beamed for a moment, her face relaxing. Then she frowned and blew out a frustrated sigh. "I'm just not sure about the bridge still. Do you think it should be in this octave"—her fingers played out a short melody—"or this one?"

"Um," I began with a sheepish shrug. "They both sound good? Sorry, you know I'm not very musical."

Tamara giggled and shook her head. "But that's why I want your opinion. You're not going to get all technical on me like one of my teachers at Herschel would—it'll give me a fresh perspective if I use your ears to decide."

"Well, er—" I reached out my hand to the keys she had played before. "This one?" I tried to repeat what she'd done, but it came out like pots banging together or something. I cringed with embarrassment.

Tamara reached out her hand, but instead of stopping me like I thought she would, she placed it over mine. "Relax your fingers," she instructed, pressing gently on my digits. "Now, the fingering goes like this." Like a master puppeteer, she moved each of my fingers slowly over the keys to produce the melody.

After a few unsuccessful attempts, I finally managed to reproduce the tune, albeit clumsily. I grinned at her, and she beamed back. She was so close—this felt so natural. My nerves began to disappear. Maybe I could finally—

"Anyone want cookies?" Bryn called from the kitchen.

It's not like I *meant* to knock the vase over. It's just that one second I was sitting there—Tamara beside me, so close, her face just centimeters from mine—and the next minute Bryn was yelling about cookies, and I was leaping to my feet in a burst of adrenaline-fueled panic. I didn't even see the end table with the vase of lilies on it—*actual* lilies, not even fake ones!—until it was careening to the floor.

At least it didn't break. It was made out of brass or something, so all it did was make an ear-splitting crash as water and flower petals went all over the torquing place.

"Isaak, are you okay?" cried Tamara.

"I'm sorry, I'm sorry... I'll clean it up..."

Bryn hurried into the room, a handful of dish towels in hand. "Here, Isaak, let me get that."

"No, no, let me." I took a couple of towels and clumsily began to mop up the spilled water. "God, I'm such an idiot."

"It was an accident," Tamara said. "It's no big deal!"

I couldn't look at her. "I'll go get some more towels," I said.

Once in the kitchen, I slumped back against the countertop and hung my head in my hands. I couldn't believe how clumsy I'd been. Tamara must have thought I was a total spaz. How could I even *face* her now, let alone try to "make a move"? That settled it. I would go back in there, clean up, apologize to Tamara and Bryn, and go home.

I reached for the towel drawer and cursed as my palmtop buzzed in my pocket.

U'd better not chicken out, bro. Or we'll have to serve YOU for dinner next time. Henry's text was followed by a grinning devil emoji.

"You bastard," I muttered under my breath. Now I couldn't run away. He knew. He torquing *knew*. I took a deep breath, begging my stomach to stop feeling so shaky. It was time to man up.

I came back into the great room with an armful of towels, telling Bryn once again how sorry I was before I got on my knees to clean up my mess.

"Don't worry about it, Isaak," Bryn told me with a warm smile. "No harm done."

I looked around. "Where'd Tamara go?"

Bryn pointed over her shoulder as she took the vase out of

the room to refill it. The large French doors that led to the deck were open, the gauzy drapes blowing in the night breeze.

I groaned. Great. She was probably all torqued off at me for wrecking her music room. Not that I could blame her.

"Hey, Tamara," I said as I stepped out into the dimness. Tamara was leaning against the railing, looking out at the bay. I closed the doors firmly behind me. "Look, I'm really sorry."

Her shoulders shook, and for a moment I thought she was crying. Then she turned to me, and I saw her face was filled with mirth. "No, I'm sorry," she said between fits of laughter. "That was just too much. We never seem to have any luck, do we?"

"We really don't." I joined her beside the railing. The breeze from the bay was sharp on my face. Hopefully it would make my cheeks cool down. Hopefully.

She nudged her shoulder against mine and smiled before turning her gaze back to the bobbing sailboats across the water. "How did we get into this whole stupid mess?"

It took me a minute to realize that she was talking about *us* as in *the four of us*, not *us* as in *me and her*. *Together. As a couple.* I sighed. "It was my fault."

"No. It wasn't. Even if you hadn't found the arch, how long would it have been before that Emil guy recognized you at the train station? It's his fault, Isaak. Not yours."

My heart swelled. For a moment, I almost said it. It was at the tip of my tongue. *"Tamara, I lo—"*

"Can you believe that thing Scylla found, though?" Tamara blurted. "I mean, it looked just like the coin. That *can't* be a coincidence. Maybe I've been hanging around Henry too much, but I swear, there is something going on out there. And I think

GSAF knows it, and they're covering it up."

I sighed. What was that she said about the luck, again?

"Y'know," I muttered at last, looking up at the sky. Both Phobos and Deimos were out tonight, shining brightly in the vast darkness. What was out there? What *really*? The answer? "I hate to admit it, but I'm beginning to wonder. But how does your mom's mark fit into it? Could—could it really be smugglers, like Erick thinks?"

Tamara bit her lip, turning fully toward me, her shoulders bathed in moonlight. *Focus*, I thought.

"Like, someone is trying to copy her work?" she asked. "Maybe they think that if her name is on it, it will be worth more money."

"I wish I still had that coin. Now that Emil's got his creepy hands on it, we may never be able to figure out—" A thought struck me, and I froze. *Emil*. What if Emil tried to come after this thing? He was so desperate to find that key, whatever that was, so anything that resembled the coin may be something he'd want.

Cristo. Thinking about Emil coming after me, putting my mom and Celeste in danger, made me sick enough. Now this was in *Tamara's house*.

"Tamara, you have to let me take it."

"What?" Tamara stared at me, mouth agape. "Why?"

"Emil—you could be in danger," I hissed, raking my hand through my hair. "Emil is a total whack job, and now you've got that thing in your house. No way. No way am I putting you at risk."

Tamara reached for me, small hands gripping my wrists and

pulling them down before I could yank my hair out by the roots. "Isaak, listen to me. It's okay." When I shook my head, she went on, "He doesn't even *know* about the object, okay? It can't be that key he wants, because your dad had that, and this was out in the middle of a heavily guarded site, buried under three meters of sediment."

"Yeah, but, I mean—he came into my bedroom, without anyone knowing, and stole the coin. I assume he did it when none of us were home, but what would happen if he came face to face with someone? With *you*? You didn't see him, Tam. He's strong, and he's a psycho." I shook my head fervently, placing my hands on her elbows. "No. I will not let that happen."

"So, what? You're saying you're the only one allowed to deal with this? Isaak, we're all in this together." With that, she raised her hands to my arms and gave them a gentle squeeze. "You are worrying way too much, okay? I'm a big girl, I can take care of myself."

The breeze picked up just then, sending her long brown hair cascading across her face. She moved to brush it away, but I stopped her, lifting one hand from around her to carefully remove the soft strands from her eyes. In that moment, the light from the two moons bathing her face, the cool breeze from the bay billowing around us, and my hand resting on her cheek, I knew I'd found my chance. "Tamara, I..."

Tamara's cheeks, I swear, reddened under my touch. She turned her chin up, looking me square in the eye.

I sucked in a breath to work up my nerve, and leaned forward, my face centimeters from hers. I closed my eyes. There was no turning back now.

And then my palmtop rang at top volume.

Tamara leapt away at the sudden blare as if she'd been burned. I cursed violently. *If it's Henry, I swear...* Swiping my hand across the screen without looking at the caller ID, I snapped, "What?!"

"Isaak, it is now nine-thirty. If you are not home in fifteen minutes, you will be grounded for the rest of your life. Do you understand me?"

I held the palmtop away from my face and cringed. "Tamara, I'm sorry," I whispered over the top of my mother's tinny rantings. "I... I gotta go."

Tamara didn't look at me. She just nodded, staring silently down at the railing as the wind whipped her hair around. I sighed and turned away.

I really *didn't* have any luck, did I?

CHAPTER 12

· ∘ ∘ • ◯ ∅ ф ∘

MY EARS WERE RINGING AS I TRUDGED INTO MY BEDROOM. WHAT Mom had lacked in coherency by the time I got home, she made up for in volume. I'd tried to tell her that I'd lost track of time, but that wasn't good enough. I was grounded for the next week.

Whatever. As if it wasn't punishment enough to have blown it with Tamara *again*.

I frowned as I switched the light on. Dad's box was still sitting there on my nightstand, covered in dirt and rust. Well, if I was stuck here, I might as well make myself useful. Tamara may have been convinced that her house was safe from Emil, but I wouldn't rest easy until I was sure he was out of our hair for good. And the best way to do that was to find him that key.

I pulled the lid off the lunch box and began rummaging through the contents, removing everything one by one. The cap on one of the containers of e-cig fluid had loosened, and sticky liquid had leaked out of it, gumming up some of the objects beneath. I pulled out his atomizers, his ring, great-uncle Hugo's watch, long-stopped. There were no key cards or even any old-fashioned metal keys. As I dug deeper, I realized with alarm that there was nothing like what Emil might have been looking for.

At the bottom of the box was an old print magazine, folded in half to fit inside the small space. The *Sports Illustrated* swimsuit edition from 2039, when my dad was thirteen. The cover proudly proclaimed, "75th Anniversary Collector's Issue," over the top of a barely-clothed blonde. Real classy, Dad.

Its back cover ripped off as I pulled it out of the box—it was practically glued to the bottom thanks to the spilled flavoring fluid. The corners of the front cover were stuck together, but eventually I managed to pry them apart. I started to leaf through the magazine's sticky pages, figuring a key card might be stuck inside it somewhere.

But that's not what I found.

There was writing on every page, scrawled in black felt-tip marker over the top of every skimpy bikini. I swallowed hard. Some of it was written in Dad's handwriting. But other pages were written in the handwriting I recognized from the note: Emil's. It was difficult to make out the writing on many of the pages. Several were permanently plastered together with the spilled flavoring. On many of the pages that I could separate, the marker had smeared to oblivion. But the centerfold was still relatively intact. I unfolded it and turned it lengthwise.

Known Atlantean Arch Locations, it read across the top. This was underlined, and underneath was a tally of sites on Earth: *Santorini, Greece. Angkor, Cambodia. Orissa, India.* The list went on, taking up the length of the centerfold. And at the bottom, *Veracruz, Mexico.* That one was circled, and below it, in my father's handwriting: *Ask Hector.*

Abuelo, too? I folded the glossy paper back up and wiped my clammy hands on the sides of my pants. It was starting to feel like my whole torquing family was wrapped up in this. Who next,

Celeste?

I glanced at the clock on my palmtop. It was quarter to eleven. California was eight hours ahead of us. I didn't know how early Abuelo got up now that he was retired, but I couldn't go without answers any longer.

So at midnight, I put on my Speculus headset and called him.

While the call connected, Abuelo's chatspace loaded around me, a full 3-D scan of the jungle around Laguna de Los Cerros—an ancient Olmec city Abuelo had worked on when he was younger. He'd taken the scan himself, years ago, so the textures weren't quite as high-res as some of the newer chatspaces, but that added a rustic, old-school feel to it. Between the impossibly tall trees, Olmec colossal heads were strewn, some on their sides, all overgrown with thick tropical vegetation. Over my head, a bird squawked noisily, and I looked up, almost expecting to see it there in the trees. But, of course, it was just ambient sound.

"Isaak."

At the sound of my grandfather's voice, I turned. Abuelo stood behind me, in the same flannel shirt and worn blue jeans his figuscan avatar always wore. "It's good to see you, *mijo*," he said. His voice was rich and deep, with the faintest hint of an accent he'd never quite lost, even though he'd come to America as a small child. Hearing his voice was like coming home.

When he moved to embrace me, I felt the familiar pang in my heart that I did every time I saw him on Speculus. As great as VR is, it still wasn't the same as having him right here with me. I could *almost* feel the hug, but it wasn't really there. It was just in my mind. It lacked the weight of reality—the smell of spices that lingered around his clothes, the rumble of his voice in his chest, the heavy solidness that I always felt when I'd visit Earth with its stronger gravity.

"You're getting tall," remarked Abuelo. "It's been awhile since I've seen you. And what are you doing calling me at this time of night? It must be past midnight where you are. Don't you have school in the morning?"

I laughed. "Yeah, I know, I know. I just... you know, wanted to talk to you. You're right, it has been awhile. School has been hard this year."

"And you've got a lot going on now," Abuelo said, nodding. He moved over to one of the colossal heads and hefted himself up onto it, gesturing for me to sit beside him. "Your mom tells me that you've been following in my footsteps, working as an excavator on the weekends."

I grinned and scrambled to the top of the stone head. "Sort of. It's a geology dig, not archaeology."

"Still, it's excavation. Are you having as much fun as you used to when you'd come down here with me?"

"Not quite," I laughed. "But it is pretty fresh. Or it was, anyway. There's been some weird stuff going on recently."

Abuelo frowned. "'Weird'? How so?"

"I dunno. It's all really complicated. GSAF keeps butting in, and—" I broke off quickly. I wasn't sure if they really were monitoring me, but I didn't want to say anything, just in case.

Abuelo just chuckled. "The old wheels of government bureaucracy keep on turning, don't they? I guess red tape is a nightmare no matter which planet you're on."

"Yeah," I agreed hollowly. "Anyway, Abuelo, I wanted to ask you something. Did, um... did my dad ever talk to you about anything? Like, maybe a key of some sort?"

His face darkened at the mention of my dad. I knew my grandparents hated him even more than Mom did, but I needed to find out.

"Your father never talked to me about much of anything," Abuelo said. "Why would he tell me where he kept his keys?"

"Well, not his *keys* keys. I mean... a different sort of key."

"*Mijo*, what are you even talking about?"

A tension headache was building in my skull. I pressed the heels of my hand against my eyes to try and abate it. "Sorry, Abuelo. I know it's random. It's just that I found this box with some of my dad's stuff in it, and... it said something about you," I said.

His eyebrows furrowed. "About me?"

"Yeah. There was all this writing about these archaeological sites, and something called the Atlantean Arch. He'd written *Ask Hector* on it."

"Ah." Abuelo hopped down off the stone head, shoving his hands in the pockets of his jeans. "Yes, Raymond did contact me shortly before he left Mars. He'd gotten wrapped up in some conspiracy theory, another of his 'get rich quick' schemes, I assume. He didn't say anything about any keys, though. He wanted information about a man who'd taught at Berkeley when I was finishing my Ph.D. there. I couldn't really tell him much—the man was a physicist, so of course I'd never taken any classes with him. Different fields. I *had* heard his name, though, because he was working with the Ames Research Center on the biological survey of Mars precolonization, so it was all over the news. David Hassan, I think it was."

"My *dad* wanted to know about that?"

"Yes, I know. I was shocked as well. I'll tell you what I told him: I never met David Hassan. Not long after I started working at Berkeley, he was discredited and lost his job with the university. It was quite the scandal. He kept insisting that the findings GSAF released weren't consistent with his research about Mars' habitability."

"You mean, like, he thought it was dangerous to colonize? But terraformation went ahead. Everything seems to be fine here."

"No, that wasn't it. He claimed"—Abuelo laughed, shaking his head—"that he'd discovered evidence of sentient life on Mars, and that GSAF was trying to cover it up."

The skin on my forearms started to prickle. "Do you know what he found?"

"No, no. I don't buy into conspiracy theories, so I didn't pay it much attention. But the fringe picked up on it for sure. You know, those people who go on the TV and insist that all of Earth's major archaeological sites were built by aliens. I think that's when the Atlantean Arch theory started to go around." He eyed me. "Oh, come on, Isaak. I know you. You're smarter than that. You're not buying into all this nonsense, are you?"

"Of course not." I forced out a weak chuckle. "I was just curious what the note I found was about. I guess it was pretty stupid, huh?"

He put his hand on my shoulder. "*Mijo*, I know what you're thinking. It's only natural to wonder about your father. No one really quite gets over something like that." He smiled reassuringly, his salt-and-pepper mustache drawing up with the corners of his mouth. "You don't have to be embarrassed. You can talk to me as much as you like. I'm just sorry that I can't tell you anything more about it."

"It's all right, Abuelo," I said, forcing a smile in return. "You've told me more than enough."

An hour later, Henry and I were in our guild hall on Speculus, poring over the internet together, searching for anything we could find about this David Hassan. Apart from archived news articles, there were a ton of websites dedicated to him—most of them old, 2-D slabs that didn't translate over to VR very well—but none of them actually had any of his data. They were all conspiracy theory sites, most with subpages about Roswell, New Mexico, the Loch Ness monster and the pyramids at Giza. I found more information about "Atlantis" than about Hassan himself.

"I don't get it," I said, closing yet another window and turning to Henry. "All these sites, they just say that the Atlantean Arches are evidence of aliens. They only mention David Hassan briefly in passing, and there doesn't actually seem to be any connection between him and the arches themselves. It's all just about the existence of aliens as tangential proof for all their other conspiracies. So why did my dad ask Abuelo about *him*, and not about the arches in Veracruz or anything like that?"

Henry sighed, swiping through another mountain of text blearily. "Search me, dude. The most I can get is that this guy may have found evidence of precolonial life on Mars. But what sort of evidence? Like, the stuff at Erick's dig site? Or something else?"

I flopped back on the virtual sofa—a large, stuffed thing, complete with mastodon-tusk embellishments. "If only we could actually talk to this guy. We could ask him ourselves."

Henry stopped scrolling. "Do you think he's still alive?"

"I dunno. He'd probably be pushing a hundred if he was."

"Maybe not. The pics of him on the news articles made him look pretty young. Like maybe your grandpa's age now, or just a little older."

"But even if he is still alive," I said, "how are we supposed to track him down? I haven't seen any record of him at all after the 2040s. He could be anywhere, on either world." I glanced at the giant steampunk grandfather's clock against the masonry wall and groaned. "It's nearly two in the morning. We've got to be up for school in four hours."

"Fine. If you're tired, go to bed," Henry said.

"But what about you?"

"I just want to check this out. You go catch some Zs. Try not to have nightmares about royally screwing up with Tamara."

I paused, my hands halfway up to my headset. "Do you just get joy out of being a dick or something?"

Henry grinned. "You know it. After all, I passed on a real chicken dinner for you."

I scowled and pulled the headset off.

Chapter 13

· ∘ ∘ • ◯ ∅ ϕ ∘

I YAWNED AS I LOOKED OUT THE WINDOW FOR THE TENTH TIME in five minutes. Somehow I'd managed to get through all my classes without collapsing, but final period was Earth Literature, and that was enough to bore me to sleep even on my best days. Through the window, the sun glinted off the river that ran alongside the school, meandering out from the delta in Gale Valley toward Escalante Bay. In the distance, the snow-covered peak of Mount Sharp disappeared into the clouds.

And somewhere in between, GSAF had our dig site under lock and key. My fist clenched involuntarily.

A buzzing sensation in my back pocket brought me back to reality with a start. I threw a surreptitious glance up at the teacher, but her attention was fixed on dissecting the quote on the pyramidal display at the front of the room. Mrs. Cheng seemed to have enough enthusiasm about *Death of a Salesman* to make up for my own disinterest with plenty to spare.

I quickly pulled the palmtop out of my pocket and held it under my desk, shielded from view by my knee. It was a text from Henry. He hadn't been at the train station this morning. I figured he'd overslept, considering how late we'd stayed up. Of course, it wasn't out of the ordinary for Henry to just not show up for school, in general. He didn't seem to share my concern over losing our Academy scholarships.

I *found it*, the text read. No further elaboration.

I rolled my eyes. *What?* I texted back.

The reply was almost immediate. *D.H.'s address.* Below this were map coordinates. I stared at them a moment, my eyes bulging.

David Hassan lived here. In Tierra Nueva.

Before my brain could process this information, Mrs. Cheng cleared her throat and loudly said, "Isaak."

I jumped. "Yeah?"

She shook her head irritably. "The alert system. You're being paged."

I hadn't noticed the red banner at the top of my deskpad. Now it was flashing on the top of Mrs. Cheng's pyramidal display as well. I'd been called into the principal's office. Why were they calling me into the principal's office? I hadn't even *done* anything—today, anyway.

"We don't have all day," Mrs. Cheng said, her voice growing testy. Apparently she didn't appreciate her lecture on twentieth-century white guys and their midlife crises being interrupted.

Twenty pairs of eyes bored into me with great interest. "Right. Sorry," I said. I shoved my deskpad into my backpack and hurried out the classroom door, ignoring their stares.

Earth Lit was on the second floor of the comparatively small and plain liberal arts building. No part of the Academy was shabby by any means, but since most of the school's funding came from AresTec, the STEM department was the real hallmark of the school. Any building would look dowdy next to the chrome magnificence of Tyson Hall, with its six gleaming stories towering alongside the red bluffs.

The administrative offices were located on the ground floor of the building, while the classrooms and labs occupied the floors above. An anxious knot built in my stomach as I crossed the sky bridge and headed down the stairs, past the Foucault pendulum and into the lobby of the administration department.

The receptionist looked up as I came in. "Hi, Isaak," she said, her voice bored. I wasn't exactly a stranger to the principal's office these days. Too much time spent around Henry could do that to a person. "They're waiting for you in the boardroom down the hall."

I blinked at her. "Not Mr. Culver's office?"

She merely shrugged. I glanced down the hall. Like the rest of Tyson, the administrative offices had been specially tailored to fit the Academy's "image," that pseudo-sci-fi look that all the GalaX trustees on Earth seem to associate with Mars. The last door on the right was slightly ajar; I could just see a large rectangular table at its center, with curved chrome legs and a smooth black Plexiglas top.

I knocked on the door hesitantly. Mr. Culver yanked it out from under my knuckles, his teeth clenched in a smile that looked more like a grimace. "Ah, Isaak," he said. "Thank you for coming."

He seemed even more uptight than usual. I realized why as soon as he stepped away from the door, giving me a full view of the boardroom. Three men sat at the table—and the man in the middle was Joseph Condor.

"Hello, Isaak," he said. "Please, have a seat."

This is just about the skeleton, I told myself as I shuffled over to the black chair across from him and sat. Mr. Culver sat beside me, like an attorney in a crime flick. *They don't know about anything else.*

"So sorry to have to take you away from your studies, but GSAF matters do take some precedence," he said.

"Of course," I replied in what I hoped was a steady voice. "Is this about Saturday?"

"Indeed."

"Have you identified the body yet?"

Mr. Culver glanced over at me, startled. Apparently Joseph Condor hadn't filled him in on all the details.

Condor smiled and lifted his chin, assessing me. "I'm afraid that's classified information, for the time being. I'm sure you have many questions, but for the time being, we need you to focus on answers. Can you give me an account of your movements leading up to the discovery of the body?"

I breathed in slowly, tracing my finger across the Plexiglas and keeping my eyes focused on the movement. *Stay calm, Isaak.*

"Not a whole lot to say. I was in Trench 17, like usual. We were just doing our dig work when we heard someone scream. Then there was a call over the radio, our TA went over to check it out, and the cops showed up a few minutes later."

"That's all?"

I nodded. "Like I said, I wasn't in the trench where the discovery happened, so I don't know what all went down."

Condor glanced at one of his companions, who quickly made a few notes on his deskpad. It was one of the newer models, the folding kind. Mama D had helped AresTec develop the membrane used for the screen.

"And had you uncovered anything that day, before the discovery of the skeleton?"

I shrugged. "Nothing of interest. Some rocks, a few seashells. The usual."

Another note on the deskpad.

Condor clucked his tongue. "Isaak, the grad student assigned to your trench—I believe his name is..." He glanced over at the man on his left. The man made a few quick swipes across the deskpad.

"Gilbert Saldaña."

"That's right, Gilbert. Gilbert informed us that you and one of the college students—one Priscilla Hwang—appeared to have unearthed a metallic object of some sort, just before the call came in on the radio. But when we went through the catalog of the day's finds, there was no record of this. And we can find no sign of such an object at the site."

"A metallic object?" I furrowed my brows and looked up at the ceiling, as if trying to remember. "I don't think so, sir. We found a couple of big rocks that day, as usual. But nothing metal."

"Are you sure?"

"Of course," I said. "If we'd found anything, we would have called you. That's protocol, after all. And it's so important for us to *work with* GSAF."

If he caught my loaded tone, he didn't react to it. "All right, then, Isaak," Joseph Condor said smoothly. "Thank you for your time. We'll call on you again if we have any further questions."

My heart pounded as I moved toward the door, and I could only pray that Condor and his goons wouldn't hear it. It seemed impossible, but I was off the hook—for now.

Then, as the door swung shut behind me, I heard: "Send in Tamara Randall-Torres."

"Isaak? What are you doing out here?"

I'd been waiting on the sky bridge between Tamara's classroom and Tyson, hoping to intercept her. There was no point in going back to class now. I had to talk to Tamara before Joseph Condor did, and then I needed to go. I was sure my grounding sentence was going to get extended now—possibly for the rest of my life, this time—but there was no way around it.

"GSAF knows about the thing Scylla found," I said.

"*What*?"

"Yeah. Gilbert saw more than I thought he did. Condor's playing dumb, but he knows we've got it. And he must have figured out that you're involved, that's why he's calling you in now."

She squeezed her eyes shut and scowled. "Dammit."

"Tamara, you've got to let me take it," I said.

"No," said Tamara firmly, her hand on her hip.

"But if Condor figures out you've got it, you guys could be in huge trouble. Your moms could lose their jobs."

"What, and you *won't* be in trouble if they find it at your house?" Tamara argued. "Your mom depends on GSAF, too. Probably more than my moms do."

I sighed. "It won't be at my house. Henry's found someone—someone who doesn't like GSAF any more than we do. He can help." I paused, then added, "I think."

Tamara made a noise of exasperation and moved over to the window, looking out at the river below us, and, beyond, the bustling valley of Tierra Nueva. "I don't know if I would trust some guy Henry found on the internet."

"I—I don't. But at least it gives us a chance. And this guy

might be able to give us the answers, which is more than I can say for Joseph Condor."

She put her hand on the glass, not looking at me. Finally, she said, "Fine. There's a spare key card in my locker. Do you remember the combination?"

I took a deep breath and nodded. "Yeah. I'll go get it now. Don't let a word out to Joseph Condor."

"Of course," she said. I started to turn away, but abruptly she moved forward and clamped a hand down on my shoulder. "Isaak... be careful, okay?"

"I will," I said.

She stared at me for a moment. Then she put her hand on my cheek, guiding my face down toward hers, and kissed me gently.

My heart about stopped.

Before my brain could even process what had happened, she pulled away, her face bright red. "I'm tired of always getting interrupted," she said.

I grinned, and she smiled back. Then she hurried across the bridge and through the doors into Tyson.

The sun was setting as I approached the rundown apartment building in South Tierra Nueva. Unbelievably, David Hassan lived not far from Henry's own apartment. All this time, the answers had been just a few blocks away.

Hassan had to have the answers. If he didn't, we were all completely screwed.

Scylla's artifact was tucked safely in my backpack, wrapped in my sweatshirt for protection. Delia had hidden it in the bottom of one of her workshop drawers—it had taken me a panic-stricken half hour to find it. I just hoped she wouldn't be too torqued at me for taking it. But it was way too dangerous for them to have it at their house right now.

According to Henry's directions, David Hassan's apartment was on the third floor. There was no outside access apart from the fire escape, but there was no doorman, either. I managed to sneak in unnoticed, apart from a haggard-looking woman and her three kids I passed on the staircase. The mom was too preoccupied with her armful of grocery bags to pay me any attention, and the two older kids were chattering loudly in Spanish about something that had happened at school that day, so they didn't even glance in my direction. Just the youngest child stared up at me with wide, dark eyes, clinging to his mom's shirttail as they passed through the door to the second floor. I smiled lopsidedly at him and kept on climbing.

Apartment 3-F had a door that appeared to have once been white but had faded to a dingy gray. Dark smudges clustered around the doorknob, and the knocker was smeared with fingerprints. I swallowed hard as I reached to lift it. What was I supposed to say to this guy? How was I going to introduce myself without coming off like a nutcase?

I pounded the knocker three times.

A few seconds later, the door opened, its hinges squealing. I stared, mouth agape, at the man who stood before me, with his haphazard shock of white hair and deeply lined face. He grinned when he saw me, brushing ink-stained hands on his pants.

"Ah, Contreras," he chuckled. "It's about time you turned up here."

It was Emil.

CHAPTER 14

·₀°•○∅ϕ○

"SO, THEN, YOU'VE FOUND IT? THE KEY YOUR FATHER STOLE?" Emil's voice was eager. That sour e-cig stench wafted out on his breath, contaminating the already stale air of the hallway.

"I didn't find anything. I wasn't looking for you," I hissed. I started to back away, looking over my shoulder for help, but the hallway was deserted. "What did you do with David Hassan?"

Emil cackled, his laughter turning into a wheeze. "I didn't *do* anything with him. I am David Hassan."

I froze, looking back at him. "What?"

"Of course, I haven't gone by that name for decades. Too much baggage associated with it. Emil was my father's name. I figured he wouldn't mind if I borrowed it, being dead and all."

"I—but—how?"

Emil rolled his eyes. "For God's sake, don't just stand there yammering. Get in here. You never know who's listening out there. And if you're looking for *David* Hassan, my guess is you want to talk about something we probably don't want GSAF overhearing."

I nodded mutely, clutching my backpack straps as Emil guided me forcefully into his apartment. He slammed the door and locked the deadbolt behind him. I shot a glance over at the fire escape. I wanted to be able to get away quickly if I needed to.

Emil sat at a small folding table in the kitchen and gestured for me to sit across from him. "All right, then," he said after I finally lowered myself into the chair. "If you didn't bring me the key, then what do you want? And stop looking over your shoulder like that. I'm not going to eat you."

I crossed my arms. "Answers would be nice. You keep demanding this key from me, but I don't have any clue what it is, what it looks like, or where to find it. You say you knew my dad, but I've never heard of you. I haven't even seen or heard from my dad in over two annums. No one even knows where he is. So why should I trust you? How do I know you didn't kill him yourself?"

Emil frowned, running a calloused thumb over his chin. "Why did you think *David* Hassan would be able to help you find those answers?" he asked.

"Answer my questions first," I said.

"Fine." He sighed. "I take it, since you know my real name, you've heard of my work with GSAF."

"Not really. I only just found it last night on an alien conspiracy website. They didn't have a whole lot of information, though."

He snorted. "Why am I not surprised? The only people who will give you a straight answer these days are wingnuts."

That was pretty rich, coming from a wingnut himself. I kept that opinion to myself, though. "So, what happened?" I prodded. "With GSAF?"

"I worked," he said, "for NASA. Back in ye olden days, before they got folded into GSAF. I was responsible for analyzing data and images sent back from their Lewis and Clark mission, one of the last rovers that was sent precolonization, to test for inhabitability. And I found evidence that indicated that not only had Mars been inhabited by lifeforms before, but that some of these lifeforms had been sentient. Intelligent. Possibly human."

I sat up in my chair. "What sort of evidence?"

Emil narrowed his eyes at me. "I think you know what sort, boy. I've been watching you. I know you've found stuff out there in the hills."

The room suddenly felt very cold. I couldn't exactly put my sweatshirt on, though, without him seeing Scylla's artifact, so I just rubbed my hands over the long sleeves of my t-shirt.

"Why did GSAF deny your findings, though?"

He snorted again. "There was a lot of money tied up in colonization. The environmental lobbies were putting pressure on Earth's governments to decrease carbon emissions. When the big manufacturers found out that they could outsource their operations to another planet, and get a tax credit to boot? It was a land rush. There wasn't time to postpone colonization to conduct full-scale research. So my findings were discredited, kept under wraps. Swept under the carpet until everyone forgot about them."

"But... but what about your peers?" I spluttered. "I mean, the other scientists that saw Lewis and Clark's data—they would have backed you up, wouldn't they?"

"A few of them did, and lost their jobs as well. The rest of them kept quiet. Economic times were tough, kid. Sometimes it was smarter to sit down and shut up so you could keep putting bread on the table."

I slumped back in my chair. Un-torquing-believable. It

seemed ridiculous, but everything I'd seen over the last two months seemed to match up. I could feel another tension headache pulsating behind my eyes.

"So what are you doing here now? And where does my dad come into it?" I asked.

Emil stood, walking over to the kitchen counter and picking up an e-cig. "Well, I sure as hell wasn't going to give up on the find of a millennium. I changed my name, and as soon as I could get a visa to come over here and work, I took it. I've worked at a dozen different factories since I've been here, a good twenty years. Salt mines by day, excavation in the hills by night. I met Raymond Contreras at the shoe plant about five annums ago. I don't remember how it came up, but he mentioned that his father-in-law was Hector Garcia." He blew white vapor out between his teeth and sighed. "There's a name with some clout attached to it. I thought he could help me, being an archaeologist and all. Maybe he'd co-author a paper with me, help me release my findings, get my reputation in the scientific community back. I didn't realize Raymond was such a dumbass—no offense—or that he and his in-laws weren't exactly speaking."

I leaned on my elbows, looking down at the scuffed surface of the table. "So you guys were excavating in secret?"

He nodded.

I glanced up at him. "What did you find?"

He flashed a yellow-toothed grin at me. "Now there's the question."

He turned off the e-cig and moved into the living room. A tall bookcase was lined with cheap paperbacks. He pulled a couple off the shelves and dumped them on the table in front of me.

"Have a look through those," he said.

I cocked an eyebrow at him, then flipped open the tawdry-looking romance on the top of the stack. The contents were not, in fact, *The Taming of the Duke*. Like the *Sports Illustrated* in my dad's box, every page was covered over with writing in felt-tip marker. Detailed diagrams of dig sites, intricate sketches of broken fragments not unlike the items Joseph Condor would close our dig site for—everything recorded in minute detail.

"Record-keeping by paper," he said. "Slow and old-fashioned, but the ideal choice when you're trying to stay off the grid. I couldn't have GSAF finding out what I've been up to."

I looked up at him in amazement. "Abuelo said you weren't an archaeologist."

He chuckled. "I wasn't. I had a midlife career switch, if you will. All self-taught."

"This data is amazing, though," I breathed. Just as thorough as Abuelo's own record-keeping. He would be impressed.

I flipped through another book as Emil looked on proudly. "And here I thought you were crazy," I said.

"Maybe this will teach you not to throw words like that around."

I colored, but nodded. He was right. Though Abuelo had always said there was a fine line between *crazy* and *genius*.

When I was done looking through the second book, I said, "So where does the coin fit into this? And the key? What is the key, anyway?"

Emil moved back over to the bookcase. "The coin and the key are, I believe, the answer to all of this." He brought another paperback over. This one wasn't a romance. It was an old sci-fi by

Robert Heinlein—*Podkayne of Mars*. He opened this and flipped forward several pages to a drawing of an arch just like the engraving on the coin. A human figure passed under the vault.

He put an ink-stained finger on the drawing and said, "I'm sure you noticed a lot of talk about Atlantean Arches on those websites of yours, right?"

I nodded.

"They're found in most major civilizations on Earth. But I've found them here on Mars, too. There is one exceptionally well-preserved example not far from here."

"At Erick's dig site?" I asked.

"No, no. Closer. There are a series of caves just past the factory district. I believe the first colonists used these caves for shelter when they came here."

I stared at him. "The *first* colonists?"

"Yes, of course. Clearly the presence of these artifacts on both planets indicates prior planetary exploration by ancient humans."

"Wait, wait, wait." I held a hand up, trying to process his words in my brain and coming up blank. "You think people from *Earth* left these things thousands of years ago?"

"Of course," Emil said. "Surely you don't think that *aliens* left them, do you?" When I didn't answer, he grumbled, "Why is it always so difficult for people to believe in the power of the human mind? Why is it so easy for us to assume that some other, *smarter* species did it? Is it because we can't bear the thought of previous generations being wiser than our own?"

"But how did they *get* here?" I said.

Emil grinned and tapped *Podkayne*. "The arch," he said

simply.

I looked down at the diagram, the person walking through the archway. "So it's, like... a door?"

"Exactly. Didn't you ever read any books growing up? I think this arch is a tesseract."

Tesseract. That was a word I had heard before. Of course, I wasn't going to tell him that I hadn't read it in a book—I'd picked it up from one of Henry's old sci-fi flix. It was some kind of object that existed in multiple dimensions. Supposedly you could use it to travel across vast distances by bending space.

"So the coin and the key...?"

"Are the devices that open the door. They fit together, not unlike a memory chip into a deskpad drive. If programmed correctly, theoretically, they can open any coordinates. You could travel from one side of the planet to the other—and potentially between planets as well."

"The coin fits into the key," I repeated. "You mean like this?" I unzipped my backpack and pulled out Scylla's artifact. The recess in the middle was about the right size for the coin to fit inside.

Emil's breath came out in a hiss. "You did have it!" he snapped.

I put my hands up defensively. "I didn't know it, though! You wouldn't stop screaming at me long enough to tell me what the damn thing looked like!"

Emil didn't answer. He just ran his hands over the key obsessively, scraping at it with his ragged fingernails, holding it up to the fluorescent light.

"How can that be the key, though?" I asked, not expecting a response. "You said my dad had it. This was buried out in the middle of nowhere—" I broke off again in horror. What if Erick was wrong about the skeleton, then? What if it really was—

"This isn't the same key," said Emil matter-of-factly.

"What?"

"This is a copy. Look at this marking." He pointed to the monogram in the corner, the one that so impossibly matched Mama D's maker mark.

"The other one didn't have that?"

"No."

I rubbed my eyes wearily. "So that means there's more than one."

Emil nodded brusquely and sat once more. "It makes sense. There were probably several dozen, if not hundreds, of these in production, to allow the Atlanteans the ability to travel freely, to several locations in one day."

I rolled my eyes. "How do you know they were *Atlanteans*?"

He glared. "It's a shorthand, Contreras. How do you know that the city Heinrich Schliemann discovered was *actually* Troy?"

I ignored him. A sudden thought overwhelmed me. "If this isn't the same key, then that means my dad still has the other one. Do you think he..." I trailed off. I couldn't begin to fathom the second half of that sentence.

"I don't know," Emil said. "It shouldn't be able to work without the coin."

"Unless he found another coin," I said. "If there's more than one key, there's got to be more than one coin."

"Dear God." Emil's voice was gravelly, somber. "Then he could be anywhere. Anywhere in the known universe. He might have wound up back on Earth, but he just as easily could have been transported to Pluto."

I gripped the flimsy table so hard my fingers ached. Emil looked at me sympathetically—as sympathetically as someone who looks like an evil version of Albert Einstein could, anyway.

"Now, don't get too upset, kid," he said. "Raymond's a dumbass, but I can't believe he's that much of a dumbass."

"Thanks, I guess." I sighed and nudged the key across the table absentmindedly. "So what are we going to do with this now? GSAF is going to be all over my back for it."

Emil frowned. "GSAF knows about this?"

"Yeah. My friend found it on-site yesterday. I thought we'd managed to sneak it out without them noticing, but they were at my school today asking about it."

Emil stood up so abruptly that his chair folded and collapsed on itself, falling to the ground with a deafening clatter. "*Why didn't you tell me GSAF knows about this?*" he shouted. His eyes had that dangerous look to them like they'd had on the train platform, and suddenly I was kicking myself for having let my guard down.

As if on cue, there was a knock at the door. In unison, our heads jerked around, staring at it in horror.

Emil crept over to the door and peered through the peephole. He cursed, then crept back over to the table. "It's them."

"What?" I whispered. "But how? Why?"

"Because of this," Emil snapped. Before I could react to his invasion of my personal space, he'd yanked my palmtop out of my pocket and shoved it in my face. "Don't they teach kids anything anymore? The government can track you at all times with these stupid things."

My jaw moved up and down noiselessly. "So what do we do

now?"

"We get the key out of here." He shoved it back into my backpack, along with the paperback books with all his data inside. "And this." He pulled the coin out of his own shirt pocket, thrusting it into my hands. Then he tossed my palmtop down onto the sofa and, quickly, dragged me toward the fire escape.

"But where am I supposed to go with this?" I said.

"Go into the hills. There's a map in that Heinlein book. Follow it and wait for me in the cave. I'll meet up with you later."

"But what are you going to do?"

Emil scoffed. "Do you think I'd have made it this long if I didn't know how to deal with GSAF? Now *get moving!*"

He pushed me out onto the fire escape and slammed the door after me. A minute later, Condor and his cronies swept into the room, fanning out through the apartment, searching for me. One of them picked up my palmtop and handed it to Condor. I saw him swipe to unlock it just before Emil's body moved to block the window.

GSAF had my palmtop. They were going to know everything. Anything I'd texted Henry or Tamara was in Condor's hands now.

I swallowed. Though, if Emil was to be believed, they'd had access to it all along, anyway. This was just the icing on the cake. I was screwed. To think that, a month ago, the worst thing in my future was working in an office cubicle for the rest of my life. Now I was probably looking at life in prison, if I was lucky.

I set my jaw.

That is, if they caught me.

CHAPTER 15

· ∘ ∘ • ◯ ⊘ ɸ ∘

MY HEART SLAMMED IN MY CHEST AS I RAN. MY BREATH WAS ragged and labored. I couldn't think straight, couldn't focus on anything except on my need to get away, as quickly as possible. Find somewhere to hide, where GSAF wouldn't find me. Somewhere to think, to figure out how exactly I was going to get myself out of this disaster that I had managed to blunder my way into.

I was nearly to the edge of town when I heard a telltale buzz above me. My head jerked skyward in a panic. Faintly, I could see moonlight glinting off the nose of a GSAF security drone. It was hot on my tail. How had they found me so quickly? I'd left my palmtop in Emil's apartment! Was there some other piece of electronics on me that I wasn't thinking of? Some other way of tracking me? Had Joseph Condor bugged me this afternoon in the office? Oh, *Cristo*, I bet that was it. Was it really so important to keep this stuff from the dig site a secret that they'd *bug* a teenager?

I couldn't stop to think about it. If I waited any longer, the drone would have me in its sights and I'd be done for. I wasn't sure if the aircraft above my head was loaded or not—I mean, really, is a high school student a big enough threat to an interplanetary organization that they'd need to take me out?—but after all the crap they'd put me through in the last two days, I wasn't going to take any chances.

I clutched *Podkayne of Mars* against my chest so tight that the corner of its spine dug painfully into the palm of my hand. But the pain just prodded me forward, into the foothills.

Emil's map indicated the entrance should be around here, but I'd never been to this part of town before. What if Emil was wrong? What if he'd set me up? Or what if GSAF had learned of the cave's existence, and sealed it the same way they did the crater? What if there were suits waiting just inside, ready to take me away and make sure that I was never heard from again?

Then I saw it—a shadow in the darkness. Under a narrow ledge, half-covered in overgrowth and bramble, there was a gash in the hillside.

The buzzing sound of the drone grew closer. It was almost on top of me. There was no time to reconsider.

I dove into the crevice. The rock walls pressed against me. I barely managed to fit in the space between them. Desperately, I wrenched my body forward as hard as I could and squeezed into the cave beyond.

It was far darker in here than it had been outside. Even without the lights of the city to guide me, the starlight had been better than the pitch blackness of the caverns in the hillside. I'd have killed for my palmtop then. How was I supposed to light my way without it?

I sat in the darkness for several long minutes, listening. The drone passed overhead. The buzz of its blades grew loud, then faded, like it was moving away.

Then there was nothing but the sound of my own breathing and my heart beating in my ears.

They're gone. Breathe, Isaak.

The silence let the thoughts flood in. My mom was going to kill me, if I ever saw her again. I wondered what would happen to Henry, and to Tamara. Henry was probably as done for as I was—most of my texts were from him. But maybe they wouldn't connect Tamara, after all. Maybe she'd be safe. *Please, let her be safe.*

I focused on the muffled sensations of the cave. Soft drips of water echoed faintly in the distance. Cold air moved gently against my face, and I realized that I could hear wind moving through the tunnels of the cavern. Just how long were these tunnels, anyway? Emil's map had shown them stretching into the mountainside, but I hadn't looked at it carefully enough to see where they'd ended. Maybe there was an exit, somewhere else in the hills.

I could only pray that I'd find my way out before GSAF found their way in.

Finally, I started to inch my way forward, back toward the crevice I'd entered the cave through. I couldn't get anywhere in the dark like this, with no way to light my path. I'd have to go back, think of something else.

I was just about to try to squeeze back out through the crevice when I heard the buzz once more. The drone was circling back. I froze, unable to move, unable to think.

The next sound I heard was even more ominous than the drone.

Voices.

Right outside the cavern's entrance.

Any second now, a light would shine through that narrow crack, and the suits would find me. There was nowhere to go, nowhere to hide. Nothing I could do. It was over.

Unless I went forward.

I felt my way through the tunnel as silently as I could manage. The rock walls were cold and surprisingly smooth. It was narrow at first, just barely wide enough for my body to squeeze through, but as I moved along, the tunnel began to widen.

Soon I saw light ahead of me. I thought that this must be an opening, an exit back out into the outside world. I rushed forward, and suddenly found myself in a larger cavern. The light wasn't coming from outside at all—there was some kind of weird, glowing luminescence all around the cavern. Blue and green speckles blinked all around me, forming strange patterns of light, like stars in the night sky. Or like magic.

It reminded me of vids I'd seen on Speculus of glow worms on Earth. Could they live on Mars, too? At this point, I didn't think anything would surprise me.

I followed a trail of the glowing dots across the cave. A puddle of water pooled on the ground. I splashed through it, the water licking through my jeans. It was as cold as ice. I scrabbled across, reaching for a thick stalagmite to pull myself back up onto dry land.

My hand didn't land on rock, though.

I gasped in spite of myself. The sound of my voice echoed across the cavern, and I froze, listening for any sounds of my pursuers approaching, drawn by the noise. There was nothing.

I turned to the stalagmite to investigate. The rock formation was about a meter and a half high, and there was something strewn across the top of it. Fabric. I picked the material up and squinted at it in the dimness.

It was a jacket, made of thick, flame-retardant material. It reminded me of the jackets factory workers in Tierra Nueva often wore. As I ran my fingers across it, I felt something thicker, like a patch. A name badge. I moved closer to a clump of the blue glowing speckles, trying to get a better look. There, I could just make out the embroidered cursive letters—

Raymond.

I nearly dropped the jacket into the puddle, but caught it just in time. This was my dad's work jacket. He'd been wearing it the last time I'd seen him, standing on the train platform that October day. I took the northbound train to school, and he went east to work. He'd seemed preoccupied. He didn't say goodbye when I hurried to board my train.

I'd thought, later, it was because he was planning on leaving that day. Heading back to Earth. But he hadn't boarded a shuttle. He'd come here.

I felt like I was going to be sick.

I clutched the jacket to myself, wandering blindly through the cavern. I was so nauseous, so overwhelmed, that I almost didn't see it. But then it was right in front of me, and I couldn't ignore it. Three meters tall and as wide as four people.

The arch.

I drew a ragged breath. It was here. It was really here. And so was Dad's jacket. He had the key. He must have used the arch. There was no other explanation. But where had he gone?!

I ran my hands over the rough stones, stacked in their

corbeled pattern. It looked just like it had on the coin. Unbelievable.

As my skin touched the stone, the arch seemed to vibrate. There was a hum, barely audible. Like some kind of long-dormant power lay buried inside. Could it really be a tesseract?

A louder sound behind me drowned out the arch's hum. I froze, listening, though my heart pounded so loudly that I could barely hear anything else.

Voices. In the cave. They were coming.

They'd find me.

I didn't have time to think. If I'd been thinking straight, I never would have done it. But I was panicking. All I could think of was Joseph Condor on one side—and my dad on the other.

Maybe he hadn't abandoned me after all.

In a heartbeat, the key was in my hand. I slipped the coin out of my pocket and, fumbling in the dark, found the round recess. Just the right size. Just like Emil said.

I pressed the coin into the divot, and it clicked.

The key was rusty and corroded, but it must have still worked, because when I pressed the coin into it, it sprang open, the hinges along the edges unfolding again and again, from a four-pointed star into a shape too complicated to name. Though its outer casing was metal and worn, the inside of the key was bright and new-looking. Diodes on the interior lit up, glowing purple and emitting a strange, humming whir of sounds, resonating with the sounds from the arch. When I touched one with my finger, it sparked.

The arch began to flicker, like a fluorescent light that's been switched off for far too long. Between the joints of the stone, bright light emanated, pulsating, crackling with electricity.

"Over here!" I heard a voice in the distance. "He must have come this way!"

The light of the arch grew brighter and brighter. It was blinding to look at. The arch had transformed into a doorway of light, and the key grew so hot it burned my hands.

The pounding feet behind me grew louder and louder.

I squeezed my eyes shut and stepped into the light.

The force of it was awful. It felt like my body was being crushed by the weight of a giant, squeezed down small enough to fit through the eye of a needle. I wanted to scream, but I couldn't feel my lungs, couldn't find my vocal cords. I was dying. I had to be.

Then suddenly the light was gone, and my voice was back, my shouted agony ringing in my ears and burning my throat. When the screaming stopped, I tried to breathe, but the air was thin—it burned worse than the screaming had.

I was flat on my back. I opened my eyes to see fiery orange clouds swirling above my head. The wind pelted me with red dust. I wasn't in the cave anymore. But this wasn't Earth, either. Where had the door of light taken me?

I struggled to my knees, trying to draw a breath but coming up empty. Around me was a desert plateau, strewn with gray boulders that were tinged with reddish-orange stripes. Above it all, I could see something—a dome-shaped building with glass walls, like a greenhouse.

I tried to move toward the building, but I felt disoriented, like I was walking through a dream world. I finally managed to stand, and the plateau loomed up toward me sideways. It was like trying to move in a fun house. If only I could breathe.

If I could get to the building, I might be able to find help. I had to get help. I was going to die if I didn't get air soon.

In front of the building—there was a person. It wasn't my imagination. There was someone standing just twenty meters away from me. She looked like an old woman, with thick white hair braided around her head in a spiral. If she would just turn this way, she'd see me.

"Hey," I tried to call out, but no sound came. The lack of oxygen stole my voice once again. I waved my arms, but another surge of nausea hit me. And still the woman did not look my way.

"Please," I whispered, falling over on to my side. My vision swam, the building swirling together with the rocks and the ground and the woman and the ever-darkening sky.

The sky. I blinked, certain I was imagining it. But it was still there even as my vision blurred to black.

Beyond the clouds, larger than the sun, a huge, bright moon burned overhead.

PART TWO
NADIN

Hope Renewed Citidome
Iamos
S.C.D. 8378

CHAPTER 16

· ◦ ° • ◯ ⌀ ɸ ◦

I CAME AWAKE SLOWLY, ENGULFED IN A FOG OF STRANGE sounds. An electronic blipping in my ear. My breath, echoing strangely and artificially. Passing voices, snatches of conversation. And, above it all, an excruciating headache.

"How is she?" said a distant, familiar voice. Ceilos.

"*Kyrin* Nadin will be fine," a woman's voice replied. "Her exposure was very limited. The Enforcers say she lost consciousness just as they arrived, and they began applying oxygen immediately. Her companion, on the other hand..." It was silent for a moment, then she went on, briskly, "He is proving a bit more difficult to resuscitate, but based on initial System scans, he does not appear to have suffered any brain damage."

My mind strained, trying to discern what it was she was talking about. What companion? I lost consciousness? I tried to draw in a deep breath and sit up, but it felt like I couldn't get enough air, no matter what I did. After a moment of confusion, I finally realized that there was a tube over my nose and mouth, regulating my breathing.

"Have you been able to identify him?" Ceilos asked.

"No, *kyrios*. We are still running tests, though. Do you have any idea what *Kyrin* Nadin was doing with him, outside the dome?"

Reality crashed back in on me, and my eyes flew open in a panic. I immediately regretted it. The ceiling spun above my head, accompanied by an intense wave of nausea. I squeezed my eyes shut again and groaned.

"Nadin?" There was the sound of movement, and then I felt Ceilos' warm fingers wrap around mine. More slowly this time, I opened my eyes. My vision swam, but after a moment, it cleared. Ceilos grinned reassuringly. "How are you feeling?"

"I can't breathe. Can someone take this tube off my face?"

The woman—a medic, I realized, and this must be the hospital level—stepped forward. "*Kyrin*, you've suffered low oxygen levels. The inhalator is designed to help you regain optimal air intake."

"How am I supposed to 'regain optimal air intake' when I can't even draw a breath?" I snapped. The electronic blipping accelerated slightly, and Ceilos squeezed my fingers. Right. Temper. "*Anger is your poison*," Gitrin had said. Thinking of Gitrin was enough to make me angry all over again, so I closed my eyes, and the beeps slowed back to their previous pace.

"Since *Kyrin* Nadin has regained consciousness and is speaking," Ceilos said in a more diplomatic tone, "it seems to me that she no longer requires the assistance of the inhalator. If you wouldn't mind?"

The medic looked as though she *did* mind, quite a bit; but she wasn't in a position to argue with two *patroi*, so she smiled accommodatingly. "Very well. But if she shows even the slightest difficulty, this will have to go back on."

I had never so thoroughly relished the taste of the cold, dank air of the caverns. I inhaled deeply, savoring it.

"How do you feel now?" asked the medic. "Any breathing trouble?"

"No. But my throat hurts."

The medic had pulled a System panel up and was making notes on it. "That's understandable," she said when she was through, waving the panel away. "If you'd like, I can get you some water."

Her smile was irritatingly unwavering. I could be as nasty to her as I felt like, and that smile would never fade. Of course, that would be very un-*gerouin*-like of me. So I attempted to smile back at her. "That would be wonderful. Thank you."

As the woman bustled away, Ceilos snickered. "There. It wasn't too hard to be civil, was it?"

I didn't dignify that with an answer.

Ceilos perched on the edge of the hospital bed beside me. "I suppose your annual gift didn't go as well as I'd hoped for," he said, the hint of an apology in his voice.

"It's all right. I wanted to see the sunset, and I got it," I said. "I appreciate you covering for me with the *geroi*. They'd never have noticed a thing if it hadn't been for that boy." I frowned, remembering his prone form on the ground. "Is that who you and the medic were talking about?"

He tugged his earlobe affirmatively. "Do you know who he is, Nadin?"

"Not at all. I've never seen him before."

Ceilos sighed. "How do you suppose he could have gotten outside?"

"I'd very much like to ask him that myself when he wakes up."

I swallowed uncomfortably. My throat felt dry and raw. That water couldn't come soon enough. "I didn't see him at all on the System. If I hadn't noticed him before I went in..."

"You didn't see him on the System because he's not connected to it."

I struggled up onto my elbows and stared at him. "What? Was he offline, like—" I broke off, not wanting to say it aloud.

Ceilos knew what I meant, though. "No, not like that," he said. "He didn't even have an earpiece. And there's no record of his DNA."

Silence hung heavy between us. If the System didn't have a record of this boy, then...

My thoughts were interrupted by the sound of approaching footsteps echoing off the stone floor. The medic with my water, I thought with relief. But a moment later, the tall forms of *Gerouin* Melusin and *Geros* Antos strode into view through the clear glass wall to the hallway. The medic trailed deferentially behind them, her smile visibly strained now. It wasn't often that the leaders of our citidome interacted directly with anyone of the lower castes. To most, the *geroi* were like gods on a pedestal—distant and untouchable. Benevolent yet firm, judging yet forgiving. They could make one's life or destroy it; but though they were strict, I'd never known them to be anything but fair. The *geroi* were more than just our leaders, they were the mother and father to all in Hope Renewed.

And biological parents to one person. Me.

Ceilos quickly stood and inclined his head, three fingers to his brow. My legs still felt too numb to rise myself, but I saluted from the bed.

"Hello, Ceilos," Melusin said as she entered the room. "And Nadin, I'm relieved to see that you are awake and seem to be doing well." Her face was serene, but her eyes were cold as they fell over me. I looked down at the sterile white sheet over my legs. She would never show it in front of an *esotoin* like the medic, but I could feel her displeasure, sharp as a knife.

"The medic informs us that you should recover quickly. That's marvelous news, isn't it, Ceilos?"

"Hm? Oh, yes. Marvelous."

"Nadin, when you are feeling well enough, Antos and I would like to speak with you in private," Melusin said.

I swallowed. "I'm well enough now."

With just a look from Antos, the medic scrambled out the door, shooing Ceilos along with her. Through the glass, I saw her put a hand to her earpiece. A moment later, the clear glass of the walls darkened, obscuring the view to the hallway. The dimmed hospital room looked eerie, lit only by the blue and green phosphates embedded in the one natural cavern wall and stone ceiling of the room.

Once the echoes of the medic's and Ceilos' footsteps had faded into silence, Melusin turned to face me, her expression grave. "Nadin, who is he?" Her voice had lost all of its pleasantness.

I furrowed my eyebrows. "Who is who?"

"The boy you met outside."

"I... I don't know. I didn't *meet* him outside, I just saw him. He'd fallen."

Melusin looked as though she didn't believe me, but there would have been no point in lying. The System would alert her immediately if I did.

After a long moment of silence, I said, "*Gerouin*, I couldn't just leave him—"

"Iamos is on the brink of destruction, Nadin," Antos interrupted me. "If our people are to survive, we must be united. That means obeying the edicts. No one is exempt from them, not even the *geroi*. You know this."

I looked down again. "Yes, *Geros*. I understand. I just... since it was my annual, I thought..."

"The anniversary of your birth does not make you above the law," he interrupted. "Especially not this one. You are *enilin* now. You should be able to make intelligent decisions, Nadin. Don't you understand how dangerous leaving the dome is, now? What if the seal had been damaged? The entire population of Hope Renewed could have been decimated." His voice was low. It made the anger in his words feel even stronger.

The *geroi* were never angry, it seemed, except with me.

"The lives of the people are in our hands," said Antos. "We are the guardians of this citidome. If even one life had been lost, the damage would be irreparable."

"But isn't it for the best, then, that I was there?" I protested. "That boy would have died if I hadn't alerted you to him."

Antos' mouth was drawn in a tight line. "We know nothing about him. He is unknown to the System. Do you understand what that means? He is, in all likelihood, an anarchist. A terrorist. And you have given him access to the citidome."

My face grew hot. "*Geros*, I didn't—"

"Nadin, in light of this evening's events," Melusin broke in, "the *geroi* have decided to reject your appeal for re-evaluation."

The breath left me. For a brief, horrible moment, I felt like I was outside the dome again, gasping in the cold, airless wind. "What? But... why?"

Antos scoffed. "Does that question really need an answer?"

I said nothing. My eyes stung, but I resolutely kept my features blank.

Melusin's face softened slightly. "Nadin, I understand how you must feel." She put a hand on my shoulder, gave it a gentle squeeze. "I'm sorry you had to come of age at a time like this. Things are much stricter for you and Ceilos than they were for other generations of *patroi*. In another time, there might have been more leniency. Room to let you learn, to make mistakes." She let go of me, leaving a cold void in the place her fingers had touched. "But Antos is right. We cannot afford that now. This simply is the way things are. There can be no oversights. You are our daughter, Nadin, but you know that does not give you privilege over the others in our care. We have to do what's best for everybody. Remember, unity through fidelity. It is the only way."

I tugged on my earlobe and absently quoted the motto of the Progression: "'All lives are one.' I am sorry, *Gerouin*."

I watched her as I spoke, standing there, hands clasped behind her back. As always, she looked collected, poised, as though she never had a moment's fear or doubt. Not even a hair out of place. I'd always wondered how I was supposed to live up to a *gerouin* such as her. Now I wondered if I'd ever even get the chance.

"You still have more to learn," said Antos. "If Gitrin believes there is nothing more she can teach you, then we shall simply have to find you another tutor." He leveled his gaze on me. "You must prove yourself, Nadin. And the best way to do so is to *not* violate the *geroi*'s edicts. If you are to be one of us, you must demonstrate that you can work with us—no matter what."

"Yes, *kyrios*."

"All right, then. We will let you rest now. When you've recovered, we will see about finding a new tutor for you and Ceilos. Perhaps in a year's time, you will be ready to take your evaluation again."

A year's time. By then, we might all be dead.

As they turned to leave, I realized that the *geroi* had said nothing about my disappearance from the System's tracker in the moments before I called for help outside the dome. Surely they must have noticed. Maybe they hadn't consulted the records yet. It seemed too good to be true that it would slip their notice entirely.

But it would be a glorious mercy if it did. Perhaps Ceilos would even forgive me for being so reckless, if it meant his unauthorized program would remain undetected.

My throat ached painfully now, raw from all the talking. Where was that medic with the water?

I sat up, squeezing my eyes shut for a moment until the wave of dizziness passed. She had probably gotten distracted by the *geroi*'s abrupt arrival. It had unnerved me, too. I hadn't expected them to come here. Usually they saved their reprimands for the privacy of our villa, where they could discipline me without risking a scandal. This mystery boy must have been a particularly sensitive issue, if they were willing to risk the rumors that were sure to be flying through the hospital level now.

I have a particular talent for getting into trouble, don't I?

The stinging of my eyes made my throat burn even more. I glanced up at the timepiece on the wall. Nearly dawn. There was no point in lying around feeling sorry for myself any longer. If the medic wasn't going to bring me water, I'd go get it myself.

The glass walls of my hospital room were still darkened, so the bright artificial lighting of the hallway was jarring. I winced, blinking it away, waiting for my vision to realign. When the sand cleared from my eyes, I saw that the room across from mine had three beds inside, each of them filled with people I didn't recognize—*plivoi*, obviously, since *patroi* would warrant their own private rooms. I watched them for a moment, a small pang of sympathy clawing its way inside my chest. Then I shook it off and continued down the corridor.

There were three beds in the next room as well, but two of these were empty. The room had been dimmed inside, and the eerie blue phosphorescence made the lone patient's skin appear to glow. I took an involuntary step closer, my hand on the glass, peering at the prone figure on the bed.

I should keep moving. There was no reason for this. It was none of my affair. My role in his story was over. The *geroi* had ordered as much. There was no point in me lingering here, staring.

But I just couldn't make my eyes move away from him. He was so *different*, so strange—so impossible.

The boy from outside the city.

CHAPTER 17

· ○ ° • ◯ ∅ ф ○

I HOVERED IN THE HALLWAY A FEW MOMENTS LONGER BEFORE finally glancing over my shoulder. The corridor was deserted; the medics in the *plivoi*'s room were preoccupied with their own patients. I was alone.

Before I could talk myself out of it, I had shoved the sliding glass aside and slipped into the boy's room.

The artificial lighting flickered on as I entered the room, illuminating his strange features. His eyes were closed, his chest rising and falling slowly. There was a breathing tube over his mouth and nose, like the one they'd fitted me with. His face had been cleansed, and a System scanner fitted over his cranium, monitoring his brainwaves. Where the rust-red dirt had obscured his features before, I could now see that his light brown skin was even and smooth. Not blotchy like exposure poisoning. This must be his natural skin tone.

My brows furrowed as I ran a hand across his forehead, brushing soft, dark hair away. I had never seen these traits before. I couldn't begin to guess as to which city would have selected them. There couldn't possibly be enough melanin in this tone to protect against ultraviolet photodamage...

His eyelids flickered under my touch, and I jerked my hand

back in alarm. Before I could move away, he'd opened his eyes, blinking at me with eyes as dark as his hair.

I stood transfixed, mouth agape. I don't know what it was about this boy that drew me in. I couldn't explain it—it was like a planet's gravity. The pull had been strong enough before, when he was unconscious. To see him awake, moving, breathing, was even more unnerving. It made him more real, somehow.

He said something, words I didn't recognize. I waited a long moment for the System's auto-translator to whisper his meaning in my mind, but it never came. All I had were disjointed syllables and a look of confusion on the boy's face.

"I-I'm sorry," I stammered, not sure what else to say.

The boy's face scrunched up and he repeated the words again, more slowly. His voice came out like a croak, parched-sounding and cracked beneath the echo of the breathing tube. I swallowed involuntarily, reminded of my own aching throat.

"Perhaps you need some water," I said, backing toward the door. "I'll see about a medic—"

The boy sat up as I moved out of his line of sight, jabbering something else. The lack of response from the System panicked me. Hearing his words but not their meaning was like being thrown into the dark. I stumbled about, blindly.

"*Kyrin* Nadin! What are you doing in here?"

I whirled around. The medic who had treated me stood in the doorway, an amphora of water in her hand.

"I was looking for you," I answered automatically. "But as I passed, I saw he'd awoken, and..." It was only a small lie, a harmless one. She was low-ranking enough that the System wouldn't alert her, but I'd learned to watch my tongue,

155

regardless, from my years of missteps.

"He—" The medic broke off, noticing her patient, fully alert, staring at her in confusion. Quickly, she hurried over to him, handing me the amphora as she passed. "We weren't expecting him to regain consciousness for a few hours still. The System was supposed to keep him in a medical coma. Why didn't it...?"

She began examining him while I drank, my parched throat greedy. The boy glanced back and forth between her and me and said a few more words. Once again, I habitually waited for the translation, but it still didn't come.

"Why can't I understand him?" I asked.

"His thought patterns are unfamiliar to the System," replied the medic. "It could take up to a week for it to finish decoding his brainwaves."

I frowned. "But how—"

The boy interrupted me with a cry of alarm. The medic had pulled open a System panel to mark down his vitals, and the boy was staring at it, wide-eyed. He reached forward, poking the air idiotically.

"What is wrong with him?" I asked. "It's just the System."

The medic waved the panel away, and the boy gasped. She tugged her earlobe thoughtfully. "It's more than the System not having a record of him. He does not appear to recognize the System at all. That could be why it was unable to maintain his bodily functions—his brain is unaccustomed to working in tandem with it."

The boy was staring at me again, making my stomach clench oddly. I ground my teeth in irritation.

"That's ridiculous. Everyone on Iamos has had exposure to—"

I stopped short. His strange appearance and behavior, no knowledge of the System...

Glancing at the medic, I said under my breath, "Simos?"

"It's possible," she said. "We'll have to run more tests to be sure."

I exhaled shakily. "Right. Someone should alert the *geroi*, then." And Ceilos. I'd have to tell Ceilos. Where had he disappeared to, anyway?

I started to turn toward the door when the boy spoke again. I froze for a moment, staring down at my feet. I didn't look at him. I didn't want to face those unsettling dark eyes.

He said the word once more, and then there it was in my earpiece, in my mind:

"Wait."

I looked at the medic in surprise. She smiled. For the first time, it seemed genuine. "Excellent. The System is beginning to decode his thought patterns. If we can keep him talking, the lexicon will build more quickly."

She looked at me expectantly, her head quirked to the side. I knew what she was thinking. The boy wanted to talk to me. I could tell by his persistent stare.

But just now, I didn't want to talk to him.

I could feel his eyes boring into my back, but I kept my own trained on the door. "Good luck, then," I said to the medic. "I have things I need to attend to."

"*Kyrin* Nadin, wait!" the medic protested. "We need to check your vitals again before we can release you—"

But I was already out the door.

CHAPTER 18

· ○ ° • ○ ∅ φ ○

MY FINGERS TRAILED ACROSS THE COOL HEWN STONE OF THE passageway. Millions of multicolored phosphates, embedded in the walls, twinkled as my skin brushed past. The upper subterranean levels of the city, where the hospital was located and the *esotoi* lived, relied primarily on the more common green and blue stones for lighting; but the deepest part of the cave system, winding below the mountains, where the *geroi's* villa was located on the *Vi'in Exelishin*—these were lit with vibrant golds, brilliant magentas. They were laid carefully into the floor in mosaic patterns, in the ceiling like long-forgotten constellations. They arced across the walls just as fragmented light through a prism.

I'd walked the long route from the hospital level through the tunnels, largely deserted now, at midmorning. Most of the *patroi* would be in the upper levels of the citidome by this time, working. I could have used the elevator, but I wanted the privacy, the time *apart*, to clear my head. I felt overwhelmed to the point of nausea. Everything that had happened the last few days—the disastrous evaluation, my annual, the doomed visit to the Outside—the boy—it was all too much.

I stopped before the fountain on the *vi'in*. The passageway widened here to accommodate a large postern, which brought warm water from the hot springs near Bright Horizon. It cascaded down in the center of the passageway like an ancient waterfall, collecting in a basin at the bottom before trickling its way on through the caverns.

I scooped a handful of warm water out from the basin, splashed it onto my face. We'd had so few communications from the party of settlers who had gone to Simos, the second world, hoping to establish an evacuation colony. The planet's magnetic field disrupted the System to the point of near unusability. Before we lost contact, they'd told us that there were other inhabitants on the planet. Seemingly human, the report had said, but I hadn't realized how much like us they'd be. Alien, but not quite alien enough.

How had one gotten here?

At the end of the *vi'in*, the passage opened out into a large cavern. Three wide steps led up to the arched entrance of the *geroi*'s villa. Even though it was deep under the ground, it had been designed to look like the aboveground manor that had once stood beside the sea. Six columns held aloft a tile roof inlaid with glistening stones, each a different color. A woven-copper gate, the entranceway to the villa's front courtyard, swung open as I approached. Where once beautiful green bushes and fruiting trees would have formed a garden, we were left with nothing but decorative stone statuary and the few scraggly vines that had adapted to life without the sun.

I glanced into the polished bronze stela in the courtyard's center as I passed. The medics had wiped my face off, but there was still rusty grime caked along my hairline. I sighed and began pulling my disheveled hair loose from its wraparound braid. My coarse white curls were stained reddish-brown. That awful tangy metallic smell wafted around me as I ran my fingers through, trying to loosen the knots.

The villa was silent apart from the echo of my footsteps across the tile. I detoured into the east wing, where Ceilos' suite was located, but no light shone under his door. Antos and Melusin were not here, either. They must be at the capitol. I wondered if they'd gotten any sleep the night before.

In my suite, I tried once more to comm Ceilos, but he did not answer. My stomach knotted with worry as I wondered if the *geroi* had taken him aside for an interrogation of his own. But even if they'd noticed that I'd gone off the grid temporarily, they wouldn't necessarily have linked it to him.

I resolved not to worry about it. Ceilos was good at disappearing. He'd come back around when he felt like it.

The hot spring had been channeled to run below the floors of the villa, and it warmed the tiles under my feet, transforming the otherwise cold cavern into a comfortable space. The floor of the bathroom opened into a large square pool, with elegantly carved steps leading down into the hot, gently flowing waters. I sank into the water, grateful for the soothing warmth on my sore muscles.

I'd barely finished scrubbing off all the grime when the chime rang in my ear, the familiar buzz that meant I had an incoming comm. *Ceilos, finally*, I thought. But when I pressed my fingers to the earpiece, it was Melusin's soft voice that answered.

"Nadin," she said, "when you're dressed, I'd like to speak with you in the atrium."

I squeezed my eyes shut, rubbing my forehead with the heel

of my hand. What had I done now?

"Yes, *Gerouin*," I said, dropping my hand from my ear.

I changed into fresh clothing, a silver long-sleeved tunic and trousers which fit snug, like a second skin, trapping warmth. I pulled my thick damp hair back, forcing my fingers to move slowly as I braided, despite my impatience—if I hurried, the braid would drift sideways and I'd have to start over. The bronze medallion came last—my unofficial pass to the city, signifying me as a *patroin*. One side was engraved with a postern, the symbol of Iamos, and the other with a diagram of the solar system. I rubbed it between my fingers. *You were born to this*, I thought resolutely. *Even if most of the time it feels otherwise.*

I pulled the long chain over my head and tucked the medallion under my collar. Then I gave myself one last cursory glance in the looking glass. Not perfect—I never was—but I would have to do.

Melusin was waiting when I arrived in the atrium. She was perched, back perfectly straight, on her favorite chair, an antique piece made of woven copper strands. Above her head, the roof of the villa opened to reveal the high cavern ceiling above us, glittering with phosphorescence like the stars in the night sky—a distant memory of what once was. Water trickled off the roof, dripping and pattering, slowly feeding the planters of black *fraouloi* that somehow grew here in the near-darkness. In the atrium's center, a heat lamp glowed amber-yellow, radiating warmth.

I stopped before Melusin, placing three fingers on my brow respectfully. She inclined her head and did the same. Then she gestured to the seat beside her.

"Are you feeling well, Nadin?" she asked as I sank into the chair.

"Yes, *Gerouin*."

"I am glad." She drummed her fingers absently on the chair arm, the glow of the heat lamp making her silvery eyes reflect gold. "Nadin, I have been doing some thinking." Her eye caught mine. "I know you wish to prove yourself to the *geroi*."

I shifted forward in my seat. "Yes, *Gerouin*. More than anything."

She touched her earlobe. "And you are correct that we are running out of time for protocol. The time has come for more... unconventional methods."

My skin felt cold despite the heat lamp's warmth. "What do you mean?"

"That boy. The one from outside the dome. Did you speak to him at all when he first awakened?"

"*Gerouin*, I didn't—" I protested, but she waved her hand dismissively, cutting me off.

"I know you don't know him, Nadin. I do trust you, even if you seem convinced that I don't."

My jaw hung open for a moment. I snapped it shut and sat back in my chair.

"It is important that this boy's thought patterns be decoded as quickly as possible. We need to know where he came from. Why, and how. Someone needs to get this information for us— preferably someone close to the *geroi*." She smiled again. "You are our best option."

"So... you want me to spy on him?" I asked.

She winced. "Honestly, Nadin, must you always use such

negative language? Merely observe him. Speak with him. Try and learn his background. We need to know everything we can about him."

I tilted my head slightly. "Do you believe he is from Simos?"

Melusin tugged her earlobe. "In all likelihood. He was carrying this." She turned in her seat, lifting a rusty object off the table beside her. A posternkey—an extremely old one, from the look of it.

I turned it over in my hands. "I thought these didn't work on Simos," I said, "because of the magnetic field."

"It appears Simos is more mysterious than we'd believed," she replied.

I took the medallion from around my neck, pressing it into the slot on the posternkey. It opened, albeit with some effort, thanks to the rusted hinges. When I ran my fingers across the diodes, the usual System panel opened, suspended in midair above it. Coordinates were already programmed into it—data the postern would use to open the tesseract to the correct location.

"*System protocol initiated,*" a digitized voice said in my ear. I started in alarm. "*Biological patterns recognized. Subject: Nadin. Decoy coordinates override. Display true data.*"

The coordinates on the System panel began to change, new numbers shimmering over the top of the old ones. My pulse sped up, and I glanced quickly over at Melusin. Her expression was blank. She hadn't heard the voice. She couldn't see this.

I was the only one who could see it.

And I recognized these coordinates.

My hands were shaking as I closed the System panel, set the posternkey aside. Melusin did not seem to notice.

"It is vital that you learn everything about how he came to be here, Nadin," she said. "If there is any chance that we can use this information to reestablish our evacuation colony on Simos, we must do so at once. Time is running out."

Her words shook me out of my fog. "I thought our evacuation colony was already established on Hamos," I said. The third planet, Hamos, was far closer than Simos. And, like Iamos, it lacked a magnetic field, which meant there would be no interference with the System, or the posterns.

"Hamos is proving to be a poor option for colonization. It is too tectonically active."

There was another meaning to her words. I could feel it, but I couldn't discern it. "The System's early warning protocol—"

"—is unreliable," Melusin interrupted.

I frowned. The System had been developed over a period of centuries. It was infallible. "*Gerouin*, what are you not telling me?"

She didn't answer at first. She picked up the posternkey again, running her fingers over the rusty hinges. "There's been an accident," she said at last. "There was an earthquake today. Ascendant Dawn's citidome was severely damaged."

"Ascendant Dawn? But that's where Ceilos'..." I trailed off, staring at her, stunned.

"*Gerouin* Clodin was critically injured. The report came in while you were outside the dome."

My chest clenched. "Does Ceilos know?"

"Antos and I informed him just after we spoke with you on the hospital level. Antos is with him now."

No wonder he hadn't answered his comm. The clenching

feeling in my chest sank down to the pit of my stomach. My fingers wrapped around my medallion as I stood. "I will do everything I can, *Gerouin*."

Melusin stood as well. "The people of Iamos are relying on you, Nadin. If you can prove yourself on this occasion... we would be willing to consider offering you another evaluation."

My heart stuttered at the words. *Another chance.* With as much composure as I could muster, I placed my fingers on my brow. "You will not be disappointed."

I turned on my heel, somehow managing to keep the grin off my face until I'd left the atrium. This was my chance to prove myself to the *geroi*—and to Gitrin. If I could just do this one thing, nothing could stop me. I was certain I would pass my evaluation the second time around. The first time had been a fluke, an anomaly. I'd become a *gerouin* in my own right, and I'd finally be free.

I hurried out onto the *vi'in*, propelled forward by my giddy confidence, not looking back, not pausing for a moment's reflection. I couldn't slow down, wouldn't let Gitrin's sharp words catch up with me. She may have been my tutor for the last six years, but she was wrong. I knew she was. I was *enilin* today, and nothing could stop me.

I kept my head held high, even as her voice still echoed through my mind, whispering insidious doubts in my ear.

"You're not ready."

The boy was no longer in the hospital bed when I returned. He was up, dressed in plain clothes like my own—long-sleeved and silver. The cranial scanner had been replaced with the smaller, standard earpiece. Dressed like this, he almost looked like he belonged here.

But not quite.

I hesitated for a moment outside the glass windows, watching him. Then the door slid open and there was a medic—a man, this time, but with the same unwavering smile as always.

"*Kyrin* Nadin," he said, guiding me through the door, "thank you for coming. I was informed you would be assisting the *esotoi* with our studies."

"You've spoken to *Gerouin* Melusin?"

"No, the message was given to me by Gitrin. She recommended the assignment as part of your ongoing studies."

I stopped short. "*Gitrin?*"

"Of course. And, *kyrin*, we greatly appreciate the offer of your invaluable time, and hope that your experiences here will be helpful in your leadership training. It is wonderful to know that even in such dire times, the *geroi* can be relied upon to care for even the smallest concerns of the Iamoi."

"All lives are one," I said, smiling automatically. Melusin had said nothing of Gitrin's involvement. Earlier she'd said that they were going to find me a new tutor. A pang twisted inside me. Most of me never wanted to hear her name again, but an irrational part of me still warmed at the sound of it. She'd been my caretaker for most of my life, more than the *geroi* had ever been, despite living under the same roof as them. I wanted to hate her, but I wasn't quite there yet.

The boy was watching me again. I noticed his gaze and squared my shoulders, meeting his dark eyes defiantly. I wasn't going to let him intimidate me again. I was here on a mission.

He lifted his shoulders in an odd manner and looked away.

"Now, *kyrin*," the medic said, gesturing to the boy. "We're working on prompting responses from the subject. If we can get him to identify commonplace objects, this will help build the lexicon. So far I've only managed to elicit one-word responses from him, but we need more than that. Complete sentences will build syntax, allow the System to more quickly recognize his particular thought patterns."

The boy was glaring now. I ignored him.

"So I just use the visual indicator program?" I asked.

The medic tugged his earlobe. "Just as you would for a child."

"Right. I will be happy to help," I said, forcing my lips into a carefully-practiced, Melusin-like smile.

"Comm if you require assistance. I'll just be across the corridor, tending to our other patients."

"Let's see," I said when the medic had gone. I pulled open a System panel, loaded the visual indicator program. "Where did you leave off?"

The boy didn't answer. He was watching me warily. I sighed.

"All right. Let's just start at the beginning. What is your word for this animal?" An image of a *gurza* hovered between us, its hefty back legs supporting its upper body weight and that of a rider.

The boy's eyebrows scrunched together, and he poked the image, his mouth slightly agape. He laughed, a scoffing half-chuckle, but he didn't speak. I gritted my teeth.

"All right, forget that one. What about this?"

The next image was a tree. I paused, staring at the image for a long moment. I had not seen a tree like this one in years. The few

167

that grew in the aboveground portion of the dome were small and scraggly. They bore tiny, bitter fruit. I ran my fingers across the image, but there was nothing but empty air. My eyes stung in spite of myself.

The boy opened his mouth as if to say something. He hesitated, then snapped his jaw shut, folding his arms and looking away.

I waved the visual indicator away irritably. "If you won't cooperate," I said, "we're never going to decode your brain-waves."

His eyes flicked over to mine, and for an instant I thought—I was certain—that he had understood me.

Then the door behind me slid open.

I glanced over my shoulder. "Ceilos!" He looked exhausted. I hurried to him, placing a steadying hand on his shoulder. "What are you doing here? You look like you haven't slept all night."

"I'm fine. After all, I'm not the one who nearly got exposure poisoning. Anyway, I needed to talk to you," he said.

I frowned. "I heard about what happened on Hamos. I am so sorry. Are you... all right?"

"Just tired," he replied. "You know what speaking with *Geros* Tibros can be like."

"Yes, but *Gerouin* Clodin..."

Ceilos snorted. "She'll live." When he saw my aghast face, he grinned—a genuine grin, not the false smile we all wore when others were around. "Come now, Nadin. You know there's no love lost between me and my parents."

I knew Ceilos often said that. But I still didn't think I would be able to laugh if Melusin or Antos had nearly died.

"You're not ready."

I shook my head, trying to clear my thoughts. "Do they know what could have caused the System's early warning protocol to malfunction?"

Ceilos glanced over at the boy. He sat sullenly in his chair, not looking at us.

"It's fine," I said. "The System hasn't decoded his thought patterns yet. He can't understand us." I hoped.

Ceilos stared a second longer, then turned back to me. "The System was hacked."

My eyes widened. "What? But how?"

"They're not sure. They're still tracing the source of the breach. But all signs seem to point to"—he lowered his voice—"the 'Liberator' and his little band of anarchists."

I squeezed my eyes shut. This could not have come at a worse time. The planet was on the brink of destruction, and these terrorists were hell-bent on bringing us there even faster. Right now, all of Iamos needed to work together. *All lives are one*—couldn't they see that?

"Listen, Nadin," Ceilos said. "There's something else I need to talk to you about. Tibros... he's petitioned the *gerotus* for a repartnership."

I looked at him in confusion. "But Clodin isn't dead. I thought you said she was expected to survive."

He didn't meet my eyes. "Not for himself. For me."

The floor dropped out from under me. There it was again, that horrible, airless feeling. "But why?" I could barely find my voice. "Because I failed my evaluation? Because—" I couldn't say it.

Because of Gitrin.

"He said that they need a new *geroi* partnership on Hamos, and he wants it to be me. But, Nadin, I told him no. I—"

I wasn't listening. My mind was whirling around, drowning in too many circumstances beyond my control. I couldn't lose Ceilos, too.

"Wait," I said, my voice cracking. "There's another way. The *geroi*..."

"Nadin, it doesn't matter," Ceilos interrupted. "I already told him—"

"No!" I grasped his hands in mine. He stopped talking, staring down at them. "Listen," I said. "I can fix this. I know how..."

I trailed off as I noticed the boy's reflection in the window over Ceilos' shoulder. He was watching us again, his eyes focused intently. The expression on his face was not one of confusion—it was one of comprehension.

I pressed my lips together. *I knew it.*

Folding my arms to match his, I whirled on the boy. "All right, that's enough pretending. You can understand me, can't you?"

He didn't say anything for a long, agonizing moment. I almost thought I'd been wrong. Almost turned away.

Then he swallowed and said, "Yes."

CHAPTER 19

· ○ ∘ • ◯ ∅ ϕ ○

CEILOS' JAW DROPPED. I INHALED SHARPLY, TRYING TO KEEP MY temper. "How long have you been eavesdropping on us?"

He lifted his shoulders again, not meeting my eyes. "I don't know," he said. His accent was heavy, his words strange, but I could understand him. What my own ears didn't pick up, the System provided for me. "An hour or two? Around when I figured out that your language was some kind of weird mix of Greek and Egyptian overlaid with half the Mesoamerican languages I know."

"What does that mean? *Greek? Meso*...?"

The boy sighed. "Never mind. I don't think you'd get it. Are you guys going to take this stupid earpod off me now?" He tapped the side of his head with his index finger.

I blinked. "You mean your earpiece?"

"I guess."

"No." I instinctively put a hand on my own, horrified at the thought of removing it. "You need it. We all need it. We can't communicate with the System without it."

He pulled a face. "What is the *System*, anyway? You people go on about it every other word. The most I can figure is that it's some kind of mind-reader. Which is not creepy at all."

I looked at Ceilos for a moment, uncertain of what to say.

How does one explain the System? The collective mind of the entire world?

"Never mind that," said Ceilos. "We still have questions for you. Who are you, anyway?"

He slouched forward, resting his elbows on his knees. "I'm just a guy."

I closed my eyes, taking a deep, soothing breath. *Don't snap*, I warned myself. "A 'guy' named...?"

"Isaak."

"Isaak," I repeated. I had never heard a name like that before. But of course I wouldn't have. Even if the coordinates the System had shown me were wrong, whoever he was, he was clearly not of Iamos. I smiled hollowly. "And I am Nadin."

"Yeah, I caught that. You're Nadin"—he gestured—"and Ceilos. And the doctor's called Heros, right?"

My face flushed. I did not know the medic's name. It hadn't even occurred to me to ask.

"You seem to know everything about us," Ceilos said. "But we know absolutely nothing about you. How did you come to be here?"

Isaak sighed. "I don't know. It's a long story. I was looking for my dad, but obviously he isn't here." He added, barely audibly, "And now I'm stuck here. Alone."

The sadness in his voice made my chest clench. There were no parents on Iamos except the *geroi*. Ceilos and I had been raised in the households of our biological parents, since we were *geroi*-born. But all other children were raised by the collective until they were old enough for an apprenticeship. It had always been that way, since the Progression.

"Isaak," I said, sitting across from him on one of the hospital beds. "I would like to help you, but I can't do that unless you tell me what happened. Where did you come from? Simos?"

"No, I'm not from Simos," he said, his expression wary. "I'm from Iamos."

"You *can't* be from Iamos. If you were, you'd know about the System. The System would recognize you."

"I didn't say I was from Iamos, I said I was from *Iamos*," Isaak snapped.

I jumped up. "What is that supposed to mean?"

He stood as well. "Listen... stop listening with that thing"—he gestured to my earpiece—"and listen with your ears. I am not from Iamos. I am from *Mars*."

I stared at him. "But what is *Mars*?"

Isaak began to pace, running a hand through his dark hair. "The planet I was born on. The fourth planet from the sun."

"Iamos is the fourth planet from the sun."

He stopped short. He stared at nothing, at his reflection in the glass. Then, slowly, he said, "What?"

Ceilos pulled his earlobe. "Iamos is the fourth world. *Ia*, four. *Mos*, world. *Wi, si, ha, ia*. Each of the eight planets in the solar system are named this way."

"The solar system," he repeated. "Can you show me? On your... System thing?"

I pulled open the visual indicator again and commanded it to display the eight planets. I gestured to the fourth one, cringing at how red the image had become. The blue of the seas had dwindled down to nearly nothing; the green of the ground was a distant memory.

"That's it," Isaak said, his voice shaking. "That's Mars." He sat down heavily, his shoulders hunched.

I knew it. I knew I recognized the coordinates on the posternkey. It seemed impossible, but I knew I couldn't be wrong.

Ceilos snapped, "Look, I don't know what you're trying to prove by lying—"

"Wait, Ceilos," I interrupted. I crouched in front of Isaak, looking up into his worry-creased face. "Isaak," I said. "When you left Mars… did you pass through a door?"

He bobbed his head up and down. "It was an archway made of stone."

"A postern," I said. "And you were holding something?"

"Emil called it the key," he said. "It was metal, ancient. So, so old. But we opened it with a coin."

I frowned. "I don't know what a coin is," I said. "But did it look like this?" I pulled my medallion out from beneath my collar and held it out to him.

He snatched it from my hands. For a moment, I wanted to rip it away from his grasp—my birthright. Something no plivos had a right to hold. But Isaak wasn't a plivos, he was something else entirely. And I needed answers more just now.

"It was just like this," he said. "Just like it. But it was old, like the key. It looked like if you buried this in the ground and forgot about it for a couple millennia."

I swallowed. "The time postern."

Ceilos gaped at me. "That's impossible!"

"Excuse me?" Isaak said. "Are you telling me I traveled through time?"

"You must have," I said, my heart starting to pound faster.

"Ordinarily, posternkeys are programmed with three sets of coordinates—dimensional data. But the key they took from you, it had four."

"Four dimensions?"

I tugged my earlobe. "The fourth dimension is time."

Isaak slumped forward, his head between his knees. "I think I'm going to throw up," he said.

I barely heard him. My mind was reeling. I needed to tell the *geroi*. Surely this would change everything. This was the answer. We could save Iamos. It didn't matter, now, whether colonization on Hamos or Simos was viable. We wouldn't need that anymore.

"Nadin, wait," Ceilos said, placing a hand on my shoulder. "Be sensible. If that posternkey really had four sets of coordinates, wouldn't the *geroi* have noticed?"

"It was encrypted. It didn't show the true coordinates until it recognized my DNA signature."

"That's ridiculous! Why would it only show *you* the data?"

"I don't know." I rubbed my temple with my right hand. "Maybe Gitrin programmed it that way. I was the one who worked on it with her the most. Maybe she's trying to tell me something."

"But why, Nadin?"

Isaak cleared his throat. His face was a sickly pale color, making him look more alien than ever. "Would you guys mind explaining some of this to me?" he asked. "Did I time travel or not?"

"Yes," I said.

"No," Ceilos said over the top of me. "The time postern is just a theory. It doesn't exist."

"Yet," I snapped. "But it *must* exist at some future date, otherwise Isaak would not be here. This proves that Gitrin's theory is workable."

Ceilos grabbed my arm, pulled me aside. "How do you know this isn't a trick? Maybe this boy," he whispered, his voice barely audible, "is with the Liberator."

I brushed him off. "*You're* being ridiculous. I know what I saw on that posternkey, Ceilos. I spent over a year working on the plans for the time postern with Gitrin. I know those coordinates better than my own face. How would the Liberator know about that? He's a terrorist, not a scientist. And besides." I gestured to Isaak. "Look at him. Have you ever seen an Iamoi that looked like him?"

Ceilos locked eyes with Isaak for a long moment. Isaak's defiance seemed to have eroded as much as the surface outside the dome. Now he looked despondent. Harmless.

Ceilos sighed. "Fine. But what do you propose we do about it?"

I reached up to my earpiece, pressing the comm button. "I need to talk to Gitrin."

"Gitrin? Are you sure that's a good idea, after last week?"

"Well, what else can I do?" The thought of seeing Gitrin again tore at me from the inside like the talons of a *gamada*, but I needed answers, and she was the only one who could possibly have them.

"*Subject Gitrin unavailable,*" the System said in my ear.

"Try again," I said.

Ceilos leaned against one of the empty hospital beds. "What's wrong?"

"She's not answering," I said. I pulled open a System panel. "Show subject coordinates."

"*Coordinates not found.*"

I stared at the blank map of the citidome, mouth moving soundlessly. "Ceilos, did you modify her earpiece?"

"Of course not. You're the only one who knows about my cloaking program."

"But look at this," I said, swiveling the panel around for him to see. "It says she's not here."

He stood, gesturing for the map of the citidome to expand. There was no record of Gitrin's presence anywhere in the dome.

"Did she transfer to another city?" Ceilos asked.

"She couldn't have," I said. "That medic..." I glanced over at Isaak and quickly added, "Uh, Heros—he said he'd spoken to her earlier today."

Ceilos said nothing. He scrolled silently across the map, looking for anything we might have missed.

"Would it be the hackers?" Isaak said. His voice was gravelly, and he cleared his throat. "You know, the Liberator or whoever?"

"Of course not," I said defensively. "What would a terrorist group want with my tutor?"

"The time postern," Ceilos answered.

I swallowed. "All right, then. We'll just have to tell the *geroi*. I'll show them the plans again, and the posternkey." I opened another System panel.

"Wait, Nadin!" Ceilos grabbed my wrist. "I don't know if that's such a good idea. If Gitrin is the one who programmed the posternkey, then she didn't want the *geroi* to know about it. That's why it was encrypted to your DNA."

I pulled my hand away. "Well, what am I supposed to do about that? I am not a *gerouin* yet. And that was Gitrin's own doing. I don't have any authority to act on my own."

Isaak stood up, looking at the map of Hope Renewed over Ceilos' shoulder. "Okay, wait. Who are these *geroi*, and why do you need their permission?"

"The *geroi* are the rulers of the citidome," said Ceilos. "And... they're also our parents."

Isaak's brows furrowed. "You guys are siblings? I thought you were—" He broke off, not seeming to know how to phrase it. Finally, he said two words in his own language. The System did not translate these, but something about Isaak's tone as he spoke them made my face grow hot.

"Ceilos is my assigned partner," I snapped. My fingers fumbled over the panel's input, and I restarted it in frustration.

"My parents are the former *geroi* of Bright Horizon citidome," Ceilos said in a calmer voice. "They relocated to the Hamos colony three years ago, and I came to live here, with Nadin and the *geroi* of Hope Renewed. Nadin and I were supposed to finish our education together, and then..." He trailed off.

And then we were supposed to form a *geroi* partnership of our own. But I had to go and ruin everything by failing my evaluation.

"*Dataset not found*," the System told me. I clenched my teeth and restarted it again.

"But if the *geroi* are your parents," Isaak said, "why don't you want them to know about the time-door thing?"

"They already know about it," I said, inputting the command slowly and deliberately this time. "My tutor and I designed it as an alternative evacuation mode. I'm sure you noticed that there's not a lot of air out there right now."

Isaak moved his head up and down. "The atmosphere is depleting. Our scientists knew that it happened, but we weren't sure what caused it. And we definitely didn't know that there were humans here when it happened."

Ceilos snorted. "The humans are what caused it. Before the Progression, people were a bit less... careful about the impact our industries had on the environment. By the time we realized it, it was too late. The *gerotus* was established to help implement policies that would offset the atmospheric degradation, but it was too late by that time. So now the primary objective is evacuation."

"The time postern would have changed all that," I said. "If we could go back in time, warn the Iamoi of what was to come—we could change history. If the people knew what was going to happen, surely they would stop. Find new methods of harvesting energy, ones that wouldn't have such a drastic impact on the atmosphere."

Isaak burst out laughing. I looked up from the System panel, folding my arms. "What's so funny?"

"I'm sorry. It's not funny. It's just... it's kind of ironic. Never mind. So I'm guessing the *geroi* nixed the time postern idea?"

"'Nixed' is not a word I'm familiar with," I muttered. I don't know why I was letting this alien boy get under my skin so much. I needed to focus.

Ceilos said, "Nadin and her tutor presented their design to the *gerotus*, but they rejected the proposal. They said it would be too much of a drain on our resources."

"They didn't believe it would work," I said. "But now we have proof that it does. I just need to show them the plans—and you."

"What do I have to do with it?" Isaak asked.

"You say you were born on Iamos." I pressed the panel's *submit* key. "Which means the atmosphere returns. Which means Gitrin's theory works."

Isaak frowned. "Actually—"

"*Dataset not found.*"

I made a noise of aggravation. "What is wrong with this thing?"

Ceilos came to stand beside me, looking at the panel. "The data isn't here," he said.

"But it *has* to be here. We spent over a year working on it. It should be *right here.*"

"But it's not."

The full meaning of his words washed over me, bringing a wave of nausea with it. It wasn't that I couldn't find it. It was that it was *gone.* "It's been deleted? But who would delete it?"

"The *geroi?*" Isaak suggested.

I glared at him. "Of course not. What purpose would that serve? The *geroi* have more important things to do with their time than whimsically manipulate the System. It must have been Gitrin."

Ceilos looked unconvinced. "But why would Gitrin—"

I waved the panel away, turning on my heel. "She must have. She is up to something, and I have had enough of her deceit."

"Wait, Nadin! Where are you going?" Isaak cried as I reached for the door handle.

His voice brought me back to reality. The *geroi* had given me an assignment. I couldn't just leave him. I couldn't disobey a directive, not after last night. I needed to prove myself to them. This was my last chance, or I'd lose Ceilos—I'd lose everything.

My shoulders slumped. "I don't know. I just... I want to talk to her. I want to know what's going on. But..." I trailed off, uncertain of what to say.

"Let me guess," Isaak said. "The *geroi* want you to keep playing flashcards with me?"

I sighed. "I do not know what that means. But yes. I am supposed to keep an eye on you."

He looked back and forth between Ceilos and me. "Then let me come with you," he said. "I mean... if you guys can build the time postern, then that means I can go home, right?"

Ceilos tapped his lower lip thoughtfully. "It couldn't hurt, Nadin. He already knows too much of what's going on. If this gets us answers..." He didn't say any more, but I could see in his eyes that he was thinking of Tibros. If I could prove myself to the *geroi*—if the time postern really was the answer—then maybe our partnership...

I lowered my head. "All right," I said. "You can help us—for now."

Isaak grinned and thrust his right hand toward me. I stared at him, baffled.

"Oh, right," he said. "It goes like this." Then he took my hand, clasped it in his own, moved it up and down. I started at his touch.

"What was that?" I asked, my face flushed.

"A handshake," said Isaak. "It means we're in this together now. We're a team."

Chapter 20

· ₀ ° • ○ ∅ ɸ ○

"WHAT ARE YOU GOING TO TELL THE GEROI IF THEY FIND OUT WE left the hospital?" Isaak asked as we stepped into the elevator.

"I will tell them the truth," I said. "That I was showing you around the city in the hopes that the audio-visual stimulation would help the System decode your brainwaves faster."

"And you'll just omit the part that I don't really need the System to communicate?" he asked with a grin.

I squared my shoulders. "A partial truth is not a lie."

He laughed. "I like the way you think."

The elevator hummed as it began to propel us toward the surface.

"So what's Ceilos doing, again?"

This was the part I was most reluctant about sharing with a stranger, even one who claimed to be on our team. I'd never had a "team"—besides Ceilos and Gitrin, that is, and look at where trusting Gitrin had gotten me. But Isaak understood far too much, even when we tried to be subtle. He read people almost as well as the System itself. There was no point in concealing things from him.

"Ceilos modified your earpiece to allow you to go offline. It's a protocol he invented and installed on the System...

surreptitiously. It makes it so the System can't track you. Then he plants a decoy elsewhere in the citidome, so that if anyone looks at the System's tracker, they'll think we're somewhere else. They won't be alerted to our absence. Ceilos and I are monitored a bit more closely than the other citizens, for obvious reasons." A stubborn strand of coarse hair slipped across my forehead. I sighed and tucked it back behind my ear. "I was offline last night when I found you outside the dome."

"I thought that was you," said Isaak. "When I woke up"—he laughed—"I thought you were an old woman."

I frowned. "Why would you think that?"

"Well, because of your hair."

"What is wrong with my hair? Everyone in Hope Renewed has hair this color. It was selected as our regional trait after the Progression. It represents sea foam. Our capital used to be on the coast." I still thought I heard the waves against the shoreline, sometimes, even though I hadn't seen the sea since I was a child.

"Ceilos doesn't have white hair," Isaak said.

"Ceilos is from Bright Horizon. They selected a wheat color because that region was an agricultural hub... before." My voice hitched on a knot in my throat. I swallowed it down.

"So, what, everyone on Iamos is, like... genetically modified?"

I tugged my earlobe. "It was a necessity for survival. The increased solar radiation from the atmospheric changes can be deadly, so we need all the protection we can get. Besides," I said, "the Progression really taught us that all of us on Iamos are a family. We didn't need differences of appearance to tear us apart."

Isaak looked like he wanted to say something, but he

hesitated.

"I'm sure you're going to tell me that I'm *wrong*," I sniffed. "Let me guess: that's not how it is on Mars?"

He looked down at his feet. "It's not. But Mars isn't Iamos. Not really. Anyway, so if things are so great here thanks to the *Progression*, what's up with this Liberator guy?"

"The so-called Liberator is an anarchist. He doesn't care about the welfare of Iamos. He just wants to see the world burn."

"Sounds like Henry," Isaak muttered. I cocked an eyebrow, but he didn't elaborate.

The elevator slowed and shuddered to a stop. A moment later, the doors slid open. We were on the ground floor of the capitol building now, a massive stepped pyramid made of stone and glass that rose from the caverns, stretching nearly to the top of the blue dome. This was the riskiest part of the venture—we were in the *geroi*'s territory. I could only hope that Antos and Melusin were upstairs in their enclosed offices. If they happened to see us here, I'd never be able to lie my way out of it.

"Put your hood up before we go outside," I said. I had given Isaak a *plivos*' cloak, made of heavy burlap, before we left the hospital. "I get enough attention when I visit the upper levels. If anyone sees you, word will surely get back to the *geroi*."

"I'll stick out like a sore thumb, huh?"

The loose strand of hair fell forward again. I tucked it back. "I suppose so."

We passed through the arched doorway of the capitol building, and Isaak drew in his breath when I opened the outer gate. The citidome spread out before us, an enormous metropolis of red-clay buildings and cloth-draped stalls, throngs of *plivoi* milling between them. The air was thick with the smell of fried food and *gurza* dung.

"Wow," Isaak said at last. "This is incredible. It's like... Ancient Rome meets Krypton, or something."

I wondered how long Isaak was going to continue using bizarre idioms like that before he realized they meant nothing to me. I pulled up the hood of my own cloak and led him into the city.

"How many people live here?" he asked as we passed through the marketplace.

"Slightly less than one million."

"Wow," he repeated. "That's even bigger than Tierra Nueva. Well, if you factor in the metro area... but all of them live inside this dome?"

"Yes. The *plivoi* live here in the upper levels. The *esotoi* live between, in the uppermost caverns which open out onto the surface. And the *patroi* live in the deepest level, far below the surface." Where the risk of radiation exposure was at its lowest. I omitted that part, though.

"That's incredible. How many domes are there on Iamos?" Isaak asked.

I swallowed. "Just six."

"Six? And they're all this size?"

"Yes. There are also two smaller citidomes on Hamos, the third planet. But that is all that remains of our population."

"I'm sorry," Isaak said. He stopped short. "Wait a minute— you say Venus is the third planet?"

"Hamos," I corrected him. I gestured skyward. The thick blue glass obscured it, but you could still see it there in the sky, shining like a second sun. "Why do you ask?"

Isaak looked up at the planet thoughtfully. "No reason," he finally said. "Everything is just so different. I wonder how far back in time I traveled."

"I would have to look at the posternkey's data coordinates more carefully to know that. Actually," I admitted, "that might be too advanced even for me. We need Gitrin."

"Well, here's hoping we find her, then," Isaak said.

The noise of the marketplace was deafening. People jostled against one another, voices shouted to be heard above the cacophony. I tried to push forward quickly, but Isaak hung back, stopping in front of almost every stall to see what was inside.

"What kind of meat is that?" he asked, staring at a tray of smoky-hot kebabs with ravenous eyes.

"*Kela*," I said.

"Is that some kind of bird?"

I sighed pointedly. "I don't know what you mean by 'bird.' A *kela* is a *kela*. Would you like to try it?"

He stared at the tray a few moments longer, as if debating whether his hunger was strong enough to risk trying a foreign meat. Finally he moved his head up and down, something I had figured out was his equivalent of saying *yes*. I fought the urge to smirk and ordered two skewers of kebabs from the merchant.

Beyond the marketplace were the insulae of the *plivoi*. Gitrin lived in one of these mudbrick structures—on a lower level, because of her status as tutor to a *patroin*. This area of the city always made me uncomfortable, though I wouldn't confess that to Isaak. Even with Enforcers on every corner, I never knew how people might react if they knew the daughter of the *geroi* was among them. Hope Renewed had been a relatively peaceful city until the Liberator got his foothold here. He made them forget that the way we lived now—the citidomes, the castes—was simply out of necessity. The *geroi* cared only for the good of Iamos, but sometimes that meant making hard decisions. It was their job—*my* job—to do what was best for the people, even if the people couldn't see it.

At the intersection of two major *vi'i* was a large public square. A massive fountain stood in its center, and throngs of *plivoi* milled around it, filling amphorae with water to bring back to their homes.

Isaak, holding his nearly-empty skewer with sticky fingers, glanced around the plaza then back to me. He swallowed and asked, "Now what?"

"Now we wait for Ceilos. He said he'd meet us here when he was done planting the decoy earpiece." I tossed my skewer into a wastebin and leaned against the fountain's concrete base. Across the plaza, a group of young women and men, not much older than myself, were playing ball on a haphazardly-constructed court. Their raucous laughter echoed off the sides of the buildings. Isaak craned his neck to watch them. I sighed, looking down at my feet. You'd never catch a *patroin* playing ball in the street.

A group of children, too young for apprenticeships, passed by us in two orderly lines, flanked by Caretakers. The child at the end of the left-hand line stopped to pull a rock from her shoe. When it was free, she glanced up at me and flashed me a gap-toothed grin. Involuntarily, I smiled back, until one of the Caretakers took notice and cuffed the girl's ear. The girl dutifully hurried back to her place in line as I stared after them.

"That game's like *ulama*," Isaak said.

I blinked, dragged from my thoughts by his voice. "I'm sorry?"

"A ballgame they play in parts of Mexico. It's based on the game they used to play in ancient times."

"I do not know what Mexico is," I said, "but we have played this game for a long time. It's one of the few things that carried over after the Progression."

Isaak laughed. "You should teach me. I bet you're Hope Renewed's star player, right?"

My face grew hot under his scrutiny. "Well, I don't know how to play. The *plivoi* play it. Some of the *esotoi*, too. But the *patroi* do not have much time for frivolities."

"All work and no play makes Nadin a dull girl," Isaak said.

I avoided his gaze, standing up to look across the plaza. "Where is Ceilos? He should be here by now."

Two of the ballplayers, a man and a woman, broke away from the group, jogging over to the fountain. Their faces were red and shone with sweat. They stopped a short distance from us, scooping their hands into the water to drink.

"We have time for one more round before we get back to work," the woman said, splashing water on her face. "Unless you want to surrender now."

The man wiped his mouth with the back of his hand. "I'm just getting started, Corin. You know my *stamina* is unmatched."

The woman scoffed. "I don't know if I'd call three minutes 'stamina'." She laughed at his wounded expression, splashing water in his direction. "I'm just joking, *yacunos*."

The man said something I couldn't hear and pulled the

woman close. She giggled and draped herself around him, her hands snaking up under the tight fabric of his shirt. I grimaced and pulled the hood of my cloak further over my face.

"What's your problem?" Isaak asked.

"These *plivoi* are like animals," I whispered.

"What's wrong with them?" He stared pointedly. I jabbed my elbow into his side.

"Stop looking at them! We're trying to be inconspicuous!" When he ignored me, I sighed and added in a low voice, "They practically mate on the streets."

The other ballplayers called to the pair at the fountain. The two broke apart, grinning and running to join them. Isaak watched them go. "They were just being affectionate," he said.

"You mean that didn't"—I paused, struggling to find the right word—"*bother* you?"

"No. Honestly, it's the first time since I've been here that I've seen anyone act human."

I glared at him. "How is *that* what makes someone human?"

"I dunno." He shifted, looking down at his shoes. "Being happy. Being in love. No one in the underground seems to love each other."

His words stung. "We all love each other," I corrected him. "We *live* for each other. It's the way of Iamos."

"Yeah, but, I mean... it's different with your partner," Isaak said. "Isn't it? I mean, don't you and Ceilos...?"

He trailed off uncomfortably. I felt something twist inside me, an unfamiliar niggle of worry. "No. We are *patroi*, Isaak." I looked back at the *plivoi*, laughing as they tossed the leather ball around the makeshift court. My stomach still taut, I said, "So... This is how *you* would behave?"

He didn't look at me. "Not with just anyone," he finally said, his voice barely audible. "But with the right person..."

"Nadin."

I started, looking over my shoulder. Ceilos stood beside us. I hadn't even noticed him approach.

"It's ready," he said.

I pulled my cloak closer about myself. "Good. Let's get moving."

Isaak took one last bite of his kebab and tossed the skewer into the wastebin, glancing at the ballplayers before moving to follow us. Something about his expression made my stomach twist into uneasy knots.

I wanted nothing more than to forget that this conversation ever took place. But for some reason, it felt burned indelibly into my brain.

The air inside the insula was cool, but it tasted stale. The strong, pungent scent of dried herbs hung heavy in the stagnant air. The interior walls of the dim corridor were made of glass, but unlike those of the hospital building, they were frosted, allowing light to filter through without sacrificing privacy.

It was so quiet after the cacophony of the marketplace, it made my ears ring. The only signs of life were the artificial lights that shone through the walls of the apartments and the occasional movement of a shadowy silhouette on the other side of the glass.

Gitrin's apartment was dark. I knocked on the sliding door, but there was no answer.

"Looks like no one's home," Isaak said.

I swallowed, unsure of what to do next. "Where could she be?"

Ceilos pushed past me, shoving the door open.

"What are you doing?" I hissed.

"We're never going to learn the truth if we just hover outside waiting for permission," he said. Isaak grinned and followed him inside.

I glanced over my shoulder. One of the silhouettes behind the glass wall moved slightly. I knew, rationally, that they couldn't see me, but I felt jittery nonetheless. I shook it off and hurried into Gitrin's apartment.

And stopped short just inside the door.

Gitrin's apartment was a shambles. Furniture was upended, her antique woven-grass chairs torn to shreds. Ceilos knelt beside a small bronze chest lying on its side. Gitrin's clothing spilled out of it, strewn in a crumpled mess across the room.

"What happened here?" Isaak asked.

"I don't know." I could barely manage the words. I didn't know what I'd been expecting, but it wasn't this. "Gitrin?" I called. There was no reply.

On the far wall, the smooth reddish-brown clay was etched with writing. I moved closer to get a better look. It was the old-fashioned hieratic that had been in use before the Progression. I struggled to remember the strange syllables from my studies. Haltingly, I read, "N'elytherios tou shenos."

"In the name of freedom," Ceilos repeated.

"What does that mean?" said Isaak.

"I'm almost afraid to find out," Ceilos said, turning to look around the rest of the apartment.

Isaak trailed after him into the bedroom. "Do you think it's that Liberator guy?"

I stared at the etched writing once more, running my hand over the carvings. Isaak had suggested that before, but I hadn't believed him. What could they possibly want with Gitrin?

"*System protocol initiated. Subject Nadin recognized. Begin transmission.*"

"Nadin," Gitrin's voice said in my ear.

I nearly screamed. I whirled around to look behind me, but there was no one else with me. No sounds apart from Isaak and Ceilos' muffled voices in the other room. I turned back to the writing, running my fingers across the word *elytherios* again. At my touch, the voice was back in my ear. "Nadin, you must listen to me. There isn't much time."

My pulse throbbed in my temples. I knew it was Gitrin. And just like when I'd held the posternkey, only I could hear it.

"If you are receiving this message, I am no longer in Hope Renewed, and there is a very good chance that the city is in danger. I know you have come here with questions, but I'm afraid you will not find the answers here. You will have to search. Seek, and you will find. Begin where we began—the answer is in plain sight, if you know where to look. The three sisters will guide the way. Touch the highest peak, and you will find me in the place where freedom lies."

She was talking in riddles. I clenched my fist against the wall, straining to understand.

"And Nadin," the voice went on, "this is very important. You must not tell *anyone* what you've heard here. Not the *geroi*, not

192

even Ceilos. This is crucial, Nadin. The future of Iamos is at stake. If you ever trusted me, *yachin*, even for a moment... Please, trust me now. I will see you soon."

I braced myself against the wall. *Yachin*. It had been her pet name for me as a child. I hadn't heard that word in a long time, and the sound of it now made my eyes burn, my vision swim. What did all of this mean?

"Nadin, what's wrong?" Ceilos asked. I hadn't even heard him and Isaak come out of the bedroom. He came up behind me now, placing his hand on my shoulder. "Are you all right?"

I swallowed down the lump in my throat. "I'm fine. Did you find anything in there?"

"No. It looked much the same in there as—"

"Hang on a minute," Isaak interrupted. "Do you hear something?"

We stood still, listening. Faintly, in the distance, I heard shouting.

"Outside. In the plaza," said Ceilos.

The three of us hurried out of Gitrin's apartment. I cast one last worried look at the engraving on the wall before pulling the glass door shut.

A large crowd had gathered in the plaza. On the steps of the insula, people stood watching the pandemonium in the square before us. I rose up on tiptoe to see over the shoulder of the tall man in front of me. The crowd appeared to be formed around an Enforcer and three *plivoi*—two women and a man. I realized, with a start, that one of the women and the man were the ball-playing couple from earlier.

"You can't do this to us!" the woman shouted, her voice

breaking. "This is our right. Our right as human beings."

"It is not your right to violate the edicts of the *geroi*," the Enforcer replied in a quieter voice. "These edicts have been chosen to ensure the survival of Iamos. All partnerships must follow the proper protocol and apply for a reproduction permit with the eugenics committee—"

"You think we haven't done that?" the man broke in. "We've been turned down six times already!"

I leaned forward, tapping the man in front of me on the shoulder. "What's going on?" I whispered.

"They got caught trying to smuggle Ferre into the city."

I inhaled sharply through my nose. More of the Liberator's doing.

The unfamiliar woman had stood quietly up to this point, but now she turned to the crowd and shouted, "People of Hope Renewed, do you not see how they strip your rights from you? Leaving the fundamental right to bear children to a faceless *committee*? Iamos is better than this! We were once a great and free people—"

The crowd around us on the steps began to shift, murmuring uneasily. I shrank back from them into the shadow of the doorway, and felt a steadying hand on my shoulder. I turned, expecting to see Ceilos, but it was Isaak. "What are they talking about? Is everything okay?"

"We should leave," I said. "Before this gets out of control."

"That is enough!" the Enforcer bellowed. "If you will not submit—*immediately*—then I will have no choice but to use force."

"Come on," Ceilos said, pushing back into the doorway.

The unfamiliar woman yelled, "We will not submit! There can be no peace without freedom! In the name of the Liberator—" Her voice broke off in a scream, and she crumpled to the ground. Around us, the crowd broke into shouts and movement, some people trying to get away, but most surging forward at the Enforcer.

"What's happening?" Isaak gasped. I gripped his elbow, trying to pull him back into the apartment after Ceilos, but he resisted me. "What are they doing to her?"

Someone in the crowd called out, "The *geroi* are the cause of this! The Liberator is Iamos' true salvation! No peace without freedom! Death to the *geroi*!"

The man who had been standing in front of us surged forward, yelling, "FREEDOM!" Then his knees buckled and he collapsed, gripping the sides of his head in agony. Around the plaza, *plivoi* staggered, falling to their knees, crying out in pain, while still others hurried to flee the area. Isaak stood frozen until the force of my fingers digging into the skin of his upper arm made him yelp.

"Now," I snapped, my heart pounding in my ears. Finally he moved, and we slammed the door to the building behind us. The shadows behind the glass were darker and sharper now, as the occupants stood close to the walls, listening. A face peered out at me from behind one sliding door. Ceilos pulled Isaak and me forward, not saying a word until we had made it through the building's back door and safely onto another street. In the distance, I could hear wailing and the thundering clatter of feet. A platoon of Enforcers rushed past us, hurrying to finish putting down the riot.

My hands shook as I struggled to catch my breath. That was far too close. This was why I didn't like to go aboveground. *"Death to the* geroi," indeed.

"What the hell just happened?" Isaak snapped. "What did that cop do to all those people?"

"The adherence protocol. The Enforcer enabled it to keep the crowd under control," said Ceilos.

"The System can do that?"

"Yes."

Isaak made a face. "Wasn't that a little bit, I don't know, overkill?"

"They broke the law," I said, my voice ragged. "Now they have to pay the consequences."

"What law?"

"That woman was smuggling Ferre. It's an illegal drug, it counteracts the mandatory birth control substances in the drinking water."

Isaak stared at me in horror. "Wait a minute—you guys put *birth control* in your *water*? And everybody *has* to take it?" When I tugged my earlobe, he said, "How do people have kids, then?"

"They apply for a permit, and the eugenics council evaluates them. How fit they are genetically to reproduce, whether there's a need for children in their caste at said time, and so on."

Isaak said something I couldn't understand. He walked a few paces away from us, running his hands through his hair compulsively.

Ceilos folded his arms. "Isaak, you don't seem to understand how serious this is. Our planet is *dying*. We can't sustain extra population. Do you understand what happens when someone has an illegal child? It puts a strain on the resources of everybody else. Sometimes you have to make sacrifices, for the good of the whole."

"Yeah, but..." He looked back at the insula. The air was still now, the street quiet. The Enforcers must have succeeded in breaking up the riot. "I mean, there's such a thing as *balance*—"

"You said it earlier, Isaak," I interrupted, scowling at him. "Iamos isn't Mars. So why don't you just keep your opinions to yourself until we can figure out a way to get you back where you came from?"

He stared at me, his eyes cold. "Fine. You got it, Madam *Gerouin*. But if we can't find Gitrin, how exactly are you planning on accomplishing that?"

"I don't know," I said, suddenly feeling exhausted. "But for right now? All I really want to do is go home." I straightened the hood of my cloak and brushed past him.

Chapter 21

· ∘ ∘ • ◯ ∅ φ ∘

MY OLD CLASSROOM—THE SIDE ROOM IN THE GEROI'S VILLA WHERE I had done all my years of learning—was cold and quiet. The dim glow of the phosphorescent stones cast multicolored shadows across the woven-copper table and chairs, the potted *fraouloi*, Gitrin's antique globe. My footsteps echoed across the stone floor.

I didn't know what I expected to find here. Answers, maybe. Or maybe I just wanted to hear Gitrin's voice again, if only in my own mind. Everything was such a disaster all of a sudden. Gitrin always used to know what to do. Figuring it out on my own was just too hard.

I paced the room a few times before finally sitting on the floor, my back against the wall, staring at the darkened classroom space. The quiet was a welcome relief after the riot in the plaza. My ears were still ringing from the protesters' screaming—and Isaak's incessant questions afterward. I was so tired of having to give him answers when I didn't know what they were myself. I was just so tired.

Maybe Gitrin had been right. Maybe I wasn't ready, after all.

I didn't even realize I'd closed my eyes until I heard the voice.

"Where is Ceilos?"

My head jerked up at the words. I was no longer alone in the room. Gitrin sat in a woven-copper chair in the room's center. And across the table from her sat another person.

Me.

I gasped, looking down at my hands, only to find I wasn't really there. The only Nadin in the room was the *other* me, sitting anxiously on the copper stool, her hands clasped tightly together in her lap. "The evaluation is supposed to be taken as a partnership, isn't it?" she asked. Her voice—my voice—sounded strange in my ears.

"You cannot rely on Ceilos for everything, Nadin," Gitrin said, a knowing smile playing at her lips. "The head will never survive if the heart is too weak."

The other Nadin frowned, her eyebrows scrunched up in confusion, but she tugged her earlobe, and the evaluation began. Questions about Iamos' history, the procedures of the *gerotus*, basic political and scientific and mathematical knowledge—all blurred together in my ears and in my memory, the standard evaluation questions I'd been memorizing since birth. I'd answered flawlessly then, as the Nadin in the chair did now. A perfect exam score. No chance of failure. I would be a *gerouin* by the night of my *enilikin*.

Then Gitrin hesitated, looking solemnly at the girl who sat before her. "Nadin, what if there was a way to save Iamos?" she asked. "What would you do?"

The other me hesitated, her mouth half-open. "The *geroi* have initiated the evacuation plan. If all proceeds on schedule, all remaining Iamoi will be safely on Hamos within one year."

"Not the evacuation. Something else," Gitrin said. "Something that could return the atmosphere to Iamos. That could prevent the cataclysm."

I opened my own mouth to respond, but no sound would come. My tongue felt weighted down.

"Surely if there were another way, the *geroi* would have already tried it," not-me said.

"But what if the *geroi* were wrong? What if *you* knew of a way to save Iamos, but the *geroi* refused to use it? What would you do then?"

I knew the answer now. I ran over to Gitrin, crouched before her, waved my hands in front of her. The time postern. That was the answer—it had to be. Why hadn't I realized it before, when it would have mattered? I tried desperately to speak, to get Gitrin's attention, but she looked right through me.

"There could be no such scenario, Gitrin," the other Nadin insisted, damning herself with each word. "The *geroi*'s first priority is the protection of Iamos. If there were a solution, they would not refuse it."

I knew how this would end. I'd lived it and relived it almost constantly for the past week. Gitrin would look me square in the eyes and tell me, "You're not ready."

But the words didn't come. Instead, Gitrin stopped and looked at me. Not the other Nadin, but *me*, though I wasn't really there. When she spoke, something about her voice was not right—it echoed, reverberated, out of sync with the movements of her lips.

"The answer lies in freedom."

The walls of the classroom began to melt around her, dripping into the dark stalactites of the cave. Hissing voices swirled around me, whispering, "*Elytherios, elytherios,*" in my ear.

I swallowed hard. My voice came back in a rush. "But what does that mean?" I cried.

"Seek, and you will find," said Gitrin. "Begin where we began."

"*Elytherios, elytherios.*"

The floor beneath my feet began to rumble and shake, cracking apart. "Wait, Gitrin! Please—"

"Find me in the place where freedom lies."

The cavern walls ripped apart with a deafening crash, an explosion of rock and blazing-red magma. The air around me now was fire, black ash and suffocation. In the distance, I could see three mountain peaks, dripping with molten lava. Balls of flame tumbled from the sky.

"Gitrin!" I called, choking for breath. She was nowhere in sight.

The voices in my ear whisper-shrieked, "*Ne'haoi ifaisteioi mesau elytherios.*"

My eyes flew open, ears ringing from the sound of my own screams. I was alone again in the classroom. I must have fallen asleep without realizing it. My mouth felt dry, and loose strands of coarse white hair tickled at my face. I brushed them away in annoyance, breathing in deeply and slowly, willing my heart to slow down to its regular pace.

"Nadin?"

I jumped at the voice, but it was only Ceilos. He stood in the open doorway, peering at me across the darkened classroom, the phosphorescent stones casting reflections of purple and blue across his skin. He stepped into the room, pulling the sliding door shut quietly behind him.

"I thought I heard voices in here," he said. "Are you alone?"

"Yes." I wiped the crust from my eyes as he came to sit beside me, on my left. "I had a nightmare. What time is it?"

"Well after nightfall," Ceilos said. "I came looking for you when you didn't come to the evening meal."

"I came in here to think. I must have fallen asleep."

"It's understandable. You've been through a lot. You haven't stopped going since you left the hospital. Your body is still weak after last night, you know. You should rest more."

"How am I supposed to rest with everything that's going on? When Gitrin..." I drew my knees to my chest, not knowing what else to say.

Ceilos put his hand on top of my foot. "Nadin, I know you're upset about it still, but... do you want to tell me about what happened with Gitrin last week? On the day of the evaluation? You've been so tense ever since then."

I said nothing, just staring at his dark fingers against the silver of my boot.

He sighed. "You and Gitrin were so close. Inseparable. She was my tutor, too, after I moved here, but I never had that bond with her. So when she passed me and failed you..."

He trailed off, watching me expectantly. I squeezed my eyes shut, resting my forehead against my knees. "I don't know, Ceilos. I don't know what happened. She said so many strange things, she was acting so bizarre. None of it made any sense." Unless she meant the time postern. But how could she have known about that, days before Isaak appeared? And then that message she left for me in her apartment. The scene from my nightmare played over again in my mind. The cracking earth, the mountain peaks. The sky engulfed with fire.

Elytherios.

"Did she say anything about the Liberator?" Ceilos asked. His voice sounded strange, and he had an odd look on his face—I'd never seen that look before.

I lifted my shoulders like I'd seen Isaak do. "I don't know. Everything she said was just *off*. I don't even remember half of it now." I stretched my legs out, leaning my head back against the wall and looking up at the ceiling. "I'm just so *tired*, Ceilos."

He frowned. "Nadin, maybe you should take a break. I can watch Isaak tomorrow—"

"No!" I blurted. He stared at me, mouth agape. "That's my assignment. I have to prove myself to the *geroi*. For..." I glanced at him, then looked away. "For our future."

He put his hand on top of mine, his palm over the back of my hand, long fingers threaded through mine. "I'm your partner, Nadin. No matter what Tibros says. You should be able to share some of your burden with me."

I smiled, but the little niggle of worry from earlier began to gnaw at the back of my mind again. "Ceilos," I said, "did you see those *plivoi* in the square earlier?"

"The ones the Enforcers arrested?"

"Yes. Did you see them before that? At the fountain?"

"I saw them when I was making my way over to you. I didn't pay them much attention."

I inhaled. "Did you think... what they were doing was... normal?"

Ceilos chuckled. "They are a bit more expressive than *patroi*," he said with a grin. "But, you know... most *patroi* partnerships are arrangements of convenience. Caste, status, genetic traits—

those are the things that matter. But I think... I think we're different, aren't we?" He shifted onto his knees, scooting in front of me. Slowly, gently, he cupped my cheek in his palm. "You're not just a business arrangement to me."

My eyes stung, but I blinked back the tears and tugged my earlobe with my right hand. "I care more about you than anyone else on Iamos," I told him.

Ceilos smiled, the kind that spread from his lips to his eyes and lit up his whole face. The smile that was only for me. "Then I think this is completely normal."

I stared at him in confusion, but then the next instant he had pulled my body up against his, softly pressing his mouth against mine just like the *plivoi* had in the plaza. He ran his fingers through my hair, pulling more strands loose from their messy braid. I didn't know how to react. I just sat there, limply, while Ceilos' lips caressed mine. But when he drew my lips apart and slipped his tongue into my mouth, I jerked back.

"Ceilos," I squeaked.

He didn't seem to notice my revulsion. His lips slid down the side of my neck, and his hands caressed my back, my thighs. His breath came out as a sigh. "I love you, Nadin," he whispered, pulling my body closer to his, and I could feel the hardness of him beneath his clothing.

"Ceilos!" I cried again, louder this time.

He pulled away, his eyes unfocused and confused. "What is it?"

"I-I..." I was shaking. I didn't know what to say. It was like I was asleep again, having some kind of horrible nightmare.

He blinked a few times, his eyes coming back into focus.

"What's wrong? Didn't you like it?"

Why would I like that?! my mind screamed, but I couldn't find my voice. I couldn't bear to see the hurt on Ceilos' face, couldn't understand what I had done to cause it.

He pushed away from me, getting to his feet. "I'm sorry, Nadin," he said, his voice impossibly small. "I thought... I thought you loved me, too."

I jumped up after him. "I *do* love you!" I protested.

"Then why don't you—" I flinched, and he lowered his volume. "Why don't you *want* me?"

I had broken him. No, I had broken *us*. I could feel it as surely as the cold air around us, as the fading atmosphere outside the dome. Something was wrong with me, and it had ruined Ceilos and me forever. We could never go back.

I couldn't stop the tears this time. They coursed freely down my face, burned my throat. "I don't know," I said.

Ceilos didn't say another word. He just turned and left me there, alone in the dark. I slumped down to the floor, my face against my knees, my shoulders shaking with sobs. This had to be a bad dream. I'd wake up in the morning and Gitrin would be home. The last week would never have happened. There'd be no Isaak, no crisis on Hamos, no conflict with the *geroi*, no argument with Ceilos. We'd never be broken.

I'd never be broken.

I told myself over and over that it would be all right, but the tears wouldn't stop coming. Because deep in my heart, I knew it was a lie.

CHAPTER 22

· ∘ ° • ◯ ∅ φ ∘

"WHAT'S YOUR PROBLEM?" ISAAK ASKED. "ARE YOU STILL torqued at me for questioning your sainted *geroi* yesterday?"

"Yes," I replied. I didn't understand half of his words, but his tone said it all. "And you need to guard your tongue. You never know who might be listening." I tapped my earpiece and looked pointedly at him. He rolled his eyes and slumped down in the hospital bed.

I sat on the empty bed next to his, scrolling through a System panel. There had to be a backup of the plans to the time postern *somewhere*. I just needed to find them. But I was having a hard time concentrating. I kept thinking about Ceilos. He hadn't been in his rooms at the villa this morning, even though the System indicated that was his location. He must be offline somewhere. He wouldn't answer any of the comms I sent him, though, so I couldn't begin to guess where he really was.

I wondered if he would ever speak to me again. The thought made my stomach queasy.

I knew it wasn't right, but a large part of me blamed Isaak for this. If it hadn't been for the things he said in the plaza, I never would have brought any of it up to Ceilos. We could have kept on as we were. Nothing would have had to change.

But someday it would have, a small voice reminded me. Clearly this had been in Ceilos' mind, though it had never crossed mine. Someday, when we were partners officially, this would have come up.

I stubbornly pushed the thought away. It might not have happened *this* way. This was still Isaak's fault.

"What are you going to do if you can't find the plans?" Isaak asked.

I whirled on him. "Why do you keep asking me questions like that? Why do you seem to think I always have the answers? I don't *know* what I'm going to do, Isaak!"

He blinked. "I'm sorry," he said. "You just... you act like you always know everything."

I flicked the System panel away in annoyance and glared down at the peeling finish on the bed's metal footboard.

In a softer voice, Isaak said, "You know, you don't *have* to always have the answers. It's okay to just say that you don't know."

"A *gerouin* should know," I said. "A *gerouin* must be a leader."

"Even the *geroi* are just people in the end, Nadin. Nobody's perfect. Nobody knows everything."

I thought about Melusin—always so poised, always so in control. For the first time, I wondered if she ever had doubts. If she ever questioned herself. If she ever fought with Antos. Somehow, I doubted it.

"So, where's Ceilos at?" Isaak asked.

My chest clenched at the words. I sighed and said, "I don't know. Just like everything else, I don't know." I flopped back on the hospital bed.

Isaak frowned, standing up and coming over to look down at me. "Nadin, are you sure you're all right?"

I squeezed my eyes shut. "I'm fine, I just—"

A beeping sounded in my ear. "*Incoming communication. Subject unknown,*" said the System.

Isaak flinched, looking around the room. "What the heck is that?"

"I'm getting a comm." Subject unknown—or just offline? I sat bolt upright and pressed the button on my earpiece. "Ceilos?"

"*Kyrin* Nadin," said a voice I didn't recognize. "Greetings."

"Who is this?" I asked.

"The two of us have been weaving quite the twisted tapestry these last few days, haven't we? Spinning round each other, warp and weft, sometimes passing just a hair's breadth apart, but never quite... connecting. I thought it was about time we closed that gap."

I sucked the breath in through my nostrils. "The Liberator?"

At that, Isaak's eyes widened. He prodded me in the shoulder. I waved him off, but pressed another button on my earpiece to patch him in.

"Well, now I'm here," I said, trying to sound more confident than I felt. "So what do you want? And where's Gitrin?"

The man chuckled, an oddly familiar sound, but I couldn't quite place it. "I think you know," he said. "But that's not what I want to discuss with you. We have very little time, *kyrin*—let's make what time we do have count. You've been ignoring the messages I left for you all over the city. But can you ignore this?"

"*Nadin, what if there was a way to save Iamos? What would you do?*"

I gasped at the sound of Gitrin's voice. Close after came another voice—higher than it sounded in my head, younger and less assured, but undeniably my own. *"The geroi's first priority is the protection of Iamos. If there were a solution, they would not refuse it."*

I cringed as the Liberator's voice laughed over the top of the recording. "Your faith in the saviors of Iamos is inspiring, *kyrin*," he said, voice dripping sarcasm.

"Where did you get that?" I tried to sound angry, demanding, but my voice faltered. "That evaluation was private."

"Nothing escapes the System, *kyrin*. But I have to wonder— how strong is your faith? Enough to sacrifice Iamos, that much is clear. But perhaps those odds aren't personal enough to you. What if it was someone closer to you? Gitrin wasn't enough to move you—what about Isaak?"

My eyes flicked over to Isaak's. His face was unreadable. He held his hand against his earpiece, as if that would help him listen—or at least understand—better. Before I could say anything, a new transmission began. I recognized *Geros* Antos' voice. He and Melusin were supposed to be meeting with the *gerotus*, the united governing body of all of Iamos' citidomes, this morning. I gripped the metal footboard so hard my knuckles ached. The Liberator had access to my evaluation, to private sessions of the *gerotus*—was there any part of the System he didn't control?

"Medic Heros oversaw the genetic testing conducted on the subject his first evening in Hope Renewed," Antos said. "Neurological behavior, blood type, genetic composition and other factors were analyzed thoroughly by the System. Medic, if you would please report your findings to the *gerotus*?"

"Yes, *Geros*," the man said. I recognized his voice as the man who had been taking care of Isaak yesterday morning, when Melusin sent me back to the hospital. "Preliminary findings indicate that though this boy demonstrates differences in physical traits—particularly in regards to skin tone, hair color, facial features and so on—anatomically and genetically, there is no significant difference between him and the Iamoi. The primary differentiation is neurological. His brainwave patterns are unfamiliar, and they show little responsiveness to the System. But while the subject was unconscious, I did some testing with an electroencephalogram. I would need to conduct further studies to be sure, but his brain seems to be attuned to the electromagnetic wavelength that the System calculates as approximate Simoi levels."

An unfamiliar woman's voice said, "So the boy is from Simos."

"It appears so, *Gerouin*," replied Heros.

I shot a glance at Isaak as a new voice broke in—I recognized this one as belonging to Tibros, Ceilos' father. "But apart from the neurological patterns, you're saying there is no genetic difference between the Iamoi and the Simoi?"

"No, *Geros*."

The transmission wavered slightly at the sound of various murmuring voices blending together. Then Antos said, "What does this mean, then? That the Simoi are actually Iamoi?"

"That seems the most logical conclusion, *Geros*. The Simoi are descended from an ancient colonization effort, and their brains have evolved to tolerate Simos' electromagnetic field."

"Or the Iamoi are actually Simoi who lost their tolerance to the field," Isaak said under his breath.

"What?" I whispered, but before he could elaborate, Melusin spoke.

"If this is the case, then it is possible we can use this boy's sudden appearance to our advantage. Simos is the most hospitable of the other planets, far more suitable than Hamos. The magnetic field has been our only barrier so far—that, and the hostility of its current inhabitants. Having one of them here on Iamos where we can study him may prove to be the key to colonization on Simos. Conquering the field, subduing the natives—this may now be in our grasp."

Isaak swallowed hard. "What are they going to do to me? They're not going to... dissect me or something, are they?"

"Of course not," I said. "Quiet, I'm trying to listen."

Another of the *geroi* asked, "How soon can more tests be conducted on the subject?"

"As soon as the *gerotus* approves the procedure," Melusin said. "He is still in the hospital level in Hope Renewed. I have assigned Nadin to guard him."

Tibros cleared his throat. "Are you sure that's wise, Melusin? Considering her... record?"

"I'm quite sure, Tibros. Nadin may be a simpleton, but she is absolutely loyal to the *geroi*. And she's desperate to prove herself—enough that she wouldn't think to question a direct order from the *gerotus*. At a time like this, that's exactly what we need."

My mouth opened involuntarily. A *simpleton*? Was this truly what the *geroi* thought of me? Not as an equal, but as a pawn?

"If there are no further remarks," Antos said, "a motion to

approve further study on the subject from Simos—"

Isaak pulled his earpiece out in disgust. "Well, are you satisfied now, Nadin? The *geroi* sure are looking out for Iamos' best interests. They think you're an idiot, and they want to fry my brain in a microwave so they can stage an invasion of Earth."

I looked up at him, eyes narrowed. "You said you were from Iamos."

He glared back at me. "I am from *Mars*," he snapped. Then he folded his arms and looked away. "But I didn't say that my parents were."

I jumped to my feet, jabbing my index finger into his chest. "You lied to me! You *are* Simoi!" I froze, my hand hovering in midair. "But you live on Iamos in the future." My hand curled limply into my chest, and I sat back down. "So what happened to the Iamoi?"

Isaak stared down at the floor, not answering for a long moment. "I... I didn't want to tell you. When we came here, Mars... the planet was dead."

And there I was again, back outside, gasping for breath in the wind-raked desert. Cold, numb and breathless. *Dead.* "Then the time postern is a failure. We're... we're all doomed."

"Not necessarily, Nadin! I don't really know how time travel works. Something could still—"

"*Enough!*" I shouted, my voice breaking. "Stop lying to me, Isaak! It's over." I couldn't even summon the energy to cry this time. I just felt numb inside. Like I was already dead.

"So, *kyrin*. What will you do now?" the Liberator's voice said in my ear. I jumped, startled—I'd forgotten he was there. I'd been so focused on Isaak, I hadn't even noticed that the transmission from the *gerotus* had ended.

"What do you want from me?" I asked, my voice feeling heavy.

"I want the same thing you do, *kyrin*," the Liberator said. "What if there was a way to save Iamos?"

I squeezed my eyes shut. "There's *not*," I snapped.

"Gitrin disagrees," the Liberator said, "and she's not the only one. Have you spoken to your partner recently?"

I froze as the meaning of his words hit me. I hadn't seen him all day. What if...

"What do you know about Ceilos?" I asked.

The Liberator chuckled. "Don't worry about him, *kyrin*. He's safe."

My fingernails dug into the soft skin of my palm. "Where is he?"

"Really, *kyrin*. Don't prove the *geroi* right now. You're smarter than that. Ceilos is with me. If you want him, you're going to have to come to me. *N'elytherios tou shenos.*"

There was silence, and then the System told me, "*Communication terminated.*"

Isaak looked up at me, twisting his earpiece between his fingers. "What's going on?"

"I don't know," I snapped. "Initiate communication. Subject: Ceilos."

"*Subject Ceilos is unresponsive.*"

My stomach twisted up. It was true. It had to be. First Gitrin, now Ceilos.

I was alone.

"Where are you going?" Isaak asked. I hadn't even realized it, but I was already halfway out the door.

"I don't know," I said. "To rescue Ceilos." I might not be able to save Iamos, but maybe I could at least save him.

"Wait, Ceilos?" Isaak hurried after me into the hallway. "You mean he has Ceilos now, too?" When I didn't respond, he said, "But how are you going to find them?"

"I don't know! All right? I don't know, I don't know." I really was just a simpleton. How could I ever be a *gerouin*, when I never had the answers?

"Wait, Nadin—" Isaak put a hand on my shoulder. It was gentler than I expected, considering how angry I felt toward him. "Maybe I can help you."

I brushed his hand away. "No one can help me. Just stay here, Isaak."

He scoffed. "Yeah, right. I'm not going to just sit around and be their lab rat, Nadin. I'll take my chances with the Liberator any day. Come on, we can figure this out together. Won't you please trust me?"

"N'elytherios tou shenos," I said, not listening to him. "Begin where we began, the answer is in plain sight..." My mind was a whirling wreck of the last day's sights and sounds, fire in the sky, Gitrin's ruined apartment, Ceilos' hands on my skin in the dark classroom.

The classroom. I stopped midstep, Isaak colliding with me, nearly knocking me over. I gripped his arm, steadying myself, and hissed, "*Begin where we began.*"

Isaak blinked. "What does that mean?"

Still holding his arm, I launched forward, dragging Isaak behind me. "It means I think I finally know where I need to look."

Chapter 23

·₀° • ○ ∅ ϕ ○

THE VILLA WAS DESERTED. MELUSIN AND ANTOS WOULD STILL BE with the *gerotus* for several more hours, and with Ceilos gone, there was no sign of life apart from myself and Isaak. Our footsteps echoed through the empty passageway. But I still had the unsettling feeling that someone was following us, watching our every move. Unseen eyes made goosebumps rise on the back of my neck. Knowing that the Liberator had been able to tap into my private evaluation, not to mention the *gerotus*, made it feel like he was everywhere—always watching, missing nothing.

I hurried into the classroom once more, Isaak following closely behind me. This time I activated the artificial lighting. Something about the dim phosphorescent glow made me uneasy—and reminded me of last night. I didn't want to think about that again, and certainly not now.

"Gitrin told me to begin where we began," I said.

"When did she tell you that?"

I hesitated. "She had... left a message for me in her apartment."

Isaak's eyes widened. "And you didn't feel the need to share that with Ceilos and me because...?"

I looked away. "She told me not to tell anyone. I shouldn't be telling you, honestly. But it feels too late, now. Anyway, she said, 'begin where we began,' and I realized"—I strode over to the antique globe—"that that was here. My first lesson, years ago, was memorizing the regions of Iamos."

Isaak came up beside me, running his fingers over the globe, the hills and valleys in gentle relief. It was old, almost a hundred years. The planet looked so different now, it was almost impossible to imagine. There was so much blue—oceans and rivers that were now almost completely dry. The continents were green and gray. The rust-red ground that covered the world now, oxidized by the violent changes in the climate, was nowhere to be seen on the globe.

"Not quite Mars," Isaak said with a small laugh. "But it's close. Some of the coastlines are shaped differently now, but you can just see the outline..." He traced his finger along the peninsula. The capital of our region had been there, on the coast. The citidome had been build nearby, nestled into the hills, but the sea had withered away. There was still some bits of ocean left, but it was several days' journey away. You couldn't see the coastline now.

"Tierra Nueva," Isaak whispered.

"What's that?" I asked.

He smiled weakly. "My home."

I felt a pang in my chest. Iamos would be inhabitable again, but it wasn't the Iamoi who would live here. Other people would take my homeworld and not even know that it was mine.

Because we'd all be dead.

I clenched my fist. "Never mind that. Gitrin said, 'the three sisters will guide the way.'" I turned the globe slightly, following the planet's curve east to the mountains near Bright Horizon, Ceilos' home citidome. "The *Haoi Ifaisteoi* mountain range. I used to call them the sisters when I was little."

"Elysium Mons," Isaak said. "And Mount Hecates and Mount Albor. The Elysium mountain range."

I quirked my head at him. *Elysium.* It almost sounded like a word in the old language. That odd sense of being watched crept up on me again. "Gitrin told me to touch the highest peak, and find her in the place where freedom lies. So, if we're looking at the three sisters..." I reached out with my index finger, tapping the tip of the central mountain. It was round and raised from the globe's surface, worn smooth with wear.

"Nothing happened," Isaak said.

I frowned, remembering the words that had been carved on Gitrin's wall. The Liberator had said them to me before disconnecting. "*N'elytherios tou shenos.*"

Two things happened at once: the globe snapped open, parting between hemispheres, revealing a cavity; and Gitrin's voice whispered in my ear, "*Nadin.*"

I gasped. Isaak grinned, reaching into the globe to pull out what was inside. My eyes couldn't focus on him. There was nothing but Gitrin's voice, telling me what I needed to know.

"Nadin?" Isaak asked, cradling the small object in his hands. "Hello?"

I blinked a few times, trying to bring my attention back to the classroom. I took a shaky breath and took the silver trapezoid out of Isaak's hands.

"It's a posternkey," I said.

"For the time postern?"

"No." I swallowed. "A regular space postern. It's going to take us to where Gitrin is. And, I assume, Ceilos, too."

Isaak furrowed his brow. "Well? Where are they?"

I looked down at the globe, slowly moved to close it. It snapped shut, seamless. You'd never know it had held something inside.

"Elytherios," I said.

Chapter 24

· ○ ° • ○ ⊘ φ ○

ISAAK HURRIED AFTER ME DOWN THE VI'IN EXELISHIN. "BUT WHAT is Elytherios?"

"It's not a *what*. It's a *where*," I said. "It's a word in the old language. That's all I could think of every time I heard it. But that's what the Liberator was expecting. Most people only use the New Standardized Language that was adopted after the Progression, at least officially. But the anarchists are using the old language for their codes."

I stopped in front of the fountain. There was no one around. Most of the *patroi* would be in the pyramid now, working. If we were going to leave, we'd have to leave now.

"So Elytherios is a place? But how are we supposed to find it?"

"Gitrin left us a key." As I spoke, I opened a System panel and began entering commands.

"And this fountain...?"

A few swipes and the water stopped flowing abruptly. I turned to Isaak. "It's a postern. It was transporting hot water from the volcanic region northeast of here. That's how we heat the subterranean villas. But right now we're going to use it"—I closed the System panel with a quick movement of my hand—"to bring us to Elytherios." As the water drained from the basin, I took my medallion from around my neck and pressed it into the posternkey. It sprang open, unfolding and unfurling, humming with blue electricity. The postern glowed in response to its commands.

Isaak grinned. "The *geroi* are the simpletons, Nadin. I'm pretty sure you're a genius."

My face flushed. I turned away from him, stepping gingerly into the shallow puddle of water that remained at the bottom of the basin. "We only have one key, so you're going to have to hold onto me," I said, hesitantly holding my hand out to him.

He nodded his head and took my hand. The postern began to glow brighter, the multicolored lights blending together until they were white and nearly blinding. I kept my fingers tightly clamped around Isaak's and stepped forward.

Traveling by postern was never pleasant, though it was quick. For one searing moment, I could feel my atoms being ripped apart, squeezed through an incomprehensibly small space, then pieced back together. My knees felt weak as the brightness dimmed; Isaak staggered forward, and I had to brace myself against him to keep him from falling. I stood still, waiting for my head to stop spinning while Isaak fought to catch his breath.

Finally, I chanced a look around. We were still underground, but these caverns looked different than the ones beneath Hope Renewed. Instead of the blue-gray rock I was used to, the cavern walls were a rich brown, rough-looking and pockmarked. Rippled lines formed irregular curves, rounded gaps in the ceiling that let light filter in. Against the wall behind us stood the tall transportation postern we'd traveled through.

Isaak let go of my hand and moved to touch the cavern wall. "Looks like sandstone." He swiveled, putting his hands on his hips. "Where do we go now?"

"I'm not sure," I said, tucking a loose strand of hair behind my ear. "Gitrin said the way would open to us, but—" I broke off at the sound of approaching footsteps. "Someone's coming."

Before I could react, a bright beam of light hit me in the face. I cringed, squeezing my eyes shut.

"Don't move, either of you," a woman's voice said. "What are you doing down here?"

As my eyes adjusted to the light, I saw a short woman with Bright Horizon's traits: green eyes and straw-colored hair. She wore her hair loose, wild curls cascading down to her mid-back and out past her shoulders. Her face and hands were covered with pale freckles, a tell-tale sign of UV exposure. A *plivoin*. I froze in a panic, unable to think. I hadn't expected to meet anyone here—no one besides Gitrin, or Ceilos, or the Liberator. I hadn't thought this through at all, I realized with a sick stomach, and now we were finished.

Before I could react, Isaak said in a steady, solemn voice, "*N'elytherios tou shenos*." I stared at him in shock—even more so when the woman grinned and turned off her lantern.

"*Degiim n'elytherios*," she responded. "Safe passage to you. My name's Eliin, I'm the guardian here. I haven't seen the two of you before. New faction members?" She squinted at Isaak. "Ah, no, of course not. With traits like yours, you must have been born on the mountain. I'm surprised they let you out, *alos*—any Progressive would notice your *anomalies* in an instant. Of course, you know what they say—it's so easy to manipulate a mind that's reliant on the System."

Isaak laughed and tugged his earlobe, making my eyes widen. The gesture made him seem so effortlessly Iamoi, I could almost look past his bizarre coloring.

"So, are the two of you returning from a mission?" She began to lead us down a narrow passageway, back the way she had come.

"Yes," I said quickly. "We were delivering Ferre to Hope Renewed."

Eliin tugged her earlobe knowingly. "No trouble with the Enforcers, I trust?"

I smiled. "Not a bit."

"Excellent. Well, I'm sure you're eager to get back home. Was this your first trip outside?"

I glanced at Isaak. "Yes," he finally said, his accent barely perceptible. "It was... different than I was expecting."

Eliin sighed. "It's gotten terrible. Every year, the *geroi* take more away. More freedoms, more rights. And the people there just accept it. The System numbs their minds to it a great deal, of course. Makes them forget what they've lost. But still..." She stopped in front of a blank patch of wall. "Here's the place," she said to Isaak. "Squeeze right inside. It's a bit tight, but of course we can't have Enforcers happening to find their way in."

I frowned, and was about to ask *where* exactly we were supposed to squeeze into considering the wall was smooth and solid, when Isaak brushed past Eliin and disappeared into the flat surface. I stared, mouth agape, as she turned to me and said, "After him, *alin*," and prodded me forward. I flinched, bracing for impact, but it didn't come. There was no wall. As I stepped forward, it disappeared entirely, leaving nothing but a narrow gully just a few paces long that opened out into a wider cave.

Isaak was waiting for me on the other side. "Did you see that?" I whispered to him.

"See what?" he asked, a bewildered expression on his face. Then I realized—he wasn't wearing his earpiece. He'd pulled it off after the Liberator had patched us into the *gerotus* briefing. He must have left it in the hospital room.

"*It's so easy to manipulate a mind that's reliant on the System,*" Eliin had said. Is this what she meant? The System had caused me to see a wall where there was none? How much had the System concealed from me in Hope Renewed, without me ever knowing?

Eliin squeezed out of the gully behind me, snapping her lantern on once more. "I have a small home here, just outside Bright Horizon. We have a stockpile of supplies for faction members traveling back and forth on missions. Do you know your way back to Elytherios?"

"No, this is our first time making the trip," Isaak said.

"Well, you'll be all right. The *gurzas* know the way. Can I offer you a meal before you leave?"

"Um, no," I said before Isaak could accept. He shot me a crestfallen look, but I didn't want to spend an overlong amount of time with this woman—just because she was believing our lies now didn't mean we could keep it up indefinitely. "We need to get back. The Liberator is expecting us."

Eliin looked confused for a moment, then she laughed. "You must mean Eos. I've never heard him called that outside of the citidomes."

"She, uh, she hasn't been with us very long, Eliin," Isaak said with a shaky laugh.

Eliin grinned and tugged her earlobe. "Of course, of course." She patted my arm affectionately and turned away. I felt an odd feeling in the pit of my stomach. Eliin's easy manner was a stark departure from the forced smiles of Hope Renewed. I wanted to get away from her as quickly as possible, but a strange part of me was reluctant to leave. And more than anything, I felt guilty for deceiving her.

She led us down another long corridor. In the distance, I could hear movement and the lowing of animals. The cool cavern air was heavy with the scent of dried grass and *gurza* dung, and sure enough, before long we had come upon a crudely-constructed pen. Six *gurzas* milled around inside it.

Isaak watched Eliin with wide eyes as she opened the gate and shuffled into the pen, talking to the animals in a low voice. "Wow," he said under his breath, and I remembered his reaction when I'd shown him the image of one on the visual indicator. They were large reptiles, with strong back legs that made them ideal for bearing loads. Their scales were multicolored, usually blue or green with thick stripes of orange and yellow. One of the animals saw Isaak staring at it, and ambled slowly up to the fence. He reached out his hand slowly. The *gurza* sniffed him, then placed its muzzle in his palm. He grinned and stroked the creature's snout gently.

"Looks like Tuupa has taken a liking to you," Eliin said to Isaak as she led another *gurza* out of the pen. She handed me the reins. "And this is Thork. He's a gelding, so he should be easy to handle if you're not an experienced rider."

I smiled. "Thank you, Eliin."

Eliin helped us get the *gurzas'* packs loaded with supplies. It would be about a week's journey—eight days—mostly through the caves, but there were sections of the trail that went aboveground. "The breathing apparatuses in your packs should have more than enough oxygen for those parts." She sighed. "It wasn't long ago that we didn't need to pack oxygen. The revivication process has done much to help the areas around the mountains, but it seems for every step Elytherios takes forward, the *geroi* drag us three steps back."

"What about the *gurzas*, Eliin?" Isaak asked. "Will they need oxygen?"

"No, *alos*, at least not yet. They're hardier than we are." She glanced at me. "Oh, I nearly forgot. I can take your dummy earpiece for you." She stretched out her hand and I stared at her blankly.

The smile wavered, fading slightly from her face.

"Your *earpiece*, Nadin," Isaak said, glaring at me over the top of Eliin's head.

My breath caught in my throat. I couldn't give her my earpiece—what if we got lost and needed to call for help? Or what if I couldn't understand Isaak and needed it to translate for me? What if Gitrin had left another message for me somewhere? I had never taken my earpiece off. I couldn't even comprehend how I would manage to function, to *think*, without the System there to help me process the world around me. It was a part of me, and I was a part of it. I couldn't go without it.

But Eliin's eyes were beginning to get a suspicious glint to them, and Isaak looked as if he was about to come over and rip it right out of my ear personally. So I forced a small chuckle. "Oh, how silly of me. I completely forgot I was wearing it."

Eliin smiled again, hesitantly. "Of course, *alin*. You wore one your whole life. But that's behind you now. You don't need it anymore."

I tugged my earlobe and quickly, before I could allow myself to think twice, I pulled my earpiece out of my ear.

Eliin turned to toss my earpiece—my *life*—into one of the baskets of tack on the ground while I gripped the reins of my *gurza* tightly, trying to keep from falling over. My vision blurred and spun, focusing and unfocusing as my brain tried to function without the System supporting it. But the strangest thing was the *quiet*. I thought I'd known quiet before, but it was nothing like this. Even when I was alone, in the solitude of my room, there had always been the distant hum of the System running in the background. I had never noticed it before. It had always been there.

But now it was gone. And it was *silent*. There was nothing but me, and Eliin, and Isaak, and the snuffling animals beside us.

Isaak nudged me. "Are you ready to go?"

I had never felt less ready to do anything in my life. But I didn't have a choice in the matter. So I nodded my head at him and said, "Yes."

PART THREE
TOGETHER

Vi'in Elytherios
Haoi Ifaisteoi Mountains
Iamos

CHAPTER 25

· ○ ° • ○ ∅ φ ○

- i s a a k -

WE RODE WESTWARD THROUGH THE CAVES, WINDING OUR WAY through a jumbled labyrinth of tunnels. The globe in Nadin's classroom had shown that Bright Horizon citidome was built in the valley east of the Elysium mountains. I remembered them from when I was little, when we lived in Elysium province, near Lake Amazonis—three giant, extinct shield volcanoes. Well, they were extinct in my time, anyway. Who even knew what they'd be like now? Considering the fact that I was currently riding on the back of a torquing horse-sized Tyrannosaurus Rex, anything seemed possible.

I still couldn't quite believe what had been through that archway. Even knowing that ancient Mars had been inhabited, I never would have anticipated anything like this. Or that I would get stuck here. It didn't feel real. I kept expecting to wake up back on Mars, in that cave, with Joseph Condor looming over me and telling me I'd slipped and hit my head or something.

I wasn't sure what would be worse, honestly.

I leaned forward in my saddle, peering at the tunnel ahead of us. Sunlight streamed in through various holes in the ceiling, casting the sandstone walls in a vibrant orange glow. We were coming up to yet another fork in the passage.

"It's a good thing the *gurzas* know where they're going," I said, looking over my shoulder at Nadin, "because I sure as heck couldn't figure it out."

Nadin didn't respond. She'd been weirdly quiet ever since we left Eliin's. Several strands of hair had fallen out of her braid, and she hadn't even tucked them back in like she was always compulsively doing. As her *gurza* passed under a shaft of light, I could see that her face was noticeably paler, and a thin layer of sweat beaded on her forehead.

"Nadin? Are you okay?"

She blinked at me, like her eyes were having trouble focusing. "I don't feel well," she said.

I frowned, tugging on Tuupa's reins to slow her down. Thork and Nadin drew up beside us. "What's wrong?" I asked. "Do you have a fever?"

"I don't know. The System always regulated my body functions before. Without it, I feel..." She sighed, slumping forward and resting her face against the back of Thork's scaly neck. "I feel like I'm going to die."

My pulse jumped. Ordinarily I'd roll my eyes at a dramatic sentence like that, but Nadin looked like she really meant it. "Do we need to go back? Maybe Eliin can help—"

"No," Nadin protested. "We can't tell her. She was already suspicious. If she finds out we lied to her..."

"Then maybe we should stop for the day so you can rest."

"We can't stop! I have to rescue Ceilos."

"Yeah, Nadin, but you're not going to be any help to Ceilos if you're dead." The word made me feel nauseous. Taking her earpiece off couldn't actually kill her, could it? I didn't believe that could be possible, but she looked so *weak*. Not like Nadin at all.

"I'm fine," she insisted. "Let's keep going. Just a little while longer."

We rode for another hour or so, until the tunnels opened up into a wider cavern, and the *gurzas* slowed to a stop. This must be a rest spot of some sort—I could see the blackened remnants of a fire on the cave's floor, beneath one of the round holes opening up to the surface.

This time, Nadin was too tired to argue with me. She didn't resist as I helped her off Thork's back. I braced her weight against my shoulder until she could sit on a large, flat-topped boulder. She drank some water, and when I handed her a blanket from her pack, she bundled herself in it and drifted quickly off to sleep.

The sky through the ceiling holes was turning a deep magenta. It was hard to tell with Iamos' weird, thin atmosphere, but I guessed it had to be close to sunset. I moved through the large cavern, looking up at intervals to see what I could of the sky above. If I stood at just the right angle, I could just make out the edge of that yellow moon I'd seen my first night here.

Nadin had said it was Venus. But that was impossible. Venus orbited between Mercury and Earth, more than a hundred million kilometers away. On Mars in my time, you could only see Venus at certain times of the year, and it was never closer or brighter than a big star. Jupiter was a lot bigger—sometimes you could even make out the stripes of its atmosphere—but nowhere near the size of this. This was bigger than Phobos and Deimos combined.

I'd thought about it last night, lying awake in the hospital after that riot in the citidome. I vaguely remembered my eighth-grade science teacher saying something about Venus' poles being upside down, about it rotating backward. Nobody knew why or how, but there was speculation that something had happened to Venus—like a super-huge asteroid collision that had knocked it out of its orbit. What if its orbit in my time wasn't its original orbit? What if... something *had* happened to it?

I hadn't thought anything about it at the time, other than a bland, *Huh, that's interesting.* But now it seemed like the worst disaster imaginable. I didn't know when that impact was slated to happen—but I did know that it would punch a big hole in the *geroi's* "evacuate to Hamos" plan. And if the whole population of Iamos had already evacuated to Venus when the impact hit...

I couldn't tell Nadin. Not after the way she flipped out when she found out I wasn't actually some far-distant descendant of the Iamoi. And maybe I was wrong. Maybe I'd misunderstood something.

But still. Ceilos' parents were up there, and who knew how many other people. Yeah, the *geroi* were creepy, but I didn't want anyone to die.

I sighed, looking at Nadin curled up asleep on the boulder. Her eyebrows were scrunched up like she was having a nightmare. I should never have made her take her earpiece off.

The cave was growing darker—and colder. Tuupa nudged me, staring unblinkingly with her yellow lizard-eyes. I should probably try to start a fire, I realized. Not that I really had the first idea as to how to go about that, but I wasn't particularly interested in freezing to death tonight.

I started rummaging around the cave, picking up the most

dried-out, woody-looking pieces of spider weed that I could find—and trying to drown out that thought that had been creeping into my mind almost constantly since I'd arrived here.

He'd used the same door as me. But no one I'd met here had ever heard of him. So if my dad had really come here... what had happened to him?

I pushed the thought out of my mind, dumping the kindling onto the burned-out patch on the floor. But as the yellow circle of Venus blinked down at me, I couldn't help remembering that freezing, airless desert outside the citidome, and the ancient skeleton in the hills.

CHAPTER 26

· ◦ · • ◯ ∅ φ ○

- n a d i n -

MY HEAD HURT WORSE THAN IT HAD EVER HURT IN MY LIFE.

Immediately after that thought, it occurred to me that I couldn't really remember if that were true. Had my head hurt like this before? Had my head ever hurt before? Had my head ever *not* hurt like this? Was my life ever anything but this headache?

I managed to pry my eyes open, blinking up at a dark, unfamiliar ceiling. It was rough, marred with shadows that seemed to grow and shrink in size in the dim, flickering light. Wind howled through crevices in the rock, whistling noisily.

Where was I?

...Who was I?

I sat up in a panic, drowning in disorientation. Slowly, as the world stopped spinning, memories started trickling back to me, little by little. They felt fuzzier than usual, gray at the edges. But they were there.

And so was the headache.

"Nadin?"

Nadin. Yes, that was my name. I turned my head, following the sound of the voice. He was crouching beside a small, poorly-burning fire. My mind struggled for a moment, trying to remember what that face was called.

He smiled, half-encouraging, half-worried. "How are you feeling?" he asked, handing me a waterskin.

I drank while I thought. As the water coursed down my throat, a few more memories volunteered themselves. Finally, I managed, "Everything hurts. But I don't think I'm going to die."

Isaak laughed. "I'm glad. I'm really sorry, Nadin. I had no idea... I didn't realize going off the System would hurt you like that."

"Neither did I." I studied the pouch between my fingers, turning it this way and that. "It's so quiet without it. My thoughts are so hard to find. I didn't realize how little of what went on in my head was my own."

Isaak flopped down on the hard rock beside me. "It seemed like such a nuisance to me. Like when you talked, I'd get feedback in my ear because the System would try to translate what I already understood. It drove me crazy. I should have realized it wouldn't feel the same to someone who'd been hooked up to it her whole life." He smiled halfheartedly. "And I guess it *was* handy when I didn't quite understand everything you were saying."

I drew my knees up to my chest, wrapping my arms tightly around them. I didn't want to say it, but I was more afraid of saying nothing. So I whispered, "I'm scared."

Isaak furrowed his brow. "Why?"

"Everything feels so fuzzy without the System. What if I start forgetting, more and more? What if someday I don't remember how to speak?"

Isaak nudged me gently in the ribs. "Come on. I've gone my whole life without the System, and I manage to get by."

"But I don't know how." My voice cracked, just slightly, but I felt like a failure all the same.

Isaak was quiet for a while. Then he said, "I could teach you."

I looked at him. "Do you think you could?"

"I can try." He smiled. "And you can teach me. Everything you know about Iamos. I think you're underestimating your own mind, Nadin. It's pretty powerful on its own, even without the System."

I tucked a hair behind my ear. "Even though the *geroi* think I'm a simpleton?"

Isaak rolled his eyes. "You know that's a lie. You're smarter than all of them put together."

I grinned in spite of myself. "All right, then. Maybe I will." I stretched my legs out, my feet just brushing the floor. "But first, pass me my pack, will you? I'm famished."

CHAPTER 27

· ○ ° • ◯ ⊘ ɸ ○

- i s a a k -

OVER THE NEXT SEVERAL DAYS, NADIN AND I TALKED UNTIL OUR throats were raw and sore—to say nothing of our backsides from all the riding. I'd never truly understood the concept of saddle sores until now. It was almost enough to make me wish we could hurry up and get to Elytherios already. But who even knew what was waiting for us when we got there? I hoped this trip wouldn't wind up being for nothing.

While we rode, Nadin told me everything she could remember about growing up on Iamos—living in the *geroi*'s shadows—which turned out to be more than she'd thought she could do without the System. She seemed to be feeling better every day, which was a huge relief. And in turn, I told her as much as I dared about Mars and Tierra Nueva. When we got too tired for long conversations, we'd just play vocab games: she'd tell me a word in her language, and I'd tell her the English equivalent. If I couldn't think of something in English, there was almost always something in Spanish, or Greek, or even Olmec. It was really weird how much like Earth languages Iamoan was—way more than it should be if there were no connection. Root words from one language, sentence structure from another... It got me thinking about what Emil had said about "Atlanteans." Whether people from Iamos had colonized Earth or vice-versa, there was an indisputable connection.

I'd lost track of how long we'd been riding the morning we reached the wide, yawning mouth of the caves, opening out to the surface. We must have been slowly ascending for quite some time, but I'd never noticed. The labyrinth of tunnels had turned me around so much, I didn't know right from left or up from down.

"We're going to need oxygen," Nadin said, peering out over the landscape before us. We'd emerged at the bottom of a deep canyon. Spindly hoodoos rose from the ground around us, rocky fingers soaring high above our heads to touch the thinning sky. Water had worn the shapes into the rock—it must have carved the tunnels, too—but there wasn't a drop to be seen now.

Nadin watched me steadily as I fished the breathing apparatus out of my pack and fiddled with it, trying to figure out which tube went where. "I hope we won't have to be outside for too long," she said. "I worry about you getting exposure poisoning."

I snorted. "I doubt it could be worse than the sunburn I got in Veracruz when I was eleven."

She came over, turning the tube-contraption rightside-up in my hands. "I just—your skin is so pale, Isaak." She had that tone in her voice, the one she always used whenever she talked about my appearance. Like she felt sorry for me for being so *weird*-looking. As if it didn't occur to her that the Iamoi looked as strange to me as I did to them. Every time she did it, I felt smaller, more self-conscious—more like I didn't belong here. Like I didn't already know that.

"*Cristo*, Nadin," I snapped, fumbling with the tubes in frustration, "what would you do if you saw Mama D, have an aneurysm? This is ridiculous. All my life, people are telling me I'm too brown. Now you're on my back that I'm too white." My fingers tripped over each other, and I groaned and flung the breathing apparatus onto the ground.

A frown crept over Nadin's face like a cloud. "I didn't understand what you just said"—her voice sounded hurt—"but I didn't mean to make you angry. I only wanted to help." She pulled her own breathing apparatus on, then picked mine up off the ground, gesturing to me where to place the tubes over my nose and mouth.

I sighed. "It's okay," I said, positioning the plastic tube and taking in a deep whiff of the sharp, clinical-tasting oxygen. "It's just... people where I come from have fought for a really long time to not be judged by the color of their skin."

Nadin didn't meet my gaze for a long moment; she just stared at the drawstring bags on the side of Thork's saddle, as if thinking. Finally, she nodded her head. "All right," she said. "I am sorry. I won't do that anymore."

"Thanks," I said, my annoyance dissipating, a smile twitching involuntarily at the corner of my mouth. She'd been doing that a lot over the past several days—nodding instead of pulling on her earlobe like she used to. I don't think she'd noticed. I wondered how much she'd been rubbing off on me, too, without me realizing.

Wind whistled between the hoodoos as we rode into the canyon, but we were relatively shielded here on the ground. The rocky trail was narrow, just wide enough in parts for one *gurza* to squeeze through. Thork led the way, Nadin perched on his back. A gust of wind whipped overhead, and the hood of her cloak slipped off before she could catch it. Her hair had fallen out of its braid days ago, and she'd finally given up on trying to tame it. Now it fell loosely around her shoulders in coarse, bushy ringlets, once-pristine white streaked with red dust and dirt. She shrugged, letting it fly free in the breeze.

I patted Tuupa's flank—she grumbled back at me, a gravelly croak in the back of her throat that sounded almost friendly— and looked up to the sky.

A few hours later, the canyon floor sloped up and the rock spire formations began to recede. A huge plain opened up before us, smooth and black. A not-so-ancient lava flow. Without the hoodoos obscuring my view, I could see that we had almost reached the foot of Elysium Mons—the central volcano, and the tallest of the three. I hadn't realized how close we were to where I'd lived as a kid. But everything looked so different. The canyon with the hoodoos wasn't there in my time—thousands of years of wind and the briny Martian water must have worn it completely away.

"How much farther do you think it is?" I called to Nadin.

"I don't know." She looked down at the oxygen tank at her hip. "Eliin said this would be enough. We mustn't be far now." She shielded her eyes, looking up at the towering peak. "Do you see any signs of life up there?"

I shook my head. "Nothing."

Her hood slipped again, and she pulled it back up. "What if

this was a trick? What if the Liberator sent us out here just to get rid of us?"

"Of course not," I said, my voice more confident than I felt. "Come on. Tuupa and Thork know where they're going. We'll be there in no time."

Without the buffer of the rock spires, the wind was harsh and freezing. I pulled my burlap cloak tighter around myself, but it still nipped at my ears and dried out my eyes. Every so often, Tuupa would glance over her shoulder at me, growling reassuringly as if to say, "We're almost there." But the mountainside looked as barren and dead as ever.

Another hour passed when Nadin slowed Thork's pace, looking up at the red-tinged skies.

"What is it?" I asked.

She pointed. "Do you see those clouds?"

I nodded. A thick bank of red-gray clouds was creeping toward us from the south. "Do you think a storm is coming?"

"I hope not." She patted Thork anxiously. "Let's try to reach the mountain before then."

Thork and Tuupa hurried forward, their muscular legs pummeling against the ground, their spines a sharp horizontal line from their heads to the tips of their thick, powerful tails. I watched the storm clouds warily—they seemed to be bearing down on us fast. I hoped it was just an optical illusion.

We were at the foot of the mountain now. The peak was high, but it was far wider than it was tall. The slope was gradual but seemed to stretch on forever. Once we'd reached it, it seemed that the mountain was all there was to the world.

A high-pitched screech rang out through the air over our heads. Tuupa skidded to a stop, looking up and whining. I followed her gaze. The storm was almost on top of us—and there was something else. Black dots, swirling around on the wind, darting in and out of the thick clouds.

"What are those?" I shouted over the roar of the storm. "They look like big buzzards."

"*Gamadas*," Nadin yelled back. "We need to get to cover, quickly!"

Thork and Tuupa seemed to understand the urgency. They plunged ahead, up the slope of the mountain, moving so fast my teeth rattled.

"That's not just any storm," Nadin called to me, her voice shaking—whether from Thork's movements or her own nerves, I couldn't say. "*Gamadas* travel ahead of sandstorms. If we can't find shelter, we could get smothered."

A huge bird streaked over my head, trilling. It was enormous, almost as big as the *gurzas*, and looked like a cross between a vulture and a pterodactyl. I clutched Tuupa's reins even tighter.

The storm clouds were all around us now, and I could see what was coming. A massive wall of red sand, surging toward us at breakneck speed. The wind was thick with dust particles. They seeped between the breathing tube and my skin, crawling into my mouth and making me cough.

"Cover your face with your cloak!" Nadin shouted.

The *gurzas* began to slow their pace. I looked around frantically. I couldn't see shelter anywhere—like the lava plain, the slope of the mountain was smooth and unmarred, a solid stone mass. The only rocks were far too small to provide any cover. We were sitting ducks.

Tuupa suddenly skidded to a halt, rearing up and squawking noisily to Thork.

"What do we do?" I called to Nadin.

She coughed loudly and yelled back, "I don't know."

Thork bucked so suddenly Nadin nearly lost her hold on him. Grasping wildly at the reins, she said, "What is it?" Thork merely bucked again, and this time she did fall, with a hard thud, onto the ground.

"Nadin!" I scrambled off Tuupa's back, trying to get to Nadin's side, but as soon as my feet hit the ground, Tuupa scuttled forward, herding me with her tail. The two *gurzas* corralled us between themselves. I crouched beside Nadin, who was already up on her knees. For a horrible moment, I thought the *gurzas* had gone berserk in the storm and were turning on us. Then they curled themselves around our bodies, Tuupa tucking her head beneath Thork's massive tail and vice-versa, and I realized what they were doing.

They were shielding us.

They tightened the circle of their bodies around us, and just as the light disappeared completely, I felt the impact of the sandstorm hit. The *gurzas* whined softly as the wind and dust pelted them, but they did not move.

Nadin gripped my hand. "Are you all right?" she asked.

I laughed halfheartedly. "I was going to ask you that. You're the one who fell. I'm fine, what about you?"

She made a noncommittal noise. "If this storm doesn't pass soon..." she said softly. "We don't have much oxygen left."

I didn't say anything in reply. What was there to say?

We sat in silence, in complete darkness, listening to the sounds of the storm.

⤙⬦⤚

I didn't realize I'd fallen asleep until I felt her shaking my shoulder. A soft, warm hand in mine. A girl's voice whispering, "Isaak."

"Tamara?" I muttered, still half-asleep.

"I don't know what that word means," said Nadin, "but the storm seems to have passed. It's quiet outside."

Sure enough, as I opened my eyes—and wiped the grit from them—the *gurzas* moved away, standing weakly and shaking themselves off. Midday sun hit me in the face, startlingly bright after the pitch-black of the sandstorm. Red dust coated the previously ash-gray mountainside. The only spot on the slope that wasn't covered with the dust was the round, crater-like indentation that the *gurzas*' bodies had left, almost half a meter deep.

I grinned, moving forward to stroke Tuupa's muzzle. Her blue scales were caked with red dust, but she seemed very pleased with herself. "You saved us, girl," I said, running my thumb up and down her snout. "You and Thork. Thank you." She cocked her head sideways, staring unblinkingly at me, and made a purr-like noise in the back of her throat.

"We're almost out of oxygen," Nadin broke in. She came up beside me, holding out her oxygen tank, a worried look on her face. "I have no idea how we're going to make it to the top of this mountain."

"You might not need to," a man's voice said. I jumped, and Nadin whipped around at the sound. A group of people was approaching us, climbing down the slope through the settling dust—three men and two women.

Tuupa made the purring sound again and hurried toward

them, nuzzling the man who had spoken. I felt a small pang of jealousy, even though I knew it was ridiculous. Tuupa was never mine. But still... I kind of wanted her to be. I wondered what Mom would say if I brought home a Martian dinosaur for a pet.

"Are you from Elytherios?" Nadin asked.

The woman to the right of the speaker stepped forward. She was older than the others, with deep lines in her face and patches of paper-white skin all over her spindly hands, like discolored liver spots. "That depends on who you are," she said, "and what you're doing here."

Nadin squared her shoulders and pulled her medallion out from under her cloak. "I am *Kyrin* Nadin of Hope Renewed citidome. I'm here to see the Liberator."

The woman laughed, moving forward to hook a bony finger around Nadin's necklace. "Well, that's a tall task, *kyrin*." Her voice dripped sarcasm. "And that trinket won't get you far here. We have little use for the *geroi*'s castes in Elytherios."

"Wait a moment, Marin," another, younger woman said. "Nadin—that's the one Gitrin said we should be expecting."

"Gitrin?" Nadin's voice sounded raw, almost wild.

They ignored her. The first man tugged his earlobe, looking at the woman who'd spoken. "Right. We'd better get the two of them back to the village, then."

He took Nadin's arm, and one of the other men grabbed mine. He glanced appraisingly at me. "Marin," he said. "Have a look at this at this one. Doesn't he...?"

The elderly woman came over and stared at me. Her green eyes were piercing. "Yes, he does," she said after a minute. "Boy, can you understand me?"

I glanced nervously over at Nadin. She looked as confused as me. I said, "Um, yes. I can."

The woman grinned, her gapped teeth magnified by the clear breathing tube over her mouth. "Excellent. You might be of some use to us, then."

"What do you mean?" I asked, but nobody answered. The five strangers led us, *gurzas* trotting happily behind, up the slope of the mountain.

Chapter 28

· ○ ° • ◯ ∅ ф ○

- n a d i n -

THE FIVE ANARCHISTS GUIDED US SOME DISTANCE UP THE SLOPE,
winding around as we ascended to the south face of the
mountain. Here the barren rockiness began to give way, and
patches of scraggly shrubs, fed by the southern sun's rays, were
visible at intervals. The smooth slope became rougher, with more
crags and crevices. The *gurzas'* clawed feet made the going easier
for them than for us humans, and they hurried on ahead of us. On
the top of a ridge just over our heads, Isaak's *gurza* looked over
its shoulder down at us, as if to ensure that we were still
following. Then it darted forward and disappeared into a clump
of thick *fraouloi.*

The man pulled me forward by my arm and I stumbled. The
slope was not overly steep, but it was still difficult to climb
without the *gurzas.* Crude steps had been cut into the ground at
intervals, but they were uneven, which did not help matters.

When we reached the ledge where the *gurzas* had vanished, I
saw that behind the tall *fraouloi* there was a gash in the
mountainside.

"This way," said the man holding my arm, guiding me into the
crevice.

247

I expected the cave to be dark, but even after the light from the entrance should have faded, the tunnel was bright. It wasn't the neon glow of phosphorescence or even the clinical white of the artificial lights in Hope Renewed, either—this looked like real sunlight, like I remembered from my childhood, before it was filtered through a thin red sky.

"You can take off your breathing apparatuses now," said the woman the others had called Marin. "We don't need them from this point on."

I stared upward, trying to find the source of the light, but the cavern's ceiling was so far above us I could barely see it. I was so focused on what was above that I didn't even notice the floor until I stepped on something soft and gasped. Under my feet, the stone was covered over with a carpet of green plant life. It was thick, crawling over boulders and stalagmites, climbing up the wall in places. Here and there, patches of ferns emerged from cracks in the floor and walls, covered in new, spiraling branches that curled and unfurled like a slithering *anguis*. Further down, a narrow channel coursed alongside the path, and thick, leafy bushes sprouted from its banks. The slow-moving stream burbled pleasantly as we passed it.

Everything was *green*. The black, gnarled branches that I'd become accustomed to in the citidomes were nowhere to be seen. It looked like images I'd seen on the visual indicator of Iamos decades ago, before the climate disaster.

"What is this place?" I breathed.

The man holding my arm smirked. "Elytherios."

The tunnel was widening, growing brighter and brighter. Ahead of us, I could hear the rushing of water. Then the high ceiling disappeared entirely behind a patch of white mist, and a whole world opened out before me.

The cavern here was so massive that you could no longer see the walls of it. I wondered for a moment whether we were even inside anymore, but nowhere on Iamos' surface looked like this. Thick clumps of trees stretched skyward, their branches—laden with new growth and small, unripe fruit—reaching toward the unknown light source. Beyond the trees, untidy rows of crops filled the landscape, tall green stalks around which climbed snaking vines. Between the rows of crops, makeshift waterspouts splashed noisily. In the distance, I could just make out the roofs of small buildings. And above our heads, wispy white clouds swirled on the hint of a breeze.

My knees wobbled, threatening to give out entirely. Only the man's strong grip on my arm kept me upright.

"Is this the inside of the volcano?" Isaak said behind me.

Marin tugged her earlobe. "It's a hollow dome, left from the last eruption. The magma chamber collapsed beneath it, just leaving the outer shell."

"And it formed a microclimate?"

The other woman chuckled. "Well, it had a little help. Elytherios' engineers are the best on Iamos."

Isaak's eyes widened. "You terraformed it?"

The anarchists looked at each other, murmured a few words I couldn't quite catch. Then they prodded us forward again.

The *gurzas* were waiting for us further down the path, beside a large pond. The one called Tuupa lifted its head, water dripping between its front teeth. It trilled and pranced ahead, leading us down the road toward the village.

As we drew closer to the buildings, I could hear voices, snatches of conversation. Figures milled between the rows of crops, occasionally calling out greetings to our group as we went by. Eventually the sea of farmland thinned, and we reached the village. The long, squat buildings were cobbled together with mud and stone and the branches of trees. The town itself seemed to have taken on a green hue—trailing vines climbed up the sides of the walls; trees emerged from the roofs of houses, creating a thick green canopy. The buildings were clustered together in circular formations, separated at intervals by the various worn-dirt paths. Here and there, small gaps between the buildings formed miniature plazas where groups of people congregated, talking and laughing while they worked.

I hesitated as we passed an open-fronted house. Inside, a woman was grinding grain with a smooth stone, while three children ran around her, squealing noisily. As I watched, one of the bigger children chased the smallest one out from under the table she was hiding beneath, and they ran, giggling, into the road.

"Look out," I said, throwing my hands out as the smaller one nearly ran headlong into me. The child wobbled on her heels, grabbing onto my hand to steady herself. Then she looked up at me, grinning wide enough to show me every tooth she had—and a couple of missing ones—and laughed.

The woman at the grindstone looked up. "Sasin, what do you say to her?"

The girl glanced over her shoulder, then tugged her earlobe in a playful, exaggerated way. "I'm sorry," she said to me.

"Oh, uh," I said, "that's all right."

The child grinned again and then ran off again, the older one chasing her at top speed.

I glanced at the woman at the grindstone. She smiled. "Children, right?" she said, if that were meant to explain everything. Then she called after them, "Sasin, Enros, if you're going to play outside, watch where you're going, please!"

"Yes, Maetrin!"

I started, staring at the children with my mouth open. *Maetrin*. That was a word in the old language—the word for *mother*. Those children... she was their mother. All three of them were her children.

Iamos didn't have parents. None but the *geroi*. But Elytherios did.

"Something wrong?" Isaak asked as we continued down the track.

I shook my head like I'd seen him do before. He smiled crookedly and tugged his earlobe in reply.

We stopped in a large plaza in the center of the village. It looked like a giant seashell, with all the roads and buildings spiraling out from the fountain in the center. Clustered around the fountain were dozens of long tables and benches, big enough to seat at least twenty people apiece. Tall trees with thick, sturdy trunks surrounded the clearing, their branches twining together like woven copper. Sunlight trickled between the leaves, creating a dappled pattern of light on the ground.

"This is our main meeting area," said the man who had been holding my arm. "The weekly forum is tomorrow morning—you'll need to be here for that." He glanced at Marin. "Anything else?"

"No," Marin said. "I'll take them to"—she glanced over at me and smirked—"the *Liberator*."

I bristled, then stood straighter, my shoulders squared. I wasn't about to let this woman mock me. But she didn't back down. Her green eyes locked with mine for a long moment, then she said, "Follow me."

She led us down another spiraling road. Isaak came up beside me as we walked and, in a low voice, said, "This doesn't exactly seem like a hive of murderous terrorists."

"It's just a facade," I replied.

"Where do you think Gitrin and Ceilos are?"

"In a prison, no doubt." I thought about the prison in Hope Renewed, in the highest level of the pyramid. It didn't hold many people. It didn't have to. Criminals were usually quickly re-educated with a System protocol, or—if they were too great of a threat—euthanized. I didn't see any tall buildings here in Elytherios, but there had to be a prison somewhere. Every city had a prison.

Marin stopped in a small, triangular-shaped clearing between three buildings. I looked around in confusion. There was no one here except two *plivoi*—well, workers, anyway; I didn't know what they called them here in Elytherios. One of them, an elderly man with age-bleached skin, was on the top of a ladder, fiddling with a large piece of glass that hung from the gnarled branches of a tree. The other was a woman. I couldn't see her face—she had her back to us, holding the ladder steady.

"*Degiim*, Eos," Marin called. "There's someone here to see you."

The man twisted the glass into position. There was a bright glare for a moment as the glass swung down, and then it was still.

Light radiated gently off it, and I realized that this was where the sunlight was coming from: mirrors.

With the mirror secured tightly, the man turned, looking down at Marin, then at Isaak and me. He frowned. "Who are these people?" he said, climbing down from the ladder with surprising agility for someone his age.

I stepped forward. "I am *Kyrin* Nadin of Hope Renewed citidome. I'm here to see the Liberator."

The confusion did not fade from the old man's face, but at the sound of my name, the woman who was holding the ladder for him turned and gasped. "Nadin!"

At the sound of her voice, the world slammed to a stop. My mouth hung open for a long moment, before I finally managed to stammer, "Gitrin?"

I stared at her for a long, wordless moment as the man on the ladder jumped the last two steps to the ground. As soon as he was safely off the ladder, Gitrin brushed past it and raced over to me, pulling me into an embrace. My stomach clenched at her touch, and for a brief moment I forgot my anger at her and I hugged her back.

"Where did you find them?" the old man asked Marin, who had hurried over to help him take down the ladder Gitrin abandoned.

"Just outside the entrance to the city. The lookout said he spotted a group with *gurzas* just before the storm blew in. We thought it was the runners back from Hope Renewed."

Gitrin clasped my face between her hands, brushing my dirt-caked forehead with soft fingers. Smiling, she said, "You understood the messages I left for you. Ah, *yachin*, I knew you would." She glanced over at Marin, who was watching with bemusement. "Bright as a star, this one. I've always said she's the finest student I've ever had. She'll be such an asset to Elytherios—"

I threw my hands up, as if to stop the tidal flow of her chatter. An *asset* to *Elytherios*? "Gitrin," I snapped, "what's going on? What are you doing here?"

She looked at me, her head cocked and her expression blank. "I thought you knew," she said. "I couldn't stay in the citidome, not after what happened with your evaluation. The *geroi* already suspected me as it was, and when things turned out... well, as they did... I knew it wouldn't be safe for me." She smiled fondly and brushed my shoulder. "But I had faith in you, and here you are."

"But the Liberator," I spluttered. "He kidnapped you!"

Gitrin looked at the old man, then Marin, then back to me. "Of course not. I left the night of your evaluation. How could I have left you those messages telling you where to find me, if I'd been abducted?"

I felt like I was losing my mind. I glanced at Isaak, who shrugged helplessly. "You couldn't have left the night of my evaluation. The medic at the hospital said that he'd spoken to you, the morning after my annual."

"I never spoke to any medic, Nadin. I didn't speak to anyone—I had to leave quickly."

I squeezed my eyes shut, my temper building explosively inside me. "Stop lying to me! I'm tired of all these riddles and these evasions. I want a straight answer. Where is Ceilos?"

Gitrin blinked. "He's not in Hope Renewed?"

"No!" I shouted at the top of my voice. "The Liberator commed me, he said he had both of you. He'd *taken* you. You and Ceilos. He said he wanted to meet with me, so I came. I came here to see the Liberator, and I want to see him right now."

Gitrin frowned. "Eos?" she said. The old man stepped forward.

I scoffed. "You? I'm supposed to believe that *you're* the Liberator?"

He folded his arms. "I am... in a manner of speaking. There is no one Liberator. That is an identity that all of us in Elytherios share. It's the name we adopt when we go on missions to the citidomes, to deliver supplies or help refugees who need a safe haven. Most people associate it with me, since I was the first runner." Something about his voice sounded wistful. Marin slipped her hand into his, an oddly affectionate gesture for someone who had seemed so cold on the mountainside. Eos smiled. Then he looked at me again. "But it's been a long, long time since I've left Elytherios."

"Well, someone must have done it," I snapped. "I spoke to a man who called himself the Liberator. He said he wanted to meet with me. He said that he had taken you and Ceilos, and that if I wanted to see you again, I would have to come here. Now I am tired of playing your guessing games. You tell me where Ceilos is *right now*, or I am going to tell the *geroi* exactly where they can find your little nest of rebels."

Eos stepped forward, straightening his back and rising to his full height. Despite his age, he was very tall—and he looked very strong. His voice was like ice as he said, "I will see you dead before you bring any harm to the people of this city, *kyrin*." He spat the word out like it was dirty. "This village is a sanctuary. It is the only free place on Iamos. We will not allow the *geroi* to taint it with their poison."

"Eos, please," Gitrin said, inserting herself between me and him. "She is only a child, and she has lost much. She doesn't know what she's saying."

I bristled. She had no right to call me a child—I was *enilin*. I was about to say as much when Isaak put his hand on my shoulder.

"Nadin, come on," he said. "Be rational. Gitrin is right here, telling you she wasn't kidnapped. And Eos says he never commed you. Think about it—why would he lie? We're totally at their mercy right now. They could throw us in the dungeon, but they haven't. They don't even have any torquing weapons pulled on us."

I glared at him. "So, what? Are *you* accusing me of being mad now? You heard the comm the same as I did!"

His eyebrows knitted. "Of course that's not what I'm saying. I'm just telling you to use some *reason* here."

My temples throbbed. I rubbed my forehead with the heel of my hand, trying to calm my temper. "Then where is Ceilos?" I asked. "Who commed me?"

"The *geroi*?" said Isaak. "I mean, I think we've basically confirmed at this point that they're pretty shady."

"But why would the *geroi* patch me in to a private session of the *gerotus*, specifically for the purpose of making me distrust the *geroi*?"

"Maybe someone else," Gitrin broke in. She turned to Eos, saying something quickly in the old language. I only caught snatches of it—without the System boosting my memory, I had to struggle to think of every word.

"Yes, it could be," Eos said. "We've heard rumors from the runners recently, when they come back from missions. Attacks on the System... and on the citidomes themselves. Things that we had no part of, but have been attributed to the Liberator. We assumed that it was just the *geroi* spreading more of their lies, trying to turn the people against Elytherios, but—"

Attacks on the System. Like the one Melusin told me about. "It's true," I said. "Someone hacked the System's early warning protocol on Ascendant Dawn, and an earthquake hit the citidome with no warning. Several people were killed, and their *gerouin* was seriously injured."

Eos frowned. "I was not aware of that. I refuse to believe anyone in Elytherios could have done such a thing, though. Our society is built on principles of non-violence. We would never wish harm to anyone, not even the *geroi*. Besides, our access to the System is extremely limited—mostly small hacks to create illusions to steer System-users away from the city. I don't think anyone here has the capability to perform a high-scale hack like that. Someone is trying to implicate us in something that we have no part in."

"So, wait," Isaak said, thoughtfully running a hand through his dark hair. "You mean there's another band of separatists out there besides you guys? Who *also* call themselves 'Liberator'? And they're the ones who have Ceilos?"

"It doesn't make any sense," Marin said. "How could all of this have escaped our notice?"

My voice faltered. "And how am I supposed to find Ceilos

now?" He couldn't just be gone. I had to find him—had to save him. I couldn't leave him on his own, not after what had happened. *I'm your partner*, he'd said. He had never abandoned me, never turned against me, even after Tibros ordered him to. I couldn't lose him now. Not before...

Not before I could at least say *I'm sorry*.

Gitrin put her arm around my shoulders. "Hush, now," she said. "You've been through a lot. The journey to Elytherios is not an easy one, and you've been worried about me and about Ceilos all this time. Come along with me, there's room for you in my household. You'll feel better if you have a chance to rest." She glanced over at Eos and Marin as if for their approval.

Marin tugged her earlobe. "There's not much we can do for now. Tomorrow is the weekly forum—we can discuss this then."

Gitrin smiled and ushered me forward. Isaak started after us, but Marin stayed him.

"No, not with them," she said. "You need to come with me."

He looked at me with alarm. I shrugged helplessly.

"It's all right," Gitrin said. "You'll see him again at mealtime. Everyone in the village comes together to eat then."

I swallowed. "Okay. I'll see you later, Isaak."

Marin, Eos at her side, led Isaak back the way we'd come. I watched them disappear down the spiral path.

"Are you sure it's all right?" I said after they'd gone.

"Of course it is," Gitrin said with a laugh. She looked at me oddly. "Nadin, who is that young man, anyway?"

I frowned, still looking beyond the buildings at the empty road. "His name is Isaak—oh, Gitrin!" I broke off abruptly, my hands flying to my mouth. *The time postern.* I had forgotten the entire reason I'd been searching for Gitrin in the first place. I sighed. "I have so much I need to tell you, I don't even know where to start. Everything has changed so fast, I feel like I hardly know myself."

"And you've changed most of all, *yachin*. You've found your independence. I always knew it was there, no matter how hard the *geroi* tried to snuff it out. I know you were angry at me about your evaluation, but I hope you understand, now, why I did what I did."

I shrugged. I still didn't, entirely. But that wasn't important anymore. I'd found Gitrin. Now all that mattered was finding Ceilos.

"Now," Gitrin said, "let's go get you cleaned up, and find some fresh clothing for you. You'll feel more yourself in no time."

CHAPTER 29

· ∘ ∘ • ◯ ∅ ϕ ∘

- i s a a k -

MARIN AND EOS LED ME THROUGH A CLUSTER OF THE SQUAT,
rectangular buildings—they almost looked like the longhouses I'd
seen in archaeology documentaries—and down a path that
wound its way along a small, burbling creek. I could hear the
noises of animals in the trees overhead, like the whistling of
birds, but different somehow. A gangly mammal with a long
striped tail skittered through the branches, watching me with
wide orange eyes.

Mom would have a field day here, I thought. I remembered
how hard she struggled to get things like tomatoes and squash to
grow in our garden, with nothing but modern, invasive spider
weeds to graft with. In the farm outside the village, I'd seen what
looked like beans climbing up stalks of maize, like they grew them
in the *milpas* on Earth. Mom had tried that in her garden without
much luck. But these plants were native to Mars, not Earth. If she
had access to native species like this, her job would be so much
easier.

"This place is incredible," I breathed. "How long did it take to
build?"

"More than the whole of our lives," said Eos. "It had already begun before I was born, and Marin and I are the oldest citizens still alive."

Marin smiled wistfully at him, her green eyes seeming to hold a secret behind them that I couldn't begin to grasp. Something about the way Eos and Marin interacted reminded me of my grandparents—the easy affection born of a lifetime together.

"How old are you guys, anyway?" I asked.

Eos chuckled. "I lost track many years ago. But I'd say I was close to your age when Marin and I first came here, and that was at least three decades ago."

Thirty years ago... If that was the case, in Earth years—annums—they must be in their eighties now, or close to it. Older than Abuelo.

"So you two are the leaders?"

"No, no." Marin waved her hand dismissively. "We have no leaders. There's no need for it. Eos and I are the eldest, so people will often come to us for advice, simply because we have that experience. But if someone chooses not to heed that advice, that's none of our concern. As long as no one is endangering the community, people essentially live as they please here."

I nodded thoughtfully. It sounded nice. Of course, everything about Elytherios seemed like a vast improvement over the torquing Orwellian scenario going on in the citidomes. I knew Nadin didn't trust the people here. And she was right that what had happened with Ceilos—and even with Gitrin—didn't make any sense. But I still couldn't help but believe that the Elytherians were telling the truth. Even apart from the fact that they wanted to use me as a guinea pig for an invasion of Earth, I could never trust the *geroi*. They were like GSAF on steroids.

"So, where are we going, anyway?" I asked as we crossed over a small footbridge spanning the creek.

"There is someone that I would like you to meet, speak with if you can," Marin said. "We have been having a difficult time communicating with him."

I frowned. "But what makes you think I'm going to be able to help you?"

Marin stopped at the door of one of the longhouses and leveled her gaze on me. "You'll see."

She pushed the door open and I stepped inside. It had a single room, long and narrow, lit by windows and several large skylights in the roof. Living trees made up the longhouse's support beams, growing into each other so fluidly that it was hard to see where one ended and another began. Two rows of beds lined the walls. In the back corner, a dark-haired man sat on one of these, looking out the window, his back to me.

"This is our guesthouse," Marin said. "It's where our new arrivals live until we can find a household for them to join. You're welcome to stay here—"

She said something else, but I didn't hear what. The man turned around to look at me and my ears just completely shut off. There was no sound. Everything was muffled, like Tierra Nueva when it snowed. No one in the room but me and him. And seeing him now, right in front of me, I wasn't sure if I wanted to hug him or punch him right in the jaw.

"Dad," I blurted. "What the hell are you doing here?"

He looked confused for a moment, like he didn't recognize me. Well, it had been *two torquing annums*. I had grown almost six inches in that time, and my voice had gotten a lot deeper. Dad, on the other hand—he didn't look like he'd aged a day. The only difference between the last time I'd seen him and now was that his face was covered with messy stubble, thick enough to almost be a beard, but not quite. He was even still wearing his factory uniform, though it was completely filthy.

He stared at me for a long minute, then recognition flashed in his dark eyes. "Isaak?" he whispered, his voice gravelly and thick, as if he hadn't spoken in days.

"Yeah," I said, clenching my hands into fists, trying to choke down the emotions roaring in my chest. I hadn't expected to feel this angry when I saw him again, especially after finding the time postern. I'd been telling myself that maybe it wasn't his fault—maybe he hadn't meant to leave us—but the built-up rage of two annums of being on my own, having to be the man of the house, never knowing *what the hell had happened to him*—it was like a living thing now. I couldn't shut it off.

Maybe if he'd say he was sorry. Maybe if he'd apologize for leaving me to grow up on my own while Mom had to struggle, working day and night to keep Celeste and me healthy and fed and clothed on just one income... if he'd just *acknowledge* it, I could forgive him. But he just stared at me, stupidly, not saying a single word.

Finally he stood up, looking me up and down like I was a stranger. "You can't be Isaak," he said.

I laughed. It came out sounding strangled, hysterical. "What do you mean, I *can't* be Isaak? I'm Isaak."

"But you can't be! How did you get so big so fast?"

"So fast? Come on, Dad, it's been two annums. Did you think I wasn't going to grow?"

"Two... annums...?" Dad choked on the words, coughing violently to clear the dust out of his chest. Then he shook his head. "No. That's not possible. I've only been here two, maybe three weeks at the most."

His sentence was like a punch to the gut. It knocked the wind clean out of me. "What?"

Eos cleared his throat. I turned, wild-eyed, to see him standing in the doorway of the longhouse. Marin was there, too, just a meter or so behind me, watching our conversation with fretful eyes. I'd completely forgotten they were there.

"Do you know him, then?" Marin asked. "I thought you might. There's... a resemblance, between the two of you."

"How long has he been here?" I asked, voice ragged.

"Twenty days or so," Eos said. "One of our runners picked him up. He'd collapsed outside Hope Renewed with no breathing apparatus. He regained consciousness not long after we got him back here, but no one has been able to understand him. He finally gave up talking altogether several days ago."

Dad was watching me, eyes narrowed. "You can understand what they're saying?" he hissed.

I glanced at him. "Yeah, but..." The room was spinning. "You can't have only been here a few weeks. You were gone all that time..." I sank down onto the bed, slumping forward, my elbows on my knees.

Dad crouched in front of me. "You came through the arch?"

I nodded.

A noise like a growl came from the back of Dad's throat. "That bastard Emil. This is all his fault."

"It's not Emil's fault, Dad," I snapped. "He didn't tell you to go through that arch. I know you stole his key. Besides, Emil at least has half a brain stem. I'm sure he wouldn't have just blundered right through a time machine without testing it first."

He crossed his arms, leaning back on his heels and glaring at me. "'Half a brain stem', huh? But I see you blundered through same as me. Looks like the apple doesn't fall far from the tree, *mijo*."

I almost did punch him that time, but managed to hold myself back. I'd almost forgotten, in two annums, what a complete dick my dad could be.

Dad ran his fingers over his chin, picking at the thick almost-beard thoughtfully. "A time machine, you say? So this isn't just some alien planet. Incredible. Wait a minute!" He slapped his hand on my knee, looking up at me with wide eyes. "Ancient stuff sells for thousands in our time. Maybe even millions. If we could bring a few things back with us—a few trinkets here and there— we'd be set for life!"

I shoved his hand away and jumped to my feet. "What the hell is *wrong* with you, Dad? These are good people. They've been taking care of you for weeks without even knowing who you are. And now you want to steal from them?"

Dad frowned. "Not necessarily *steal*, just—"

"No, you know what? Shut up. Do you know I've spent the last two annums worrying about you? I thought you might be dead, or sick, or hurt. When I wasn't torqued off at you for ditching us without a word, I was completely miserable at the thought that something might have happened to you and we'd never know what. And now, after all this time, I've finally found you"—my voice caught on a lump, but I forced it down—"and you don't even say that you're glad to see me. You don't even ask me how Celeste is, or Mom, or anything. Why did I even waste my time?"

I stormed off, across the longhouse and out the door. "Isaak! Wait, don't be like that," I heard Dad yell, but I ignored him.

"Isaak," Marin called, hurrying out the door after me. "What's the matter? What did he say?"

I froze midstep, realizing I didn't know where I was going, where I was running to, anyway. I just wanted to get away from him.

"Isaak," Eos said in a softer voice. "Who is he?"

I didn't look at him. I kept my eyes trained on the road ahead of me, snaking between the longhouses. In the distance, I could hear the familiar trill of a *gurza*. I wondered if it was Tuupa. If I followed this road, maybe it would lead me to their stables. It wasn't Escalante Bay, but I realized with a sudden certainty that I'd rather spend the afternoon with a friendly T-Rex than with that man in the longhouse any day.

"I'm sorry to say he's my father."

Eos didn't reply. He merely tugged his earlobe, and his expression seemed to say it all. I nodded, then turned to make my way down the road, following the winding creek and the sounds of the animals.

CHAPTER 30

· ₒ ° • ◯ ∅ ɸ ○

- n a d i n -

THE SUN HAD LONG SINCE SET, AND THE LIGHT FROM THE GIANT mirrors had dimmed along with it. The village had grown dark, though the yellow lights filtering through windows cast a soft glow here and there. They flickered like starlight, making the night seem vast and unfamiliar. In the canopies of the trees, I could hear animals settling down to sleep, and others awakening, readying themselves to roam the night. An unfamiliar animal looked down at me from its nest, its eyes wide and orange. Its soft, black-and-white-striped tail wrapped tightly around the branch, steadying it. The two of us stared at each other, silently, for a long while, before the creature gave up and scurried off on its way.

I dipped my hand into the creek, feeling the cool water swirl around my fingers. A small *psara* swam up, nibbling my fingertip before darting away. I smiled softly. There was more life here on the inside of the mountain than the entirety of the Iamos I'd known.

The anger I'd felt earlier had dulled by now into a small, dimly-glowing ember. I'd spent the afternoon talking with Gitrin about everything—the time postern, Ceilos, the *geroi* and their plan for Isaak. She'd shown me the village, and the farmland, and the forests that framed the cavern's edge; and slowly, reluctantly, I had come to realize that maybe this wasn't the den of terrorists the *geroi* had insisted the anarchists were. Many of the refugees I met today were scientists like Gitrin, whose research had been halted by the *geroi*. They didn't want to destroy Iamos—they wanted to heal it. And they had the technology to do so, right here and now. They knew how to reverse the atmospheric degradation, to revive the world, make it like it was before. But the *gerotus* had told them *no*. Just like when Gitrin and I had shown them our plans for the time postern. And today, finally, after all this time, I realized why.

Because healing Iamos would mean that the *geroi* weren't needed anymore. And they couldn't have that. They would rather have no world at all than a world where they didn't hold the power.

It made me feel sick.

The one thing I didn't understand was how Ceilos fit into all this. If the Elytherioi didn't have him—if Eos was not the one who had commed me—then where was he? Who was behind his disappearance?

As I sat beside the water, thinking, I heard footsteps on the worn-dirt path behind me. I glanced up. Isaak stood under an arch of tree branches, tangled together at the entrance of the clearing. He waved halfheartedly as I got to my feet.

"You didn't come to the evening meal. Where have you been all day?" I asked him as he drew closer.

He snorted, a small, forced laugh through his nose. "Hiding from my dad."

"Oh. Yes, Marin told me that the man they'd found was your father. But you weren't happy to see him? I thought you were looking for him."

"I was," Isaak said sheepishly. "But I realized afterward that maybe some things are better left not found."

I looked down at my feet. "I think I know what you mean."

Isaak moved to the creekside, crouching and peering into the dark water. "Any news about Ceilos?"

"None."

"Figures. Did you get a chance to ask Gitrin about the time postern?"

I sighed. "Yes. I thought she might have saved a copy of the plans, but she left all her research behind in Hope Renewed."

"Whoever broke into her apartment probably has it now, then." He glanced up at me. "The *geroi*, do you think?"

"I don't know." I shrugged. Isaak grinned at the gesture, and I self-consciously rubbed my arms, half turning away from him. "She said she could probably recreate the plans relatively easily, but sending you back home might be harder. The posternkey that you used to get here would have the space-time coordinates stored on it, but Melusin has that now."

His shoulders slumped. He breathed in slowly, staring at the creek so long I worried that I'd upset him. Then he finally nodded, seemingly resigned. "So there's no way for me to get home without it?"

"I don't know." Hesitantly, I stepped forward and placed my hand on his shoulder. "There might be another way. What about your father? Does he still have the key he used?"

He shrugged and stood up, brushing off his pants and walking a few paces away.

Something inside me curled in on itself, and I suddenly felt exhausted. "I'm sorry, Isaak," I whispered.

He looked at me. "It's not your fault."

"It feels like it is. Especially after—" I broke off, swallowing hard. I wasn't ready to go into that with Isaak, everything that had happened with Ceilos, everything I'd done to cause this disaster. "I thought everything would fix itself when we got here—that I'd suddenly have all the answers. But I feel like I understand less now than I ever have before. There's just more and more questions, and never, never any answers."

As I spoke, something wet hit the side of my cheek. I felt it again, on the top of my head this time. Startled, I looked at the sky. The clouds above us were thick and dark. As I gazed up, another water droplet hit me in my eye.

"What is that?" I asked.

Isaak glanced up. "Oh, it's sprinkling," he said, as if it were the most uninteresting thing in the world.

I cupped my hand, and a few more droplets plinked into my palm. "Rain?"

"Yeah."

I stepped away from Isaak, my shoulders shaking. I could hear it, now—the raindrops falling into the slow-moving creek, making tiny splashes. The air smelled wonderful, like cool, damp earth. I couldn't take it. I could feel water streaming down my cheeks, not just from the rain. It was like the opening of the clouds cut me open, and now the tears wouldn't stop coming.

"Nadin, what's wrong?" Isaak said.

I swallowed, trying to find my voice. "It's too much. How is this real? How can this be..." I trailed off, looking up at the dark clouds, letting the cold raindrops soak my face.

I turned. Isaak had come up behind me, and now my face was level with his shoulders. I couldn't look up at him. My eyes focused on nothing as I said, "You know, earlier, Gitrin..." I took a shuddering breath, and started over. "I always was afraid of *this*. How I feel right now. I was afraid of being weak. The *geroi* never show their emotions. They're always calm, always poised. Perfect. I thought the reason Gitrin told me I wasn't ready was because I couldn't keep myself together. I wasn't a real leader—I was too angry, or too scared, or too sad. Just volatile. But tonight, Gitrin said"—I sniffled, wiping my face off with the back of my hand— "she told me that wasn't it at all."

"*There's nothing wrong with having emotions, Nadin,*" she'd said to me, gently squeezing my hand. "*It's natural. The sterile world of the geroi, that's what's unnatural. That's what I wanted you to see. What I was testing you for. If I used the geroi's own standards, you were ready at your enilikin. But I don't think you really want to be just like everybody else. You have the potential to be a great leader, to really help Iamos. Our people deserve for you to live up to your full potential.*"

My eyes stung with fresh tears. "But I don't feel like a leader, Isaak. Especially now." I ran a hand through my damp hair, looking down at the ground. "All I feel is scared."

Isaak put his hand on my shoulder. I froze, then finally dared to look up at him. His mouth was pulled up into a crooked smile, one that made my heart beat inexplicably off-kilter. "Come on, Nadin," he said, gently brushing my shoulder with his thumb. "You're putting too much pressure on yourself again. Stop worrying so much about what *might* happen. Just take it one day at a time." He grinned at my expression and swiped at my cheek playfully. "Besides, you don't have to do any of this by yourself. You've got Gitrin, and Eos and Marin. Everyone in Elytherios. And..." He hesitated, then said, so quietly I could barely hear him, "And me."

Those two words somehow managed to make my heart soar and break, all at once. Because he *was* here, now. But he didn't belong here. He had to go back to his own world someday. And he knew it. I could hear it in his voice, in the unspoken words at the end of his sentence. I had him—for now.

And it occurred to me, for the very first time, that losing Isaak would kill me as much as losing Ceilos.

I reached up, my fingers brushing his chest, hooking around the folds of his shirt like an anchor. He looked startled, but he didn't pull back. Instead he smiled and pulled me close to him, arms wrapped around my waist in an embrace.

My pulse staggered, and for a panicked moment I was afraid he was going to try to put his mouth on mine the way Ceilos had. But he didn't. He just held me, until my heartbeat steadied, and my tense muscles relaxed, and my fears evaporated one by one, leaving nothing but calm. Safety. I breathed in the smell of him, warm and familiar, and for once in my life, I didn't worry about anything. I didn't think of what could be, what was coming. There was only here and now: Elytherios, and the rain, and Isaak.

I never wanted it to end.

"Isaak," I said. My voice came out muffled against his shirt, and I felt his chest vibrate as he laughed. Grinning, I leaned back, looking up at his face. "I know—"

"Nadin."

Isaak jumped, dropping his arms from around me and stepping back. The air felt suddenly cold without his warm presence filling it.

Gitrin stood at the edge of the clearing, holding a lantern. Her expression was unreadable in its flickering amber glow. A second, taller figure stood beside her, but I couldn't make out his face.

"There's someone here," Gitrin said. "To see you."

I peered through the shadows, and the figure stepped into the light.

Ceilos.

CHAPTER 31

· ₒ ∘ • ◯ ∅ ϕ ○

- i s a a k -

THE DOOR TO THE GUESTHOUSE BANGED OPEN MORE LOUDLY
than I intended it to—my face was still burning, my mind racing
with what had just happened, so I wasn't paying attention. It
didn't really matter, though. There was only one other occupant
in the guesthouse just now, and I didn't really care if I
inconvenienced him.

My dad was lying on his side in his bed, and he rolled over to
look at me as I came in. I shut the door more gently and looked
around before deciding to flop onto the bed furthest from him as
possible. I reached down to pull off my shoes—slick boots made
of an unfamiliar material that Nadin had brought me in the
hospital—and tossed the first one in a heap on the floor.

"What's eating you, kid?" Dad said, sitting up and watching
me intently. He acted like nothing was wrong—like I had no
reason to be mad at him.

"It's nothing," I muttered.

"Heh, are you sore about that Ceilos guy showing up and
ruining things for you with the alien girl?"

I froze, my right boot halfway off my foot. "How do you know
about Ceilos?"

Dad grinned, looking obnoxiously pleased with himself. He rose from the bed and strolled over, stopping directly in front of me. "Well, I figured that was his name when you all kept saying it over and over."

"That's not what I meant," I said, my voice unreadable even to me. "Were you... were you *spying* on me?" I thought about the way I'd turned tail and fled the minute Gitrin turned up with Ceilos, and my face got hot. That was the last conversation I wanted my dad eavesdropping on.

The grin faded off Dad's face. "I wouldn't call it *spying*, necessarily. Oh, come on, Isaak, don't look at me that way." He sat on the foot of the bed next to me, putting a hand on my knee. "After what happened earlier... I wasn't sure if you were going to come back here at all. I wasn't sure if I was ever going to see you again. And..." He trailed off, then said in a small voice, "I didn't want that, Isaak. So I just was looking for you. That's all."

Guilt crept up from the pit of my stomach. Maybe I was being too hard on him. He didn't know what we'd all gone through over the last two years. Maybe... maybe he really was trying, and I needed to give him a chance.

"It's okay, Dad," I said, smiling tightly.

He smiled back, ruffling my hair like he used to when I was little. Then he said, "So, does this mean you're not slobbering over Tamara anymore? Or are you just sowing some wild oats?"

I groaned, my shoulders slumping. "Dad, don't be gross."

"Ah, come on, *niño*. You're not still on about that oddball demigod thing, are you?"

"Demi*sexual*, Dad," I corrected him through gritted teeth. "And it's not an 'oddball' thing, thanks so much. It's normal. Lots of people feel this way."

275

Dad rolled his eyes. "Right. And that's why you have to make up a weird, complicated name for it."

I jumped to my feet, pushing away from him. "It's not weird, and I didn't make it up! I've told you a million times. It's completely simple: I just don't feel sexual attraction that much. Not unless there's a bond first. That's all there is to it."

He gave me a look that said he still didn't believe me. I knew what he was thinking—there was no such thing as a guy who didn't want to bang everything in sight. But it was the truth, and I was getting really sick of having this argument.

"Here we torquing go again, Dad!" I snapped. "I haven't seen you for two annums, and already you're on my back. Can you go for even five minutes without harping on me? Is it really any of your business what I do with my life, how I handle my relationships?"

"Of course it's my business," Dad snapped. "You're my son."

"Really? Because it sure hasn't felt that way in a long time. The last time I saw you was before my fifteenth birthday. You haven't been there for me while I was growing up, what makes you think you get a say now?"

"That's not fair, Isaak. I didn't leave you on purpose."

"Are you sure? Because I saw what you left in that box in the garden. Where's your wedding ring, Dad?"

He blinked at me, then glanced down at his left hand. But he didn't say anything.

"Yeah. That's what I thought. Maybe you weren't planning on coming to Iamos. But you were still going to leave all the same."

"I wouldn't have abandoned you, Isaak," he said softly. "I would have kept in touch with you."

"Really? Are you sure?"

"Of course I'm sure." He stared at me for a long moment, then sighed. "Look. Things weren't working out with me and your mom. Everyone knew it. But that doesn't mean that I don't care about you and Celeste."

"I don't want to hear it," I said, turning my back on him and looking up at the green, leafy roof of the guesthouse. "Look, forget it. There's nothing going on between me and Nadin. She's engaged to Ceilos, and she's my friend. That's all there is to it. So let's just drop it and get some sleep."

Dad nodded, getting up to move back to his own bed. When he was safely out of my space, I moved back, sitting down on my bed and trying to fight off the scowl that was still pulling at the corners of my mouth. I wish I'd never come out to him to begin with, back in ninth grade. Everyone else in my life—Mom, Abuelo and Abuela, even Henry—had been totally stellar about it. Everyone except Dad. He just couldn't comprehend a life that didn't one hundred percent completely and totally revolve around sex. He'd been all over me about Tamara before he disappeared, and I could just tell that he wasn't going to let this Nadin thing go, either.

Still, I couldn't get it out of my mind—that spark when she put her hands on my chest like that. I ran my hand over the soft woven coverlet thoughtfully. I'd never felt like that before— except with one other person.

This was ridiculous. Nadin was my *friend*.

But Tamara had been my friend, too. That's how it always worked for me. Normally I didn't even think about it, but at times like this it felt like a torquing curse.

"Hey, Isaak," Dad said suddenly from across the room. I looked over at him warily, dreading what he was going to say now.

But I didn't get a chance to find out. Just then, the door to the guesthouse swung open, and Eos entered, carrying a lantern.

"Sorry to disturb you," he said. "We just found out that we've got a few new refugees joining us tonight, so they'll be staying here with you and your father." He ushered in two people, a man and a woman, who looked strangely familiar to me. It took me a moment before I recognized them—the couple who had been playing *ulama* in the plaza last week.

"This is Corin," Eos said, gesturing to the woman, "and Gios."

I grinned. "I saw you two before, in Hope Renewed. How did you get away from the Enforcers?"

"One of our best runners was with them. We weren't about to abandon them," said Eos. "And we've developed... certain *techniques* over the years. Enforcers usually can't hold our people for long."

"It's easy to trick a mind that's reliant on the System?" I said. Eos tugged his earlobe.

Dad broke in, "Mind telling me what's going on here?" He was glaring at Gios and Corin, who stared back at him in confusion. I rolled my eyes, and was about to start translating when Eos cleared his throat.

"There's one other thing, Isaak."

My eyebrow arched, and Eos pushed the door open wider—revealing a man with a shock of white hair and a crooked, hawkish nose standing just behind him.

"I think we're going to need your help again."

CHAPTER 32

· ° • ○ ∅ ϕ °

- n a d i n -

"CEILOS," I SAID ONCE ISAAK AND GITRIN HAD GONE. MY BREATH hitched in my throat. "I don't understand... what are you doing here?"

He turned his hands out. "I'd like to know that myself." He came closer to me, and I could see through the shadows that his face looked haggard. I thought I could see the fading remnants of a bruise along the edge of his jawline.

My hands curled into fists. "Who did this to you?"

"I don't know. I didn't see much of him. He kept me blindfolded."

"The man who called himself the Liberator?"

Ceilos tugged his earlobe. "After what"—he swallowed, looking away from me—"happened in the classroom, I couldn't think straight. So I went out for a walk. Through the caverns at first, then finally up into the dome." He took a deep breath and sighed. "He was waiting for me. I didn't even see him coming. I wasn't... paying very much attention."

My fingernails dug into the soft flesh of my palm. I had caused this. What had happened to Ceilos really was all my fault.

"When I woke up, I didn't know where I was. But I could hear his voice. The Liberator. I didn't see his face, but I will never forget that voice." He shuddered. "I had no way of knowing how much time had passed. I didn't know what he wanted from me. He just taunted me, relentlessly. About what he'd done to Clodin, about what he was planning to do to the *geroi*—about you."

I reached over to put my hand on his shoulder, but I hesitated. The memories from last week still burned painfully inside me. And knowing that what had happened to Ceilos was all because of that...

"Finally he took me outside somewhere. Said I wasn't of any use to him anymore. I didn't know where we were, but it was freezing cold, and there was no air. Like you said it was outside the dome. Being out there, unable to breathe—I understand now. It's the most terrifying feeling in the world. I thought I was going to die. But the next thing I knew, I was waking up here in Elytherios. That woman from the citidome—the one who was smuggling Ferre—she found me on the mountainside and brought me here." He laughed humorlessly. "She of all people."

"Ceilos," I said, my voice shaking. "I am so, so sorry."

He looked at me sidelong. "I... heard what he commed you. The *gerotus* session."

"The *geroi* are *gamadas*," I spat.

Ceilos chuckled. "I've said that all along. I told you there was no love lost between me and my parents." He sobered. "It just took a threat to Isaak to make you see it."

I stared at him. "What are you talking about?"

"I saw what was happening just now."

My face flushed. "Nothing was *happening* just now, Ceilos. Isaak was just trying to comfort me because I was upset—about *you.* I've been frantic to find you. That's why we came here."

He didn't look at me. He kept his eyes riveted on the burbling creek. I followed his gaze, just catching the silver glint of a *psara* tail plinking through the water. "So Isaak can comfort you when your partner cannot?"

"Isaak didn't *touch* me in a way I didn't want to be touched," I snapped before I could stop myself. I didn't want to be angry with him, not when I'd finally found him—not now that he was safe. But he was making it impossible. I hadn't done anything wrong, and still he didn't trust me.

Ceilos turned to me, his eyes fixed on mine. They looked so hurt. Guilt washed over me, and I started to open my mouth to apologize, but the words died on my tongue. I didn't *want* to apologize. All I'd done was tell the truth.

Finally, Ceilos was the one to say, "I'm sorry, Nadin. Listen, let's not fight, all right? We're together again. That's all that matters."

He reached his hand out to me. I stared at it for a long moment before slowly moving to take it. His fingers were warm in mine. He smiled at me, and, reluctantly, my own lips turned up as well. "Yes," I said. "That's all that matters. I'm so relieved that you're safe."

He pulled me close to him, and I automatically put my arms around his waist. The rain trickled down around us, cool and fresh, and I tried as hard as I could to ignore the hollow feeling growing in my chest.

CHAPTER 33

· ∘ ° • ◯ ∅ ϕ ∘

- i s a a k -

"EMIL," I STAMMERED, LOOKING BACK AND FORTH BETWEEN HIM and Eos so fast I thought my neck might snap. "What the hell? What are *you* doing here?"

"Looking for you," he said matter-of-factly. He glanced past me at Dad, who had jumped out of bed and was staring at Emil like he'd seen a ghost. "And you."

"You know him, too, Isaak?" Eos asked.

I blinked at him for a minute, my brain—still feeling like it was short-circuiting after the sudden appearance of Emil—trying to process jumping back and forth between English and Iamoan so rapidly. "Yes," I finally said. "He's... I know him."

Emil fixed one of his piercing black eyes on me. "You speak their language?" When I nodded, he said, "Tell them I say thanks for the lift."

I translated this to Eos. Then I asked, "Where was he?"

"The same place we found your father, and where Nadin says she found you—in the hills outside Hope Renewed. But this one was prepared. He was carrying an oxygen tank."

I laughed. Of course he torquing was. Emil was nothing if not thorough. He'd obviously thought this through much more than my dad—or I—had.

"How many more visitors from your world should we be expecting, Isaak?" Eos asked wryly.

"I don't know," I said, frowning at Emil. He looked like he was itching to jump into the conversation. Knowing him, he'd probably start taking notes the second someone got a pen into his hands. "I'll let you know if I find out."

"Very well," Eos said. "I'll leave you to get reacquainted, then, while I get the others settled." He started to guide Corin and Gios to the second row of beds, then paused, glancing at me. "There's something else, too. Have you seen Gitrin tonight?"

"Yeah," I said. I started to nod, then thought better of it and pulled on my earlobe instead. "I know about Ceilos."

"Yes, Ceilos." He frowned when he said his name, and his eyes seemed to darken for just a moment. I wondered what that was about. Eos wasn't the one who got busted with Ceilos' girlfriend. My face flushed again at the thought. What the heck was wrong with me?

"He will be staying with you tonight as well. The weekly forum is going to be held in the courtyard in the morning—try to be there if you can, because we're going to be discussing your living situation." He smiled and shut the door, and I turned to Emil, who looked like he was going to positively bust.

"Incredible," he said in his gruff voice. "I knew that the ancient Martian settlers were advanced, but this is beyond even my wildest dreams. And believe me—they were pretty wild."

"You figured it out, then? About the arch being a time machine?" I asked. On the opposite side of the room, Gios and Corin were pulling back the coverlet on their bed, talking quietly to each other and tossing uneasy glances in our direction.

"Well, obviously. I'd already started to suspect as much, when Delia and I were studying the plans from her 3-D scanner. But it's obvious as soon as you take a look outside. The atmospheric degradation, the red oxidation of the rocks—the presence of the Elysium mountains—it doesn't take a rocket scientist to figure it out."

My dad bristled at the jab. He opened his mouth to say something, but I cut him off. "Wait a minute, *Delia*?" I said, my voice rising in a panic. I noticed Corin and Gios had stopped talking and were staring at us with interest. I smiled tightly at them and whispered, "She's not here, too, is she?"

"Oh, no, no. She didn't dare take the risk. Things back home—they've gotten kind of crazy since you disappeared, kid. GSAF has been watching her family like a hawk. But that friend of yours, the Pakistani kid—"

"He's *Indian*, Emil," I interrupted.

"Yeah, yeah, whatever. He told me that you'd given the key to Delia Randall-Torres to scan, and that it had her maker mark on it. Once again, it didn't take a rocket scientist to figure out that she must have a copy of it. Well, she didn't have one made. But between the two of us, we were able to put one together. And let me tell you—it wasn't easy, getting past GSAF to the arch. They have guards everywhere. But I made a promise to Delia that I'd try to find you, see if I could bring you back." He put his hands in his pockets, shifting awkwardly from foot to foot. "And besides... if I have to say it, I was sorry I'd gotten you mixed up in all this. Raymond here may be a dumbass, but you didn't deserve it."

My dad flipped him off, and offered a choice expletive to go along with it.

"Wait a minute, Emil," I said. I was almost afraid to ask what was weighing on my mind, but I had to know. "How long have I been gone, anyway?"

"At the time I left, I'd say it had been about sixteen months."

"Sixteen... months?!" It felt like the floor had dropped straight out from under me. "As in *almost an annum and a half*?"

He nodded grimly.

"Oh my God," I said. It was all I could say. Sixteen months gone. Celeste would almost be in second grade now. And Mom—Mom would kill me! Being gone for two weeks was bad enough, but almost a whole Martian year?!

"Now you know how it feels," Dad said, his voice bitter. He crossed his arms, leaning against one of the trees growing out of the longhouse's walls.

"Am I missing something here?" Emil asked, his bushy dark eyebrows furrowing.

"Time passes differently here," I croaked. "I've only been here, like, two weeks. Dad was here less than a month before that."

Emil's eyes widened, but then he nodded thoughtfully. "Yes, I suppose that makes sense. Our timelines aren't synced—the only thing determining our arrival date is the coordinates programmed into this." He reached into his pocket and pulled out a bright, silver key—brand new and untarnished. Freshly printed in Mama D's basement workshop.

I stared at it blankly for a moment, then something clicked in my brain. "Emil," I hissed. "You're a genius."

"Obviously."

"No, you don't get it! We can go home with this." I snatched the posternkey out of his hands. "We can fix everything! Gitrin can just program it to take us back to the moment I left—"

"Are you mad, boy?" Emil ripped the key away from me, clutching it protectively to his chest. "*Think!* If you return to a time before the date when I left, you'll be opening an alternate timeline!"

"What does that mean?" my dad asked.

Emil rolled his eyes. "The *best*-case scenario is that we'll be existing in a reality different from our own. The worst case—and the most likely one, if you've done any research on the subject— is that you'll create a paradox with the power to destroy the entire known universe."

"So?"

"So?!" Emil roared. "So I'm saying that you cannot change history, Contreras! Under absolutely no circumstances!"

"But if we can't change history," I said, "then the Iamoi..."

"Who are the Iamoi?" Dad interrupted.

"The people here. The ones who brought you here. The ancient Martians."

"Well, what about them?"

"They wanted to use the time postern to fix their planet," I said. "So that the atmosphere wouldn't... you know."

"That's impossible," Emil said firmly. "They cannot be allowed to alter history any more than the three of us. The stability of the universe depends on it."

"But Emil, we can't just leave them here to die!"

"Look, kid. I don't like it any more than you do." Emil's voice softened, almost imperceptibly. "But that doesn't change the fact that this planet was a barren wasteland when we got here.

History says they died, so they have to die."

I stared down at my feet, my ears ringing. I couldn't let them die. All the people I'd met here, everyone in the citidomes— everyone here in Elytherios. Eos and Marin, Eliin, Corin and Gios, who just escaped from the *geroi*, were just starting a new life. The people and the plants and the animals—the *gurzas*—everyone...

...Nadin.

"We don't really know what history says, Emil," I said slowly.

He stared at me. "What are you talking about? Of course we do. My team found the evidence here back in the thirties. Relics from their civilization were everywhere. But the planet was dead, and they were gone."

"*Gone*," I repeated. I looked across the longhouse to Corin and Gios, curled up together in the small guest bed, seemingly asleep. "But *where* did they go? Maybe they didn't die. Maybe they just... left."

"Yeah, but where would they have gone?" my dad scoffed. "Venus?"

"He's right, as much as I hate to admit it," said Emil. "There's no evidence of life anywhere else in the solar system besides Earth, Isaak."

"And Mars in our time," I said.

"Exactly. In our time..." Emil trailed off as the meaning of my words hit him.

"Maybe it's not a question of *where* the Iamoi went," I said, folding my arms. "Maybe it's *when*. What if they came forward?"

Emil nodded his head slowly.

To our time.

Chapter 34

· ∘ ∘ • ◯ ∅ ϕ ∘

- n a d i n -

I FOUND ISAAK ON THE EDGE OF THE VILLAGE, WHERE THE GURZA pens were located. The morning air was chilly and damp—water droplets from last night's rain beaded on leaves, and small puddles dotted the worn-dirt track.

I leaned against the wooden fence, watching him quietly for a moment. He reached into a trough, pulling out a large *kela* steak and tossing it to Tuupa. The *gurza* reared up on its strong legs, catching the meat in midair and noisily tearing into it. Isaak laughed, then turned his head slightly and caught sight of me. I thought his smile wavered, just for a moment, but then it passed and he came over to stand beside me.

"Hey," he said. "How are you feeling? Better?"

My cheeks burned with embarrassment. "Yes. I'm sorry about... you know, last night."

He looked at me. "Why are you sorry? You didn't do anything that needs apologizing for." When I didn't respond, he said, "How's Ceilos? I must have already been asleep by the time he came in last night. I haven't had a chance to talk to him."

I ran a finger along the knotty wood of the fence. "About as well as can be expected." I told him what Ceilos had said about

288

the man who called himself the Liberator.

Isaak frowned, climbing up on top of the waist-high fence and staring thoughtfully at the *gurzas*. "It doesn't make sense. Why would this guy target Ceilos, but then let him go?"

"I've been wondering that myself." The two of us glanced up to see Ceilos approaching us down the dirt path. He came up beside me, putting a hand on my shoulder and looking at Isaak. Isaak didn't react, but I squirmed internally. It felt like Ceilos was trying to mark me. He obviously still didn't trust me. I shrugged his hand off, moving several paces away from both of them, not meeting his eyes.

"So?" Isaak said. "Do you have any theories?"

Ceilos stared unblinkingly at me. "One. But I don't like it." He folded his arms and sighed. "What if I wasn't the real target? What if it was..." He thrust his chin in my direction.

My eyebrows furrowed. "Me? But why?"

"I don't know. But that comm he sent you seems to indicate that he was more interested in you than me."

I looked down at my feet. It didn't make any sense. I was a nobody. True, I was the daughter of *geroi*, but there were two others here on Iamos and a third on one of the two colonies on Hamos. They were all younger than me, though—I was next in line for the *gerotus* before I failed my evaluation. But what did that have to do with anything?

"What if it's because of the time postern?" Isaak interrupted. I looked up at him. He'd swiveled on the fence, looking down at me seriously. "I mean, all of this started right after the people from my time started turning up. And you and Gitrin were the only ones who knew about it."

Ceilos made a noise in the back of his throat, gravelly and thoughtful. "That's a possibility."

"The time postern is a dead end, though," I said. "Without the plans, without a key—there's nothing we can do."

Isaak shifted uneasily. "Well, actually, Nadin, there's something I wanted to tell you."

Before he could say anything else, the air around us filled with a metallic sound, like the knell of a gong.

"What's that?" Isaak asked.

"The call to the weekly forum," Ceilos said. "Gitrin said that we needed to be there today." He looked at Isaak. "Can what you were going to say wait?"

Isaak shrugged. "No point, really. You'll hear it at the meeting."

He had a fretful look about him, but before I could ask him what was wrong, Ceilos took my hand in his. "Come on, Nadin," he said. "Let's go together."

"Right." I glanced over my shoulder at Isaak. "Together."

The central courtyard was filled with people—more than had even been at mealtime the night before. They crammed together at the long tables and milled around the edges, some men and women carrying tiny children. This had to be the entire population of Elytherios, or close to it. I'd never have imagined that so many people lived here. I saw traits I recognized from the various citidomes around Iamos, but they weren't uniform. One man near me had the hair of one region and the eyes of a second. Another had a skin tone nearly as light as Isaak's, and a hair color I'd never seen before—a rich reddish-brown like the oxidized dirt outside. The people here were a patchwork of different traits, a stark contrast from the uniformity of the citidomes. I swallowed, realizing that this is what Iamos would look like without the eugenics committees. What the world was like before the Progression.

Elimination of differences was supposed to bring unity. But Hope Renewed never felt as unified as Elytherios did just now.

In the middle of the courtyard, a group of people stood with Eos and Marin. I realized with a start that I recognized some of them: the *plivoi* couple from the citidome, and the Ferre smuggler. I couldn't begin to guess how they had gotten away from the Enforcers. Gitrin was also with them, and two men that I had not seen before.

Isaak saw them and started to move away from Ceilos and me, but I stayed him. "The man with the dark hair is your father?" I asked.

He nodded. "And the other one is a... friend of his, I guess. He's also from my time. And that's what I wanted to tell you—he has a copy of the time posternkey."

My eyes widened. "That means you can go home! But what about..." I trailed off, glancing at Ceilos. His fingers were still laced tightly through mine. "What about all the rest of us?"

Isaak smiled tightly. "I have an idea about that."

Before he could elaborate, Gitrin hurried over to us. "Good, good, you're here. You'll have to sit by me—I'm sponsoring the two of you for citizenship."

"What, already?" I asked.

She tugged her earlobe. "Every week we vote at the forum on where to place the new refugees. Everyone is taken into a household, where they learn about Elytherios and how we live here. It's just a formality. The other members of my household agreed to allow you and Ceilos to stay with us, so we'll be voting on that."

I glanced over at the two strangers. Isaak was talking to them in English—I caught snatches of their conversation, but they were far away, and the language was too new to me to understand much. "Isaak's father has been staying in the guesthouse all this time?"

Gitrin frowned, following my gaze. "Yes. He was here before I arrived. They hadn't placed him yet, though, because no one knew what to do with him. It's irrelevant now, I suppose. Now that we have the posternkey, we'll be able to send them home soon enough. With the data stored on there, you and I can make the modifications to one of our shipping posterns."

I started to nod, then caught myself and tugged my earlobe instead. The chatter around us was starting to die down, and Gitrin ushered Ceilos and me over to a crowded bench near the courtyard's center. The woman I recognized as the smuggler from Hope Renewed stayed standing, and she cleared her throat, looking out over the crowd. When her eyes ran over mine, I shrank into myself, remembering the way the rioters had shouted, "*Death to the* geroi!" I could already tell that that reflex would be difficult to overcome.

"*Degiim*, friends," she said in a much gentler voice than that she had used the first time I'd seen her. "*N'elytherios tou shenos*. We have much to discuss at this week's forum, so thank you all in advance for your time." The crowd murmured agreeably, and she went on, "We'll start with our first pair of new refugees, Corin and Gios. These two are a husband and wife from Hope Renewed who were attempting to have a family. After being declined by the"—her voice hardened—"*eugenics committee* multiple times, they attempted to use Ferre to have a child extralegally. I was running a shipment to them when we got caught by the Enforcers, so Syrin and I ran an emergency evacuation."

Another woman with short, light-brown hair and amber eyes—traits I recognized from Radiant Tomorrow citidome, on the far side of Iamos—stepped forward. This, I assumed, was Syrin. "We'd be happy for them to enter our household, if the citizens are amenable."

Eos tugged his earlobe and stood. He called something out in the old language. I couldn't quite translate it, but I remembered it from my studies with Gitrin—a phrase from one of the old regional republics, before the Progression. At his words, the people around us all stood. Apart from the other outsiders, I didn't see anyone who remained seated.

Ceilos leaned over to me. "Stand to be counted," he whispered. I tugged my earlobe. Like Gitrin said—it was a vote.

The Ferre smuggler smiled. "Wonderful. Thank you, friends." She turned to the *plivoi* couple and said softly, just barely loud enough for me to hear, "Welcome. After the forum, Syrin and I will get you settled in our household."

As they took their seats again, Gitrin rose beside me. Like the smuggler, she began, "*Degiim*, friends. Our next refugee pair also comes from Hope Renewed. They are two youths, raised in the underground, who are in desperate need of sanctuary." I noticed that she didn't name us, nor did she mention just who we were. I wondered if that was deliberate. "Like most of us, they have been persecuted by the *geroi*. They have escaped from a very dangerous situation, and risked much to come here. I would like to request they be allowed to stay in my household, if the citizens are amenable."

The crowd before us had fallen silent. Unfamiliar eyes stared at me, their expressions wary. The smiles and pleasant murmurings that the *plivoi* couple had received were nowhere to be found. I shifted awkwardly in my seat, and Ceilos put a hand on my knee.

Finally, a woman near the back stood. She glanced at me, then said, "Gitrin, you cannot conceal it from us. We all know that these children are *geroi's* blood."

Marin stood up. "Come now, Giulin," she said, a smile pulling at the corner of her lips. "We are not the *geroi*, with their sects and castes. The doors of Elytherios are open to all who wish to embrace a life of liberty and equality. Remember who I was. Everyone can change, and they deserve that chance."

A man rose from the bench across from us, holding a sleeping child against his chest. "But you were not *geroi's* blood. These two will not be permitted to simply disappear. The *geroi* will be looking for them—they probably already are. If they find them here, we'll lose everything." His arms tightened protectively around the child. "Every moment we allow them to stay here, our families are in danger."

The crowd began to whisper among themselves. The eyes boring into the back of my neck burned with suspicion. My pulse raced, and I kept hearing the rioters screaming in my ear. *Death to the* geroi.

"Friends, please," Gitrin implored. "They are *children*. They cannot help their parentage any more than the rest of us can."

Before I could think twice, I had leapt to my feet. "Stop calling me a child, Gitrin," I snapped. "I am *enilin* and I am old enough to take responsibility for my own actions."

The crowd fell instantly silent. The man across from me turned his shoulder, shielding the child he'd been holding—as if I were an *anguis*, plotting to rip her from his grasp and devour her whole. I bit my lip. "I understand that the *geroi* have done much to hurt you. But they have hurt Ceilos and me, too. And all of Iamos. Our top priority should be saving this planet—for all of us. After seeing the life you all have made here... I believe Elytherios holds the key to that. So I will gladly renounce the *geroi*, for the good of our people."

Saying the words aloud felt like a release. Several people in the front row turned to one another, murmuring inaudibly. My hands shook, but I inhaled through my nose, determined to steady them. Ceilos stared up at me, eyes wide, as if he didn't recognize me. Over his shoulder, I could see Isaak grinning at me and nodding encouragingly. I gave him a tight smile and sat back down.

Eos stood once more, looking around at the crowd. "Very well. I think everyone has made their point very clearly. Let's put this to a vote. All in favor of allowing Nadin and Ceilos to remain in Elytherios, in the household of Gitrin?" Then he said the words in the old language, asking the Elytherioi to stand and be counted.

I held my breath.

Gitrin stood, proudly and defiantly. Marin also stood without hesitation, and I smiled despite myself. Throughout the crowd, a few others rose to their feet. Near the back, I saw the woman from the day before—the mother who had been grinding the grain. She looked directly at me as she stood. I inclined my head to her, three fingers on my brow.

Two dozen people stood. And that was all.

Eos gazed around the courtyard fretfully. "Very well. Nadin and Ceilos shall not be allowed to remain in Elytherios."

The ground dropped out from under me. I could feel the cold of the outside on my skin all over again, taste the airlessness. The memories of the night of my annual, of the sandstorm, of my nightmare all swirled together until I couldn't breathe, couldn't think.

Ceilos looked at Gitrin, his eyebrows drawn. "What does that mean?" he asked. "If we can't stay here, where are we supposed to go? Back to the *geroi*?"

Gitrin didn't respond. Her mouth just moved wordlessly. Marin leaned over her and said, "We can't allow that. Elytherios' location must remain an absolute secret." She frowned, looking at her age-bleached hands. "This has never happened before."

The words stung worse than I thought they would. I had come all this way, fought so hard, learned so much—only to have the door slammed in my face.

"They're going to kill us," I said resolutely.

Ceilos put his hand on my shoulder firmly. "Of course not—"

"They are, Ceilos," I snapped. "There's no other alternative. We know too much. If we can't stay..." I swallowed. "We'll have to go."

Ceilos didn't reply. I knew he knew I was right.

Eos was talking again, saying something about Isaak and his

father. I tried to pay attention, but the panic in my mind was drowning everything else out.

"*Our final group of newcomers is not seeking sanctuary in Elytherios. They are instead asking for our help to return to their home —*"

I'd sworn that night—the night of my annual—that I wasn't going to give up. I didn't want to die. I refused to die. But I was going to die all the same.

"*I know it's probably hard to believe, but the three of us actually are from Iamos —in our time, it's called 'Mars' —several thousand years in the future.*"

I wish I had never gone out that night. I had wanted to see the sunset, but for what? To prove to myself that everything really was as bad as it seemed?

Several voices of disbelief rose up over the top of Isaak's in a smoky cloud of noise. Gitrin stood up beside me, trying to talk over the top of them, but I couldn't bring myself to listen. I slumped forward on the bench, staring down at the spinning ground beneath my feet. Twigs and fallen leaves and pebbles and mud blurred together before my eyes as Isaak and Gitrin tried to explain what I'd already accepted days ago.

Gitrin had asked me, "*What if there was a way to save Iamos?*" And I had told her that there wasn't, I'd told her everything the *geroi* had always taught me to believe. But the truth was, I didn't believe them. I believed Gitrin. That's what I was really looking for, that night—the answer that we had overlooked. The way to save Iamos, the one that Gitrin had hinted existed.

I thought I'd found it in Isaak.

Ceilos put his hand on my back, running his palm back and

forth across it reassuringly.

I wish I'd never met him.

Even as I thought that, I knew it was a lie.

I looked up as Isaak said the word "paradox." That was like a word I remembered from the old language—the word for *contradiction.* I knew what he meant, and it turned my stomach sour all over again.

"What is that supposed to mean?" the woman with the short brown hair—Syrin—asked. "That it doesn't matter what we do? We're all destined to die, and we're supposed to just sit back and accept it?"

"Of course not," Gitrin snapped. "Would you quiet down long enough to let the boy finish?"

Isaak took a deep breath. "When Gitrin and Nadin developed the time postern," he said, "they were thinking they could use it to go back in time to change history. To undo the climate disaster. That won't work—but there's nothing to say you couldn't still use it to travel forward."

The courtyard fell silent. I stared up at Isaak, eyes widened.

"You think this would be possible?" Marin finally said.

"I don't see why not. The planet's habitable, but the population isn't too big—our continent Cimmeria hasn't even been terraformed yet. The technology you have here in Elytherios would be a huge help to our scientists. And besides"—he shrugged—"it is your planet, after all."

"Why should we believe any of this?" a man's voice called out. "How do we know this isn't a *geroi* trick, trying to lure us out of the mountain and back into captivity? After all, this boy came here with the *geroi's* blood."

"Teros, be sensible," Marin said. She gestured to Isaak's father. "That one's been here for weeks. He can't even speak our language!"

"That's what they'd want us to believe."

Gitrin scoffed. "Friends, *listen* to yourselves—"

"That's enough, Gitrin," Eos broke in. "It's a valid concern. It wouldn't be safe for us to simply blindly evacuate our entire population when we don't know what's on the other side. We'd have to send an envoy ahead into what could potentially be an extremely dangerous situation. I refuse to agree to something that could harm any of our citizens. Not to mention that it would take hands and eyes away from the revivication project, which is our top prio—"

"I'll go."

My voice felt so quiet that I thought for sure no one would hear me, but Eos stopped mid-sentence and stared at me. "What?" he said.

"I'll go," I repeated, louder this time. "As a way to prove myself to all of you. You didn't know what to do with me anyway, right? So I'll go through the time postern. I'll learn more about the future, find out if it would be feasible for us to evacuate there. If it is, then I will return with proof. And if not... well, then, you'll be rid of me. Your hands will be clean."

I could feel Isaak's eyes boring into the side of my head, but I didn't look at him. I kept my gaze riveted on Eos.

Beside me, Ceilos stood. "I'll go, too." I looked at him in surprise. His mouth was drawn in a thin line. "I'm not letting you go alone," he said firmly.

"I will also go," said Gitrin. "They are my students—my

family." She stared at Ceilos for a long moment, and something seemed to pass between them that I couldn't quite understand.

The crowd around us began to murmur. I saw a number of people tugging their earlobes, and a glimmer of hope began to burn in my chest.

"Very well," said Eos. "Shall we put this to a vote, then?" He called out the words in the old language once more, and this time, nearly everyone in the courtyard got to their feet.

My skin prickled, and I rubbed my sweaty palms together. The world's rotation seemed to be slowing back to a regular pace. It didn't seem possible, but somehow I'd managed to evade death's jaws again.

"It's decided, then," Eos said. "Gitrin will accompany the outsiders through the time postern and report back to us. How long will it take you to build the device?"

"Not long, now that we have the key. Maybe a week?"

As Eos tugged his earlobe, I felt a hand on my shoulder. Isaak.

"Are you sure you want to do this?" he asked, his brows scrunched with worry.

I forced a smile. "Of course."

"Yeah, but... I can't guarantee that everything's going to be okay for you in my time. Our government isn't exactly..." He trailed off, struggling to find the right word. "...super fantastic or anything."

I laughed humorlessly. "That's nothing I'm not accustomed to." Isaak didn't laugh back. He didn't even smile. I nudged him. "Don't worry, Isaak. This was your idea, after all."

"Yeah, but I wasn't thinking *you*—" He broke off, then added, barely audibly, "and Ceilos... I mean..."

My spirits sank like a stone through water. "You don't want me to come?"

"I didn't mean that! I just—"

Before he could finish, Gitrin pushed between us. "Nadin, I'm going to need your help getting the postern prepared. Think you're up to it?"

My eyes didn't move from Isaak's. He was staring at me, brows furrowed, expression unreadable, waiting for my response.

I turned to Gitrin. "I am. Just tell me when."

CHAPTER 35

· ∘ ° • ○ ⊘ ϕ ○

- i s a a k -

"SO, HOW DOES THIS WORK?" I ASKED, STARING AT THE JUMBLED pile of tools and supplies Gitrin had dumped out on the table between us. In the midst of the clutter sat Delia's 3-D printed key. Nadin had opened it with her medallion, and I ran a finger absently over the irregular curves and corners of the unnameable shape and glanced over at her.

She was mad at me. She still wouldn't even look at me. I didn't know why I'd said what I said after the forum. It wasn't that I didn't want her to come. After all, like she'd pointed out, this whole thing was my idea. It wasn't even that Ceilos was coming, too—although, if I was honest with myself, that was part of it.

It was that I didn't know what was waiting for me when I got back. I was wanted by GSAF, and so was Emil. I'd been gone for sixteen months. And now I was going to be turning back up accompanied by three aliens and my prodigal dad, and I'd have to explain to everyone where the hell I'd been, hopefully without winding up in jail and/or some kind of mental institution. I'd promised the Iamoi a means of survival, and I had no clue how I'd be able to deliver on that.

And then there was Tamara.

And, yeah. That was part of it, too.

So you couldn't really blame me for being a little bit antsy about the whole thing. But I didn't know how I was supposed to explain that to Nadin. I wished I'd never said anything at all.

One of the diodes on the key sparked purple, and I yanked my hand back with a start. Gitrin laughed and made a *tsking* noise at the back of her throat. "It's going to be a bit harder to program without full access to the System," she said, strapping on a pair of goggles that looked uncannily like my Speculus headset back home, "but it's not impossible."

Emil, sitting on the bench to the left of me, prodded me hard in the ribs. "Well? What's she saying?"

I rolled my eyes and grudgingly translated. Emil had demanded to be part of the building process, since he'd spent so long decoding the technology with Mama D, so I got roped into translating for him while they worked. Most of it was going right over my head—hacking and programming was never my strong suit. That had always been Henry's territory.

I wondered what he would think about all this. He'd cracked jokes about my "Little Green Men," but I knew deep down he was dying to know what it was that GSAF had been covering up. I wished he could see this now.

"We can't just use Emil's key to go back," Nadin said. Her head was bent, rummaging through a second box of supplies that Gitrin had brought from the engineer's longhouse, and she didn't look up as she spoke. "Because of what he said about the paradox. His key is the one you and your friends unburied in your time, and what you used to travel back. Its counterpart is with the *geroi* now. Which means"—she pulled another posternkey, more tarnished than Emil's but otherwise almost identical—"it has to stay here until we can leave it in the place where you found it. So we'll copy the coordinates from Emil's key onto this one."

Emil moved to poke me again, and I leaned away from him. "Yeah, yeah, I know." I quickly repeated what Nadin had just said in English.

He nodded thoughtfully. "Does it have a record of the time and place that I left from?"

"It does," Gitrin answered after I translated. "But it is not exact. The postern that he used recorded a timestamp on the key, so we can estimate the date. But the spatial data will be harder to calculate. The planet is constantly in motion—in its orbit around the sun, and in its own daily rotation. If we had a static connection between two posterns that would make things easier. But those need to be established beforehand—the receiving postern must be programmed to the key's frequency. Without it, we have to just make a guess. If we calculate wrong, you could rematerialize in the middle of solid rock, or the vacuum of space."

"So we're talking potential death here," I said, frowning.

Gitrin tugged her earlobe. "The safest alternative is to direct the key to transport you to a wide open area, one where there aren't likely to be many obstructions. Your keys were programmed to bring you to the plateau outside Hope Renewed. I'll have to program Emil's key with that information, too, for when you find it in the future—but that will be easier. I know the exact date and time each of you arrived here, and I know the exact spatial coordinates for the plateau on each of those dates. Your time, though, is an unknown to me. How has the planet's surface been altered? Have there been any changes to the planet's rotation or solar orbit? Emil's key gives me a clue, but it's all just guesswork."

"We have to make sure we arrive at a later date than when Emil left," Nadin pointed out. She looked at me—for the first time since the end of the forum. I felt my face color under her scrutiny. "If his arrival and departure overlap with each other, that could also create a paradox."

"So there's no way we can get back any earlier than sixteen months after I left," I said glumly. "And we could wind up getting back even later than that."

As I spoke, Ceilos entered the courtyard carrying a large clay jug with steam coming out the top. Small earthenware cups hung from hooks on the jug's side. "*Sokol*," he said, placing it on the table. "From Marin." He sat next to Nadin, putting a hand on her knee. She smiled tightly at him, and moved to pour some of the hot beverage into one of the cups. I put a hand on the back of my neck and looked down.

"Once we arrive in Isaak's time," Gitrin said, taking a cup from Nadin's outstretched hand, "our first priority should be to establish a stable connection between the two posterns. Once we have that connection, we can move freely between them without experiencing a time skip. That will also eliminate the concern about miscalculations."

"That makes sense. It's like interplanetary travel in our time as opposed to at the turn of the century," Emil said after I translated. "Now it's easy for shuttles to move back and forth between Mars and Earth—there's spaceports on both planets, a stationary place for the pilots to travel back and forth between.

But in the old days, before there were humans on Mars, the space agencies just had to calculate and hope for the best. Maybe they'd land in the right place—or maybe they'd burn up on entry." He took a sip of the hot red liquid and winced at its bitter taste. "It's not going to be easy, though, even if we make it back in one piece. GSAF has the caves totally sealed off. Delia bribed a guy to get me in the last time—I doubt she'd be able to manage again."

"But surely this *Gee-Saph* will listen to reason," Ceilos said, setting his empty *sokol* cup down on the table. "The posterns belong to the Iamoi. This is our planet. They can't keep it from us."

Emil snorted. "I wouldn't be too sure about that."

"But we can try," Nadin snapped back at him in English. All four of us stared at her. My mouth involuntarily pulled up into a grin. Her accent was lilting but slight—much fainter than I was sure my own Iamoan accent was. I guessed my teaching might have paid off after all.

Emil stared at her appraisingly. Then he nodded, slowly. "You're right. There's nothing else we can do."

Nadin's face softened slightly. "All right. Let's get to work, then." She pulled her medallion out from under her shirt and opened the second posternkey.

"Isaak," Ceilos said. I started, my face reddening as I realized I'd been staring at Nadin. I could tell by Ceilos' expression that he had been watching me. "You should probably go tell your father what's going on."

I scoffed. "I doubt he cares," I said. He'd flounced back to the guesthouse after the forum. I was sure he wasn't really interested in the specifics of the time postern. But I stood up anyway. I'd been dismissed.

I smiled at Nadin as I passed, and to my surprise, she smiled back. Then her face colored and she looked down, tucking a hair behind her ear. My heart skipped for a second, followed by a wave of crushing guilt. What was I doing? I didn't even know anymore. Everything was a torquing trainwreck.

I trudged back to the guesthouse, still feeling Ceilos' eyes burning into my back long after I'd left the courtyard behind.

Chapter 36

· o ∘ • ○ ∅ φ ○

- n a d i n -

THE WEEK PASSED IN A BLUR, WITH GITRIN AND I SPENDING MOST of our waking hours working on programming the posternkey. It was decided that the area we were going to aim for was an open space in the hills outside what Isaak called Tierra Nueva. It was close to the caves where the one working postern we knew of was located, but Emil insisted that the area had been sealed off from the public, so it should be deserted when we arrived.

We didn't know how long it would take us, but we knew when we would return. Gitrin programmed the key to bring us back three minutes after we departed. Once the stable connection to the postern in Isaak's time was established, we could pass freely between the two timelines. To the people of Elytherios, it would be as if we never left.

But I wondered how much time it would be for me.

The morning of our departure was cold and damp. The clouds hung low over the village, shrouding the trees and buildings with white mist that I could barely see through. The shipping postern was located on the edge of the village, where the buildings began to give way to crops. As we passed, people watched us from the doorways of their houses, silent and stony-faced.

When we arrived at the postern, there was no one to see us off apart from Marin. I wondered if any of the Elytherioi expected us to return, or if they were hoping this was the last they would see of us.

"Are you all ready?" Marin asked us.

I glanced at Ceilos. I didn't feel ready, but if I wasn't by now, I was never going to be. He smiled back at me, and I turned to Marin and said, "Yes."

Isaak's father said something in English. I couldn't quite catch the meaning, but Emil snorted and Isaak shook his head. "We're ready, too," he said.

Marin took a shaky breath. "Well," she said. "Safe travels to you. You're sure you won't need anything for the journey?"

"No, we have stuff in my time. We'll be fine," Isaak said. Under his breath, he muttered, "I hope." I don't think he meant for anyone else to hear. I shivered, looking down at the cold ground and trying not to worry. The breath came out of my nostrils in steamy puffs.

"Now, remember—" Marin began, but she broke off. In the distance, there was the sound of the gong. It rang out three times before falling silent.

"What is that?" Gitrin asked.

Marin frowned. "I'm not sure. Forum isn't until tomorrow."

"Should we go check on it?" Ceilos asked. His voice sounded oddly strained. I furrowed my brows at him—something seemed different about his face, but I couldn't quite place it. He seemed off, somehow.

"No," Marin said. "You go. I will go check. If all goes well, I will see you again in just a few minutes."

She hurried back down the path toward the village. I watched her go, an anxious knot forming in my stomach. From the village, raised voices rang out, but I couldn't hear what they were saying.

"Maybe this isn't such a good idea," Isaak started.

"What's going on?" his father interrupted in English. "We're not backing out, are we? Because I'm not sticking around here any longer."

Isaak clenched his jaw. "No, Dad, but don't you hear—"

"Let's go," Ceilos said firmly. I looked at him in surprise. "Marin is right. We'll be back in just a few minutes. Whatever is going on in the village, they can handle it."

"I don't like it," said Gitrin. "But I'll leave it up to you, Nadin."

"Me?" I looked around at the group, then turned to face the postern. The sounds from the village had faded slightly. Maybe it was nothing. And, after all, we were not citizens of Elytherios—yet. We still had to prove ourselves.

I looked at Isaak for a long moment; then at Ceilos, his expression firm. "I... I think we should go," I said at last. I held the posternkey out to Isaak.

"You want me to carry this?" he said in surprise.

I nodded. "Yes. Keep a firm grip on it. We can't break our links, or we'll get separated." I reached out for Ceilos' hand, and he took it, wrapping his fingers tightly around mine. Gitrin took Ceilos' left hand, and Emil's in her own. The old man's face flushed, and Gitrin smirked.

Raymond hooked his hand around Isaak's elbow. "Hold on tight, Dad," Isaak told him in English. Then he turned to me. "You ready?"

The postern began to glow, tracks of light forming geometric patterns between the stacked stones.

I nodded and reached for Isaak's hand.

The light of the arch grew brighter and brighter. The doorway was opening.

"All right, everyone," Isaak said. "Let's go."

We stepped forward, and the world exploded.

It wasn't just the force of the postern. We hadn't passed through the arch yet, but the ground beneath my feet began to rumble. My ears were filled with the sound of an explosion. Then something thrust me forward, knocking me into Isaak, and we toppled into the light.

I opened my mouth, but no sound came out. My voice was ripped from my throat as my atoms began to disassemble themselves.

The last thing I felt before being torn into nothing was Ceilos' hand slipping through my fingers.

Chapter 37

· ∘ ° • ◯ ∅ ɸ ○

- i s a a k -

AS ALWAYS, TRAVELING THROUGH THE POSTERN WAS ABOUT AS pleasant as getting squeezed through a meat grinder. I gasped for breath as my atoms reassembled themselves, agonizing pain giving way to normalcy. I was just about to congratulate myself on managing to not collapse after rematerializing this time when a body staggered hard against me, knocking me over. I slammed into Dad and the group of us tumbled onto the ground.

"What the hell was that?" Dad muttered, rubbing his ribs.

"He let go."

I lifted my head to look at Nadin, splayed sideways over my chest. She shakily pushed herself up onto her knees, looked around the empty crater around us. "Ceilos?!" she called.

I sat bolt upright. We were in one of Erick's dig trenches, but the excavation crew was nowhere to be seen—even their equipment was gone. But that's not what caught my attention.

It was that there were only three of us.

"Where are the others?" I asked, dreading the answer. "Emil? And Gitrin and Ceilos?"

Nadin's eyes were frantic. "Isaak, he let go."

"Who let go?"

She swallowed. "Ceilos. He had my hand as we were stepping into the postern, and just as I passed through, just when I heard that noise... he let go."

"What's she saying?" my dad demanded.

I ignored him. "What does that mean?" I asked. "Where did they go?"

"I don't know," Nadin said, her voice breaking. "If the postern closed before they made it through, they'll still be back in Elytherios. But if Ceilos let go of my hand after they were already in the postern..."

Silence hung over us for a long, grim moment. Then Nadin leaped to her feet, ripping the posternkey out of my hand. "We have to go back!"

"How are we supposed to do that? First we have to get to that cave that my dad and I—"

"Then let's go!" She pulled me up to my feet, frantically dragging me over to the trench's edge.

"It's not going to be that simple," I argued. "Emil said that GSAF—"

"Freeze. All three of you."

The voice came from behind us. I recognized that voice. It was the last person I ever wanted to see again—the one whose unnerving eyes had been haunting my nightmares for the last month.

Slowly, we turned to see Joseph Condor standing above us, looking down into the trench. On either side of him was an armed suit, pointing a military-style weapon at us.

"Well, well," Condor said, his mouth twisting up into a grin. "Isaak Contreras. Just the person I've been looking for all this time. And if there was ever such perfect timing, I've never seen it."

I couldn't say anything. My tongue felt like it was made of lead.

The two GSAF agents gestured with their guns, indicating a rusty metal ladder leading out of the trench. Slowly, I trudged over to it, Nadin and my dad following close behind. Even behind his aviator sunglasses, I could feel Condor's eyes on me, never leaving my form for a second.

As I climbed off the ladder, Condor grabbed my elbow, pulling me uncomfortably close to him. "You're just in time for your own party," he hissed in my ear.

"What's that supposed to mean?" I asked, but he didn't reply.

The three men led us down the familiar path of Erick's dig site, over to the wide open area where the shuttles always used to park. As we walked, I could hear a tinny voice, echoing as if from a loudspeaker. I couldn't catch most of the words, but I realized with alarm that one word popping up with regular frequency was my own name.

Then we rounded the corner, and I sucked in my breath.

A huge crowd filled the former parking area. Many of them held posterboard signs saying things like *Free Mars* and *End the GSAF Coverup*. But the one that made my heart stop was the huge banner with a pixelated image of my face on it—a printout of my last yearbook photo—that read, "WHERE'S ISAAK?"

A makeshift stage had been erected along the viewing area that looked out over Tierra Nueva. A man wearing a faded t-shirt with a nice-fitting suit jacket over it was standing at a podium, addressing the crowd. He had a stocky build, with deep brown skin and short-cropped black hair. Neatly-groomed stubble lined a jaw that had become defined and square, and uncannily adult.

When our eyes met, the man froze mid-sentence. We stared at each other, silent, neither able to believe our eyes. It couldn't be him. He couldn't have changed this much in the few weeks since I'd seen him last.

But it hadn't been just a few weeks for him. And that's when the full impact of what Emil had been trying to tell me all this time hit me—the time I'd lost, I could never get back. I'd stayed the same, but they'd all moved on. And there was nothing I could do.

"Isaak?" Nadin said in a soft voice. "What's wrong? Who is that?"

I couldn't answer. I couldn't find the words.

The man at the podium was Henry.

Glossary

· ∘ ∘ ● ○ ∅ ϕ ○

- the words of the iamoi -

ALOS/ALIN – an affectionate term for a child

ANNUAL – birthdate

ELYTHERIOS – a word in the old Iamoi language, dating to before the Progression. It means "freedom." The Liberator's faction has co-opted much of the old language, including this word.

ENILIKIN – a person's eighth annual (approximately sixteen in Earth years), signifying the transition from childhood to adulthood. A person who is now an adult is called an *enilin* or *enilos*.

ESOTOI – the middle caste of the Iamoi, who work alongside both *patroi* and *plivoi*

FRAOULOI – known in Isaak's time as the "spider weed"; a resilient, woody black plant that can grow in almost any condition

GEROI – the governors of a citidome (singular: *gerouin* [feminine], *geros* [masculine])

GEROTUS – the united body of all *geroi* on Iamos and Hamos, similar to a senate

HAMOS - Venus

HAOI IFAISTEOI – "The Three Mountains"; the Iamoi's name for the three Martian shield volcanoes we know as Elysium Mons, Hecates Tholus, and Albor Tholus

IAMOS - Mars

KYRIOS/KYRIN – a formal term of address, its closest English equivalent being "lord" or "lady"

PATROI – the most prestigious caste of the Iamoi

PLIVOI – the bottom caste of the Iamoi, considered to be the "drudges"

S.C.D. – "System Collective Date"; the annual-count system of the Iamoi, dating back to when the System estimates human civilization first arose on Iamos

SIMOS – Earth

YACUNOS/YACHIN – beloved, sweetheart

Acknowledgments

First and foremost, I want to thank my family for all their love and support. An enormous thank you especially to my sister, without whom this book never would have happened. If it weren't for her talking me through the rough spots, brainstorming with me, and making me "Mars-flavored" smoothies at the drop of a hat, I never could have done it. Much love and many thanks also go to my mom, who has been my diligent first reader for my entire life and still hasn't disowned me yet.

I also want to thank my best friend and fellow writer, Selenia Paz. She has seen almost as many different versions of this story as my sister, and she remained supportive of the book even when I was positive that it was completely terrible. Once again, without her, this book never would have existed.

Thank you to everyone who has helped made this book a reality. Thanks especially Ayah Assem for all her support, from coordinating writing sprints to talking me into joining the Camp NaNoWriMo cabin that finally got this book finished; to everyone at Snowy Wings Publishing for providing such an awesome community and home for the series; to Rose Anne Roper and Brenda J. Pierson for their editorial feedback; to Elise Marion and the amazing team at Mosaic Stock, who were able to find fantastic models to match my vision for Isaak and Nadin; and to Najla Qamber, for the beautiful cover design—it came out so much more spectacular than I ever could have hoped, and I couldn't be happier.

A huge shout-out to my fellow ace authors at The Pack of Aces, for supporting my writing as well as the creative ace community in general: Claudie Arseneault, Joel Cornah, Darcie Little Badger, and especially Lauren Jankowski, who brought us all together in the first place. They are all awesome and you should check out their books, I'm just saying.

And finally, the biggest thanks of all must go to my former students at Lawrence Elementary School. Your love of science—and especially of Mars—is what put the idea for this book in my head in the first place. I wrote this story for all of you, and I can only hope that it's something you will enjoy. Keep reaching for the stars, because I believe that each of you has the ability to change the world.

About the Author

Lyssa Chiavari is an author of speculative fiction for young adults, including the critically-acclaimed *Fourth World* (Book One of the Iamos Trilogy) from Snowy Wings Publishing, and *Cheerleaders from Planet X*, a quirky sci-fi romance published by The Kraken Collective. Her short fiction has appeared in *Ama-gi* magazine, *Wings of Renewal*, and *Brave New Girls: Tales of Heroines Who Hack*. She's also the editor of the anthologies *Perchance to Dream* and *Magic at Midnight*. When she's not writing, you can usually find her exploring the woods near her home in the Pacific Northwest or losing an unreasonable number of life balloons on *Donkey Kong*. Visit Lyssa on the web at lyssachiavari.com.

BOOKS BY LYSSA CHIAVARI

the iamos trilogy

Book One: *Fourth World*
Book Two: *New World*
Book Three: *One World*

Different Worlds – An Iamos Novella

other novels

Cheerleaders from Planet X

anthologies

*Perchance to Dream: Classic Tales from
the Bard's World in New Skins*

Magic at Midnight: A YA Fairytale Anthology

PRAISE FOR FOURTH WORLD
book one of the iamos trilogy

★ A LIBRARY JOURNAL SELF-e SELECTION

"*Fourth World* is a gem. Exciting and interesting while covering the span of archaeology, time travel, government conspiracies, overcoming diversity, individualism, and friendships that defy odds, Chiavari paints us a vivid colonized Mars with such beauty it's effortless to believe."

- Brenda J. Pierson, author of JOYTHIEF

"Striking characters evolving in a beautifully-described Mars, coherent and entrancing world-building, a mystery that builds relentlessly, one question after the other..."

- Claudie Arseneault, author of CITY OF STRIFE

"This book fires perfectly on all cylinders."

- Jaylee James, editor of VITALITY magazine

"The world-building of both the Martian colony and Nadin's world, Iamos, is nothing short of spectacular. Full of mysteries, intrigue, and fantastical new discoveries, *Fourth World* is the kind of book that's hard to put down."

- Mary Fan, author of STARSWEPT